MW00917695

AN UNLIKELY BRIDE

BILLIONAIRES' BRIDES OF CONVENIENCE
BOOK 7

NADIA LEE

FOUR ISLES PRESS

An Unlikely Bride

Copyright © 2017 by Hyun J Kyung

This book is a work of fiction. The names, characters, places, and incidents are products of the writer's imagination or have been used fictitiously and are not to be construed as real. Any resemblance to persons, living or dead, actual events, locales or organizations is entirely coincidental.

All rights reserved. No part of this book may be reproduced, scanned, or distributed in any manner whatsoever without the prior written permission from the author except in the case of brief quotation embodied in critical articles and reviews.

1

LUCAS

WHY ARE YOU SO DIRTY?

What did I say about touching me when you aren't clean? Mother's voice is always so impatient, so full of exasperation. The muscles in my shoulders pull tight, and I start to feel small and pathetic. *Don't try to manipulate me, Lucas!*

My feet are encased in the most expensive and scientifically advanced running shoes money can buy, but they can't do anything to minimize the damage of my fucked-up gait.

Slap, slap. Slap. Slap, slap.

Fool, fool. Fool. Fool, fool.

Even the rhythm's uneven.

The day after Ava ended what we had, I stop across

the street and stare at the closed door that keeps us apart.

You're toxic.

We're done.

Ava's words superimpose on my mother's, and suddenly the pain in my left leg cuts through, hovering over my pumping heart.

"Get cleaned up, Lucas." Mother looks at Elliot, closes her hand around his shoulder and pulls him in for a quick sideways hug. Elliot tries to shrug her off, but she is stronger and prevails.

I ignore her command and hug her on my way to the bathroom. She pulls away, her nose wrinkling. "Lucas, look at my dress now! What have I told you about mud?"

"He's muddy too!"

"But Elliot didn't dirty my dress, now did he?"

My perfect twin. Lovable and worthy...and somehow I'm not. Never was.

There's something fundamentally wrong with me that goes beyond DNA—something in my soul, perhaps. Or maybe in the way atoms clustered to form me, or the alignment of the stars when I was separating from my twin in the womb. If Ava had known Elliot, she would've sensed the defect in me more clearly and chosen him too. He's always been the better choice.

My mom often told me that I was the greedy twin, the one who stole all the blood from Elliot, that he lived only because of the best care money could buy. *If your father had been poorer, your brother would've ended up dead right in my womb!*

If I want to keep Ava, I should just whisk her away someplace where nothing and no one can reach us. Why not just...take her? Who'll know? I promised to abduct her to Paris anyway. The plane can be ready to take off anytime.

All I have to do is kick down Eva's door. Convince her the test was bullshit, we should be together and that I'll do everything in my power to prove I want *her*, not the fucking painting, not helping out my siblings.

I start to take a step, but a sliver of sanity holds me back. She'll hate me even more if I do that. She'll despise me, wither away. How can she thrive around something she finds toxic? If I were just a little bit more like Elliot, just slightly less offensive...

Suddenly I can't bear it anymore. Blood roars in my head, and coherence is no longer possible. I turn and run back to my place as fast as my legs can take me. Not slowing down, I smash open the door and rush all the way to my office. There are the photos of me and my family on the mantel. A rough swipe of my arm brings them crashing down on the hardwood floor, the glass shattering. I grab one that didn't break and hurl it against a wall, watch the expensive frosted glass frame explode into a million fragments.

In the picture, the ten-year-old versions of Elliot and me are smiling. I have no scars, and we look so alike it's almost scary.

Wrong.

I rip it in half. Then I grab the left side—the one with me in it—and tear it again. Blood smears the glossy

3

paper, the image of the unlovable, fucked-up child. The greedy one. The clingy one. The one who almost cost his twin his life. The one nobody can ever love.

Vaguely I sense my housekeeper Gail rushing inside. Her old, mottled hands grab at me, and I shrug them away.

"Lucas, stop. What's wrong? You've hurt yoursel—"

"*I hate this!*" I snarl, tearing the picture one last time before flinging the pieces away.

They flutter and fall, coming to rest on the shard-strewn floor. I run a hand over my face, feel the salty sting of tears and the rough scar on my cheek.

I hate this. I *hate* this and I hate her and I hate him and most of all I hate myself for hating my twin and tainting all that I touch.

~

– CLEANSING –

The water runs, hitting the bottom of the white porcelain sink with a hiss. It's extremely hot, almost scalding the boy's delicate young skin. He grits his teeth and does not complain. His mother set the temperature, and he dares not adjust it and add to her anger.

His mother is furious, almost disgusted. His hands, after he's played in the garden for a while, are filthy. Dark grime covers his palms, and some managed to get under his small, neatly trimmed nails.

He breathes harshly through his nose and teeth. He

does not understand why his mother is so upset about a little dirt. It'll come off the dress. All she has to do is give it to the housekeeper. The housekeeper always gets stains out. But Mother is upset that he touched her with his gross, dirty hands at all.

After he's finished, he shuts the water off and wipes his hands on a clean white towel. Nothing comes off on the pristine, fluffy cotton, now slightly damp. Satisfied, he runs to his mother in the living room.

She sits in a plushy armchair, her slim legs crossed. She's changed into a new dress—a pretty cream-colored one that makes her look sweet and loving. In her hands is a fancy fashion magazine. His mother loves good clothes.

Maybe that's why she was upset. She cares about her outfits.

"Are you finished?" she asks, not looking up.

"Uh-huh!" He reaches out for an embrace. Surely, his mother will appreciate how well he's done.

She pulls back. "Let me see."

Proudly, he shows his hands, palms up. She leans forward without touching him. Her nose wrinkles as she studies his palms, then has him flip his hands so she can examine the fingernails. After what feels like forever, she slowly straightens. "Lucas, you didn't wash very well. You see that little spot under your fingernail?" She gestures. "That's dirt. It shouldn't be there."

"Where?" He brings his left hand close and stares as though he can will himself to see what his mother sees.

"Right *there*. I don't understand why you can't see it." She sighs and goes back to the magazine. "You never see anything."

The boy returns to the sink. He turns the water on, as hot as it was before. Then he grabs the bar of soap and finger brush and starts all over again.

2

LUCAS

THE WATER RUNS, HITTING THE BOTTOM OF THE white porcelain sink with a hiss. It's extremely hot, almost scalding. I grit my teeth and scrub. The water has to be hot, or it won't be effective. I know that from experience.

The cuts from two days ago reopen and bleed, but I slather more soap on my skin. The burn from the water and open wounds blend together, and I smile grimly. Burning means it's working.

After I'm finished, I wipe my hands on a white towel and study it. It's damp but pristine. Narrowing my eyes, I examine my hands with care—backs, palms, the tips of the fingers where a lot of people miss, the nails...every line I can see.

But I can't stop seeing Ava, retreating from me,

wiping her hand—the one that I touched—on her jeans, as though she couldn't bear the grime.

I turn the water back on and start washing again. If I'd been more careful, if I'd just been *clean*, would she have been less aloof? Would she have been more receptive, tried to understand things from my point of view?

Would she have smiled when I told her, "I'm in love with you"?

She couldn't have seen my defect, not the way Mom did. Otherwise she wouldn't have shared herself with me in the way she did... Never like that.

Despite my not sleeping much, two days have given me some clarity and a plan of sorts.

Surely I can fix what's broken if I just present my case better. And I understand the importance of presentation. Elliot and I would've never gotten the funding for our company if we didn't know how to convince tight-fisted venture capitalists we deserved their money and confidence.

I just have to do the same with Ava...and pray that she never sees how fucked up and undeserving I am. I can probably hide all my flaws with the right props— some charity work, maybe...and spoiling her rotten until she can't imagine going back to a life that doesn't have me to pamper her.

But first, I have to be absolutely immaculate.

My hands are red from the hot water, and my skin stings. Still, I don't feel clean enough.

Unable to help myself, I start the shower and strip everything off. My clothes end up on the bathroom floor in a heap. As soon as I'm naked, I hop under the water, the temperature punishingly hot.

I take soap and scrub myself, my hands rough and impatient and desperate. I have to get *all* the dirt off me. I have to.

And after I'm really clean, I'm going to try again. I'm going to make Ava see that I did not approach her for some fucking painting.

I keep washing, feeling like a hamster on a wheel. I'm trying so hard, but the effort... I don't know if I'm getting the result I'm striving for.

Maybe, before I see Ava, I should run Dad's Wife Number Three over for leaking the family's deal to the press. It's the least the bitch deserves for ruining the best thing that's ever happened to me. A grand gesture like that might please Ava. I think. I hope. I can't decide anymore. My head is a jumble of ideas about how to fix what's broken between us.

"Jesus, what the fuck?" Blake's sharp voice shatters my concentration. "Lucas! What the hell's going on?"

"Go away," I say tersely. "I'm washing." I have to be clean so I can make another run by her place. Maybe I'll get a glimpse of her this time. I can go see her, ostensibly to give her the Lexus back. I had it detailed and waxed again this morning. It is probably the cleanest car in the state of Virginia, if not the entire country.

"I can see that." He scowls at me from the other side of the glass stall. "The question is why?"

"Why do people wash, Blake?"

"You tell me, genius." His lips pull apart in distaste.

"Much more scrubbing and you won't have any skin left."

He opens the door and reaches inside, getting water all over his expensive cashmere sweater. "Goddamn it. Are you trying to cook yourself?" With an impatient, deft twist of a wrist, he shuts off the water. "Get out." He tosses me a towel.

When I merely grip the soft cotton in my hands, he takes my wrist and drags me out. "Lucas, focus. You've been washing for three days now."

"How did you get here?" I ask numbly.

"Rachel called."

"Rachel?"

"Yeah, your assistant? Remember her? She was worried about you. I'm pretty sure she would've preferred to have Elizabeth here, but our sister's a little busy. Not to mention, I don't know if it's a good idea for her to see you like this." He gestures at me. "Dry off, for fuck's sake. You're dripping water everywhere."

I scowl, but run the towel along my body. Dripping water is bad. It makes a mess, and nobody likes a mess. I wince at the stinging sensation; it feels like I've got a head-to-toe sunburn. "Why not?" I say, referring to our sister. "She always does the delicate work in the family."

"Because she, against my advice, gave you that information about where your ex was."

I drop the wet towel in the laundry basket and come to a halt just outside my closet. I've been so focused on getting Ava back that I never stopped to consider who sent me the mysterious package that got us together again. "Elizabeth knew about Ava all this time?"

A careless shrug. "Maybe. She has her own ways of finding things out. Never uses Benjamin Clark or any of the other usual PIs, so"—he spreads his hands—"how the hell should I know?"

I narrow my eyes. I don't know who she uses either, and she won't share the man's name...if it even *is* a man. She guards the person's identity as though it's the Hope Diamond. But whoever it is, they're scarily good.

"I told her to stay out of it. When people don't stay together, it's usually for a reason. And I was right as usual. Look at you. Just... What the fuck."

Blake sounds disgusted, which doesn't surprise me. Of all my siblings on the Pryce side—three total—Blake fits the image of the old-moneyed and influential family the best. Not only does he have the Pryce features—the dark hair, the classic profile their men are famous for, the arrogant tilt of his eyebrows and that insolent gaze that says he's entitled to whatever he wants—he also has the temperament to match.

"You lied to me about not knowing Ava." He denied categorically that he and Ava ever met or had words.

He holds up a finger. "I said I didn't remember who she was. I don't keep track of people's love lives. There are better uses for my brain cells. I'm sort of aware that you had an ex you broke up with two years ago, but even that's only because of Elizabeth. She thought perhaps you'd be more amenable to smoothing things out with the girl and marrying her for a year."

Damn Elizabeth. I know she wants Grandfather's portrait of her... "That's going way too fucking far." She should've at least had the guts to tell me about Ava herself rather than sending an anonymous envelope.

"You should've never revealed you aren't going to marry. It's making some people very antsy."

"Are you saying it's my fault?"

"Yes, because you give away too much. It's always best to play things close to your chest."

Fucker. It's annoying how coolly he speaks, but he isn't saying anything untrue. Everything's my fault, and even though I find Blake abrasive at times, I'm glad he's here to pump some sense into me. There's no one quite like him to ground a person.

"People who don't give a shit tend to get what they want," he adds. "Just look at Dad."

Point taken. I should've never been so needy and pathetic, telling Ava all the things I felt about her. Did she curl her mouth in distaste when I wasn't watching? I can just imagine...

Blake steps past, goes into my walk-in closet and tosses a blue shirt and some worn jeans my way. "Get dressed, unless you plan to parade around naked. It may thrill your housekeeper, but I've seen enough."

"Good god. She's in her sixties." Not to mention, she seems to believe it's her number one responsibility to mother me. She cleaned up the mess I made in my office even though I told her to not bother.

"So? She's not dead yet, is she? Where else is she going to see a man in his prime prancing around naked?"

I snort, then my gaze falls on the ugly scars on my left leg, and my mood darkens. Ava caressed them as though they didn't repulse her. She even ran her cheeks along the white, bumpy lines. And for that one moment, all the pain and weight I carry just...vanished.

Was she upset about the implied end date to our relationship? The fucking tabloids were thorough—they didn't forget to add that the fake marriage was to last a year.

She shouldn't have shut me out. I told her I loved her. Why didn't she try to negotiate?

Or did I fuck it up by bringing nothing but the pathetic terra-cotta pot? Maybe I should've prepared something sparkly and expensive. Diamonds usually work pretty well. Their dazzling display would've hidden what's wrong inside me. Ava might not have even noticed the pot.

I cover my eyes with a hand. They'd have made a perfect present, and I'm an idiot for not having seen it sooner. But I was foundering in my own thoughts at the time.

Blake grabs a fresh shirt from his small suitcase and changes out of the wet sweater. Once we're both dressed, my brother drags me to the living room. It has a couple of plushy mahogany-colored leather armchairs and two matching loveseats. A few coffee table hardbacks on Monticello and Jefferson's legacy lie on the low wooden table in the center. Rachel had the place decorated, and whoever she hired did well.

Gail comes out from the kitchen, wiping her thin hands on a paper towel. Her hair is gray, and her eyes a murky green, although still perceptive behind a pair of glasses. She's put on a UVA shirt—her children went to the University of Virginia—and jeans and a pair of those sensible white sneakers.

She takes one look at me and nods. "Good to see you finally rejoining the ranks of the living."

"It wasn't that long."

"Three days is plenty. Demolishing pictures in your office? Jogging three times a day? Washing before and after you go out? My Lord. I thought you'd lost your mind!" Gail presses her lips together until they practically vanish. "I do confess you had me worried. Wasn't sure what to do."

That explains why Rachel called for reinforcements.

I go to Gail and squeeze her weathered hand. "I'm sorry. Really. It won't happen again."

Blake sits back in an armchair, doing what people are starting to call manspreading. "That's right. I won't let it."

"Good. Now, would you like something to eat?"

"Something warm. And maybe a sandwich?" Blake asks hopefully.

"I can manage that." She points at the other armchair. "Sit down, Lucas. You're making me nervous." She waits until I actually take the seat and then disappears into the kitchen.

"'*I won't let it.*'" I snort. "Smug SOB, aren't you? You can't stay here forever to keep an eye on things."

He shrugs. "You can't stay here for too long either."

"Why the hell not?"

"Don't you remember your rather open-ended promise to Nate Sterling?"

Obscenely wealthy and well connected, Nate Sterling is a relative—through marriage—on the Pryce side of the family. Although he and I are friends, I can't imagine making a blank promise to him. I absolutely hate owing anyone anything. "What promise?"

Blake shakes his head. "I knew it. I even told Nate you probably forgot, since you're no liar."

I inhale sharply as a fresh wave of pain cuts through me. My asshole brother thinks I'm not a liar... but not the woman I love.

Not just a liar, but a greedy, greedy bastard.

Just like the way I was a greedy fetus.

I rub my hands together, feeling grimy.

Blake's flat tone pulls me out of my headspace. "You told him you'd help in any way you could if he ever opened a clinic for the poor."

Finally, I remember. When I learned how much Ava and her mother had suffered growing up, a clinic for people who fell through the cracks was something I wanted to do, and Nate seemed like the perfect partner for that type of venture. "And? Don't tell me he's going to build one now." I no longer have the drive or the proper state of mind for a project as ambitious as this.

"He has, and it's already open. The Sterling Medical Center in L.A. Well, 'open'... He'll make it official in about a week or two, I imagine."

"Then he doesn't need me."

"Wrong. He wants you to help with fundraisers."

What the hell? "That's not my area. Why doesn't he ask Elizabeth?" There's no wallet she can't crack with that smile of hers.

"She told him she was too busy. It's not like she has nothing to do with her time."

Goddamn it.

"And it's not like there's anything keeping you here."

But there is.

I didn't go jogging three times a day for shits and giggles. No matter how convoluted a route I took, I always made sure to pass Darcy and Ray's house... which I guess makes me a stalker. It wouldn't surprise me a bit if Ava's taken out a restraining order. I've been behaving like some of the psychos who've harassed my sister.

If I were a better man, I'd just accept Ava's decision —no, that's not right. If I were a better man, she wouldn't have rejected me in the first place.

But...I'm not. So I kept going by her place to see if she was all right without me. To see if she'd found someone else.

I wish she were a tenth as miserable as I am, so

she'd want me back to make the hurt go away. But I haven't seen her at the house and she hasn't called. Wanting her—*missing* her—has become a tangible thing that wraps around and squeezes until I feel like I'm about to burst.

The only bright spot is that she doesn't seem to be dating anyone new.

Blake, as usual, sees a bit too much. "It's that girl, isn't it?"

I merely stare at him.

He steeples his fingers. "Stop rubbing your hands together and tell me what happened."

– NEVER GOOD ENOUGH –

Ava

THE SECOND I OPEN THE SCARRED DOOR TO THE small public apartment Mom and I share, I wrinkle my nose. The stench is overwhelming—something acidic and rotting.

Dropping the school bag, I stomp inside and open the windows to air the place out. We don't have any pets—animals cost money—and I know what's caused the gross smell. My stomach sinks as I rub a hand over my mouth, bracing myself for another difficult scene.

I go to the bedroom and see Mom passed out at the

foot of the bed. She's half sitting up, back against the bed and slumped over to one side. Puke covers her chin and shirt. This close, the odor is much worse, laced with stale alcohol.

I sigh. She should be at work. She'll probably lose her job for missing another shift—if she hasn't already. But I don't have the energy to be upset with her. It isn't the first time Mom drank until she passed out or threw up. This is the only way she knows how to deal with Dad's betrayal, and we're too poor and unimportant to be helped. I know because I've called every clinic in the area, asking if they could do something for her.

"Mom." I put a hand on her shoulder and shake gently.

Her eyes flutter a bit. "Wha...?"

"Let's get you cleaned up."

Mom looks down at herself, makes weak movement with one hand. "Wha...?"

"Come on." I wrap an arm around her torso and pull her up.

"I'm fine. Don' need anyone."

"I know."

"Hafta go to work..." She glances at the clock, registers the time. It galvanizes her. "Shit, I'm late!"

"Your shift is probably over by now."

"No, no, I have to get to work."

"Mom, you can't go in like this. Let's get cleaned up first. Then we'll call your supervisor and say you were sick." That isn't really a lie. Mom *is* sick. Sick in her soul, her body.

All because Dad turned out to be an asshole.

I half carry her to the bathroom and turn on the water. Mom huddles on the floor, not caring that her clothes are gross, and starts crying into her hands. "I got nothin'," she sobs. "My God, Beau."

I look away, unable to bear her misery but at the same time too angry to be kind. When she makes no move to get into the shower, I push her toward the tub. She resists, sitting like a sack of flour on the cold tiles. "What am I gonna to do? What am I gonna *do*?" she wails.

"How about you get into the damn shower?" I glare down at her. "You know what? I'm *glad* Dad's dead! My only regret is that he didn't suffer, because he sure should have."

Mom lifts her head and stares. From her slack expression, I don't know if she's registering half of what I'm saying, but I'm too furious to care.

"If somehow he comes back from the dead, he better not show his face here or I'll kill him again!"

She moves so fast I almost don't see it. Her palm cracks against my cheek hard enough to make my head snap to the side. Stunned, I put a hand on the stinging spot.

"*Don't you dare say that, you little bitch!*" Spittle flies from her mouth, her eyes wide and bloodshot. "He's my everything! You're nothing! Nothing, you hear!"

That hurts far more than the slap, but I swallow my tears. "I'm your daughter."

"No daughter of mine disrespects her daddy!"

"If he'd acted like a real father, I might've given him some respect!" Disgusted, I walk out of the apartment and stand leaning against the door. My cheek aches, and there's probably going to be a bruise. Tears bead in my eyes, but I blink them away. What will they accomplish? I'll cry when tears can put food in my belly and take me away from this...hell.

Resentment is a tight ball that chokes me. I kick the dilapidated door with all my strength before spinning around and leaving, going somewhere that doesn't have this miasma of misery.

Mom should have never let a man as selfish and undeserving as Beau Huss ruin the rest of her life. She shouldn't make her child suffer because she can't pull herself together enough to be a mother.

If I were her, I would've moved on a long time back. Just *left*, so he'd know how little he meant to me, how little I needed him to live a happy, fulfilling life. I would've never wasted tears on him.

"You've got no pride! No self-respect!" I yell in the apartment's direction. My stomach knots with hunger, but there's no food at home. Just a woman who's coming apart at the seams and doesn't care that she has a daughter who needs her.

I will never let any man have this much power over me. *Never.*

3

Ava

Three days.

Sometimes three days can pass you right by, quick as a bullet. And sometimes that much time feels like an eternity. You'd think that when time is flying, you'd remember less. After all, everything's going so fast, and surely your senses can't absorb it all, your brain can't process the whole skein.

But it's the opposite. I remember every second of the happy days I had with Lucas... The three sweet, heartbreaking days at the bed and breakfast that ended far too soon.

The way he made my body sing.

The way he held me in his arms.

The way he made me feel like I was something special, precious to him.

Time's been crawling since Lucas's final visit. The last three days might as well have been a decade. But I remember very little of what happened after he came back with the barren terra-cotta pot.

I'm in love with you.

My heartbeat stutters at the memory. The five words I would've given anything to hear from his lips. He said them when he came by that last time. But I didn't want to hear them that way—a gambit to get me to capitulate, to look away from all the things he's done. A lot like how my dad used to bring gifts to make my mother forget all the ways he treated her badly. If she'd been thinking more clearly, maybe she would've seen the signs faster.

Still, my heart is foolish and impetuous, easily impressed.

I'm in love with you.

How I wanted to give in, wrap my arms around him and tell him I loved him too. I'm so much like my mother it's scary. So I tossed out the only response I could—"You're toxic"—and shut the door in his face. I couldn't trust myself not to be impulsive.

Was I too harsh? I only wanted to make a point, make him go away so I could move on—again. But the utter devastation in his gaze still haunts me. It's as though *I'm* the villain, not him.

And I despise myself for feeling this way.

Forget him. He only wanted to use you to get that ridiculous painting.

Why didn't he just tell me honestly from the beginning? Then things could've been different. Instead he fed me lines about how he wanted to keep me a secret, hidden away from everyone because he was afraid to lose me, that others might covet what he had. What he meant was people might covet the multimillion-dollar painting he would get if we were together.

What humiliates me the most about our reunion is that I opened up to him. I told him things I would've never said because I believed he was making himself vulnerable to me. How stupid. Men don't work that way.

I won't let the past hold me down. What I've learned from the bitter disappointments in my life is that the only way to heal is to move on.

I'll be damned if I end up like my mother.

Which is why I find myself in LAX waiting to board a late-night flight back home. Maybe I'll get an offer from the medical center. The final round of interviews with Robbie Choi, my would-be boss, is done. The third son of Korean immigrants from Busan, the man's super nice. Although he's only in his forties, he's gone prematurely gray and his ash-white mane is quite shocking on a face that looks so young.

You have to tell me everything! Bennie messages me on Facebook.

They liked me, I think.

Well, duh. Why else would they bring you all the way out to L.A.? What did you think about the hospital?

It's really nice. It doesn't look like the crappy public clinics we used to go to. They were usually understaffed and overcrowded, housed in buildings that looked as sad and worn out as the patients who waited inside.

Apparently the Sterling Medical Center isn't just a safety-net clinic, but a fundraising organization. Every penny raised goes toward treating anybody who walks through the door, I write, regurgitating information from the first interview.

That's so noble it's positively obscene. They're probably trying to hide something.

I snort a laugh. Only Bennie would be this cynical. But then, we didn't have the kind of childhood most people have. When your parents fail you over and over again, it's hard to trust anything—or anyone.

And Bennie hasn't seen the facility. The brand-new six-story building gleams—big windows letting sunlight pour in, spotless floors and pristine walls covered with glossy posters promoting various ways to stay healthy on a budget. The air has a hint of disinfectant—like every other hospital in the world—and the sound system delivers soothing classical music at a low volume.

Robbie gave me a tour of the center. Doctors in white coats moved briskly, nurses and staff entering information onto slim tablets as they readied for the official opening. Everything at the medical center said *money* and *top-class* and *our patients deserve the best*.

"We take what we do very seriously," Robbie said during the tour. "It's a shame that in a country as wealthy as ours, we still have people who can't afford basic medical care."

"I know," I said. "My family really struggled when I was growing up. Not much of a safety net."

Well, Mom and I struggled. Dad lived fine—he was a rich man who pretended to be poor so he could have my mom as a cheaply kept mistress to fuck whenever he was in the mood. He had a family he provided for in style—his *real* wife and his *real* daughter.

If we'd had better medical care, would Mom have let herself go? Died of an overdose? If she'd received help for depression, anger issues and substance abuse...would she have survived the heartbreak? She couldn't handle it once she realized Dad would never marry her—that she was nice enough to fuck, but not good enough to wed.

Don't be a cynic, B, I type and hit send. *I want to work there.*

You are so gonna work there. I can feel it in the soles of my feet.

I smile at his confidence, although I secretly think he's probably right. During the initial phone interview, I asked, "Why are you recruiting someone who lives so far away? There must be people in L.A. who can start immediately. Not that I'm ungrateful—I love your mission and what you do, but I'm genuinely curious."

It isn't something I would've asked normally, but after the whole fiasco with Lucas, knowing that he was using me to acquire *art*, I really had to know. The hospital didn't have to take Erin's referral.

"We liked your résumé," Robbie answered without missing a beat. "I especially liked your international experience, and the fact that you've overcome a lot to be where you are now, as you mentioned earlier. We want someone who's seen and experienced what the people we're serving have seen and experienced. We want someone with drive, but who's also capable of empathy. Does that satisfy you?"

It did.

If they offer, you should take it, Bennie says. *Unless you have something better in Charlottesville?*

Nope, I respond. Actually, that isn't entirely true. I have my foster parents Ray and Darcy McIntire...and Mia...but they aren't enough to help me move on. And Lucas lives in the same closed community they do. Behind the same gates, within the same walls. Being that close to him...

I clench my jaw as pain blossoms again, starting from the center of my heart. It's been weeks since I discovered his lies, but I hurt as though it just happened moments ago.

The worst thing is that I miss him. Every idle moment I think about throwing away my pride and self-esteem and running to him with open arms for another slice of sweet, poison-laced heaven.

What does that make me other than a contemptible, weak-willed creature? I swore I'd never let a man reduce me to that, but as long as Lucas is within easy reach, I'll give in. I just know it.

I have to leave.

4

AVA

THE ROAD IS DARK AS I DRIVE. IT FEELS FAMILIAR somehow, but I'm not certain if I've ever driven here before. The grass along the edges is shaggy, like hair badly in need of a trim.

Then I see a car—a black Mercedes. Instinctively I know it belongs to a woman, someone beautiful, sophisticated and worthy of a man like Lucas.

My soul shrivels as it stops in front of his house, the engine cutting off. The door opens. I look away, not wanting to see...

Suddenly I'm back on Darcy and Ray's porch, my feet cool on the wooden planks. The day's bright; early morning sun shines through a wispy shroud of clouds. The sight of the black Mercedes dims my mood. What's it doing here?

Lucas stands before me, a pot in his hands.

"I'm in love with you," he says.

I can't see what's inside the pot, but surely nothing's there. He doesn't want me, not the way I want to be wanted. He's just saying that because he needs me to get the painting.

But I'm not strong enough to resist his words—the five most precious words in the world.

Tell him he's poison. Tell him it's over. There is nothing between you. Only *you* think you have something, and you'll end up suffering because it's just not true. When are you going to wake up?

But I can't. I'm too weak to resist him.

Tears spring to my eyes. I let them fall as my legs fold. "I love you too, Lucas."

His face splits into the most blinding smile I've ever seen. Unable to stop the tears, I soak up its radiance on my knees, enraptured like the humblest worshipper before her god.

He brings the pot forward. In the center of the dirt is a small green sprout, so precious, so full of potential. Suddenly my heart is bursting with joy. What we have isn't a one-way trip to misery, like I feared. There is something we can nurture and grow. In time it'll become stronger, nourish our souls.

The black Mercedes vaporizes, turning into tendrils of coal smoke. Everything vanishes, leaving only two of us. And it's enough. I need nothing so long as I have Lucas.

I raise my hands to touch him. But somehow he's

beyond reach. I stretch, but he's just at my fingertips. We're so close I can graze my nails against his skin.

"Lucas." His smile only grows more brilliant, and my desperation mounts. "Don't move. Let me hold you."

The beatific expression still on his face, he shakes his head. "Ava, surely you know this can't last."

Apprehension frosts my mind. "What do you mean?"

"Look at us."

And I do, really do. He glows like the sun, while I'm dim and drab in cheap, clearance-rack clothes. My hands are work-rough, and I know without having to look that my teeth are nicotine-stained, like my mom's.

"How can there be anything permanent between us? When are you going to wake up?"

"Lucas... You said you loved me."

"Love doesn't last." He holds out the terra-cotta pot. The green sprout is no more. In its place is a brittle brown thing, withered and without hope or future.

Lucas gazes somewhere beyond my shoulder with tender longing, and I turn and see Faye walking toward us, her eyes on him. Stylish stilettos exaggerate her pelvic swing, and she looks like something out of a movie. She is soft, all feminine curves, with a sweetness that says she's lived a pampered life. Diamonds on her throat sparkle as she lays a hand on his arm. "Darling."

He takes the slim hand and kisses the knuckles. "Love."

Something inside me shrivels and dies like the shoot in the pot. Somewhere Mia cries, and Lucas stares at me *dispassionately.* "*You should've known better. A baby was never going to be enough. There's nothing of worth you can give me. You just aren't good enough, and nothing's ever going to change that. When are you going to wa—*"

I jackknife up. Sweat has beaded on my skin, and my clammy nightshirt sticks to it. It's barely six. I rub my eyes, take a deep breath.

It was just a bad dream, nothing more. I should go back to sleep. My plane didn't land until almost midnight in Dulles, and I drove over two hours to reach Ray and Darcy's home afterward in a rental car. It was easier than trying to get a flight that would bring me all the way to the small airport in Charlottesville.

But sleep is the last thing on my mind.

I put on workout leggings, a shirt and a pair of running shoes. If I can't sleep, I might as well get some exercise.

It's still a bit dark, but the streetlights illuminate everything. The air is crisp but feels cleansing as it saws in and out of my lungs. I put my body on autopilot, letting my feet take me wherever as I focus on the rhythm of each stride.

Some time passes, and I suddenly realize I'm in front of Lucas's house. In its driveway is the sleek black Mercedes—not Lucas's—I saw last night coming back from the airport. Although Lucas's home isn't on the way, I made a detour because...well, I don't know what I was trying to accomplish. It's not like I was planning to resume what we had.

I swallow. Maybe I needed a sign that he's fine without me. Concrete, undeniable proof that he lied when he told me he was in love with me.

And here it is. Whoever came in that car last night has clearly stayed for breakfast. My muscles tense, and I'm forced to admit my restlessness wasn't because I haven't exercised in a while or the nightmare unsettled me. It's because I kept thinking about this damn car.

Whose is it? The license tag is Virginia, and the first three letters are YME. Why couldn't it be a vanity plate? Then I'd be able to guess what kind of person owns it.

My instinct is to say Faye Belbin—the woman Lucas took to high-society functions while he was fucking me in my shabby college apartment. I can't remember if Faye had a Mercedes when she came by a few weeks ago—I was too upset to notice—but she could have. She's a wealthy woman and knows how to treat herself. A black Mercedes would be perfect— expensive and luxurious, just like her.

Imagining Lucas with Faye, laughing and rolling around in bed, sends jealousy spiking through me. My eyes start to tear, and I slap both cheeks hard to stop myself from crying. What is wrong with me? This just gave me the affirmation I sought—he lied to me when he said he was in love with me. I was smart to rebuff him. The alternate scenario—the one from my nightmare—is too horrifying.

Telling myself I'm fine—because really, I am—I

spin around and start running again. I can survive Lucas Round Two. I've survived worse.

A couple of blocks away from Darcy and Ray's home, my lungs are burning and the stitch in my side is too excruciating to keep running. I pause with my hands on my knees. As soon as I can breathe without feeling like I'm going to pass out, I'm going to walk the block and stretch.

The sandstone-colored sidewalk looks orange under the slanting rays of the just-risen sun, and some ants are already busy dismembering the carcass of a beetle. A car slows and stops behind me. The door opens and closes, and apprehension runs a finger along my spine as I straighten up. Charlottesville is a very safe town. But that doesn't mean it's totally crime-free. Even a city as safe as Osaka has its share of criminals.

"Ava Huss?"

I turn and face a tall, dark man. He's dressed in a cream-colored cashmere sweater and black slacks that lie neatly over his long legs. His dark hair is cropped with care, framing his handsome but unsmiling face perfectly. It's so familiar that I feel like I've gone back in time.

I must be hallucinating. There's no other explanation for me seeing the son of a bitch from the hospital two years ago. "Blake?"

A corner of Blake's mouth tilts up into an arrogant smirk. "You're not too terrible looking. I guess I can see the attraction."

I clamp my mouth shut so I don't blurt out the first

thing that pops into my head: who's sharing Lucas's bed? It doesn't matter who. What matters is he's not alone.

"Are you here to harass me the way you did two years ago?"

He frowns.

I cross my arms and continue before he can get a word in. "Well, you better think twice. Google told me you people are loaded. I'm sure you don't want to be sued or have your names dragged through the mud. That would make it harder for you to marry in the next few months, wouldn't it?"

He comes closer, until he's less than a foot away. I stand my ground, knowing that if I take a step back, I'm conceding to him. I'd rather die than concede anything to this bastard.

He stares into my eyes, and I meet his gaze head-on. His lips twist. "You really are a viper, aren't you? It amazes me that Lucas doesn't see that."

"Don't you dare call me names. He lied to me."

He snorts, rolling his eyes. "You're such a self-centered little bitch, you can't even admit you did anything wrong."

My hands clench into fists, and it's all I can do to restrain myself. I would give half my savings to knock that superior expression right off his face. "*Me?* You have no idea what Lucas did to me. He got me fired from one job, and an offer rescinded for another, all in order to drag me back home. He lied about being in love with me while he had another woman waiting on the side. And it was all about those damn paintings—the paintings that you guys are going to inherit by marrying."

"Ah." He cocks an eyebrow. "So that's why you set him up to fail. Did it make you feel good to see him work his ass off over that stupid pot? I guess you gold diggers have an instinct for nice guys. I sure as hell wouldn't have done it." He raises a forefinger. "Before you get all self-righteous, understand one thing. He never—*never*—needed you. Any of us can get a woman off the street to marry for a few bucks—which, by the way, is exactly what he should've done. You're no better than we are."

Blood roars in my ears. What gives him the right to talk to me like this? Does he think because he's Lucas's brother, he's exempt from courtesy and minimal decency? "I *am* better than the lot of you. I would never use and discard people like garbage just because I had more money than them."

He laughs. "How would you know? You don't have enough money to treat anybody like garbage, my dear, and you never will. It takes millions before you can. You know why I hate all my father's wives?"

The sudden change of topic makes my head spin.

"They're all fucking users. I don't understand why Lucas picked you—a woman who's just like any of my father's tarts *du jour*. He should've just bought you the minute he found you again rather than trying to cater to your sense of...romantic bullshit."

I laugh in his face. "You'll never find enough money

to 'buy' me. I'm nothing like you people or whatever women your father married. If I'm so greedy and unethical, I could've just stuck around to squeeze a bunch of money out of Lucas."

Blake smirks. "Could you? Really?"

"You have no idea." I'm certain this smug bastard doesn't know I was pregnant back then. "Asshole."

"I'll take that as a compliment and give you a *friendly* warning. I'm not going to sit around and watch you punish my brother for something he didn't do." He finally smiles, but it lacks warmth. "We'll meet again, Ava Huss. Unlike Lucas, I'm not a particularly nice guy. Unlike him, I don't fight fair."

Sweat dampens my palms as he walks away. I told him what Lucas did to bring me back to the States—how he lied to me, manipulated me, stripped me of the means to support myself. But apparently none of that matters to Blake.

When people threaten me, I generally shrug them off. Blake's different. His quiet, measured tone states that he's the dominant one with all the power. Destroying me would be as easy as flicking lint off a finger, and the instincts that kept me alive and relatively unharmed in the poor, rough neighborhood where I grew up clang a warning bell.

Blake climbs behind the wheel of the car. It's black, and as he drives off the license plate starts with YME.

I watch the car disappear, my hands and legs trembling.

Then it hits me... Lucas never spent the night with another woman.

I shake my head. It just means he didn't spend last night with Faye. It doesn't change anything.

I can't let it.

5

LUCAS

I FEEL ALMOST HUMAN AFTER SOME SPICY TOMATO soup and scrambled eggs. Blake had a few bites, claiming that he wasn't that hungry due to jetlag. Then he disappeared, telling me to eat to start making up for the last three days. "You can't win a war on an empty stomach."

Bossy bastard. But I have to admit he's right about eating. I stand up and stretch my legs. Maybe it's the full belly or maybe it's something else—the weather is absolutely gorgeous this morning—but I feel more grounded. Stray thoughts are no longer tumbling around inside my head, and for once I have a bit of clarity.

Just then, the door opens and Blake walks in, bringing the cool breeze from outside with him.

"Where have you been?"

He dumps his keys on the narrow table by the door where Gail places the mail. "Just checking out the community. It's surprisingly nice. Cheaper than Boston, too."

I narrow my eyes. Blake's passion is for technology startups, and I doubt that's changed in the last two years. "Don't bullshit me. Houses aren't your thing. That's why you have a special advisor handling your real estate portfolio."

"A man is entitled to indulge his curiosity." Blake comes into the living room and takes a seat. "Guess who I ran into?"

"Who?" I have a bad feeling about this. Blake is entirely too pleased.

"Ava Huss."

"What the—? You went to her *house*? What the hell were you thinking?"

He snorts. "I don't even know where she lives. Besides, do you think I'd be crass enough to do that? She was outside, jogging."

I don't understand. Ava hates jogging. She told me so.

Blake continues, "There's nothing wrong with striking up a conversation."

"So...how is she?"

"Fine. Better than you actually. At least her skin hasn't been scrubbed raw, and she doesn't look like she hasn't eaten in the past week."

I ignore the jab, relieved that she's been taking care

of herself. Knowing her terrible childhood, I don't ever want her to go hungry. Then it hits me: he actually spoke with her, which makes no sense at all. "How did you get her to talk to you?"

"I said hello like any normal human being. You should try it sometime."

I shake my head. "She hates you. Said you were nasty to her two years ago."

"She mentioned something about that. The thing is, I really don't remember. So yeah, I might've said something to her. Who knows? Couldn't have been that important."

His arrogance is breathtaking. "It's because of you that I had so much trouble in the first place. You made her leave."

"I didn't *make* her do anything. She chose to go."

What the hell? "You think she still would've left if you hadn't said those things to her?"

He stretches his legs out and lays linked hands on his belly. "If she thought what you guys had was worth fighting for, yeah, she would have stayed no matter what I might've said. But she didn't. Doesn't that tell you something? Wake up, Lucas. Ava thinks you're the enemy, and you're treating her with kid gloves. That has to change."

"Are you fucking serious? I'm not going to treat her the way you treat the women you sleep with." Women are like condoms to Blake—one-time use only. "She's special."

"Uh-huh. And how did your special snowflake treat

39

you when you showed up with that pot full of dirt? Did she light up and say hello? Or did she pull away like you were a slime monster?"

Dirty.

Don't touch me.

What did I say about touching me when you're dirty?

Don't be greedy.

You're toxic.

I press the heels of my hands against my eyes, my teeth clenched tight.

"What do you really know about her?" Blake's question cuts through the ugly voices in my head.

I sigh. "Where are you going with this?" With Blake, there's always a particular conclusion he wants to lead you to.

He continues, "You say she's special, but you don't really know much about her past, do you?

"She's loyal. Caring. Capable of putting others before her. I don't need more than that." Those are the qualities that drew me to her in the first place. I'm not going to lie; her looks also had something to do with my attraction...but if I hadn't glimpsed those other aspects, I would never have fallen for her as hard as I did.

Blake regards me patiently, like I'm five. "Anyone can fake that stuff. Look, you need to adjust the way you view this whole"—he gestures at me, in the direction of Darcy and Ray's house, the whole neighborhood —"situation."

"You're giving me relationship advice now?"

"Somebody has to. And I'm not letting you continue with what you've been doing to yourself anymore."

I cross my arms.

"Unless, of course, you think that what you've been doing is working."

Touché. "Fine. Let's hear it."

"Unless you know your enemy really well, you can't win."

Some advice. Blake should never be a relationship counselor. "Ava isn't the enemy."

"Really? Then why don't you have what you want?"

"What the hell kind of question is that?"

"A pertinent one. You have an answer?"

I have no good response to counter his crazy logic. "She's who I want, except she thinks that I betrayed her. Goddamn tabloids!"

"Tabloids have little to do with it. Fuck decency and what the world says is fair. To win and get what you want, you have to be willing to go the distance. You have to use every weakness your enemy has, and you have to be ruthless. Zero mercy. Then you can win."

"What the hell, man? If I go that route, she's going to hate me."

He shrugs. "She already hates you."

The four simple words stop me. Her contemptuous expression drips through my consciousness like acid. She found my effort pitiable, my hands grimy, my very presence about as pleasant as a pile of dog shit left on her nice front porch. My mouth dries, and I surreptitiously wipe my hands on my pants.

Blake isn't finished dispensing wisdom. "Why did you go see her in the first place? When you got Elizabeth's package. Surely it wasn't to win her back, was it?"

No. I wanted to take back what I lost when she left me—my warmth and vitality. And she gave me a glimpse of something even better in that one week. Now that she's taken it back again, I feel colder and emptier than ever.

"You changed course, you let your guard down, and what happened?" Blake grows serious. "You should never let anyone who doesn't love you in. And most importantly, you should never love anyone who doesn't respect you enough to be honest about what she's doing. She played you like a dancing monkey, the same way Betsy used to. Jump this high. Good, now higher. If you jump high enough, I'll give you what you want! You'll be rewarded!" He pauses. "Were you ever rewarded?"

My throat closes. Suddenly my mind is flooded with memories of how my mother used to make me promises—be good, stay clean, don't touch her...then I'll take you to Disneyland...I'll take you to the movies...I'll take you to see Santa...

Except she never kept her promises, no matter what I did. She always found something to object to. I walked too loudly. I was sweaty after playtime in the park. I was standing too close to her.

Blake continues, "Ava set you up, Lucas. She wasn't going to give you a chance no matter what you did, but she made you jump through the hoops anyway."

I shove my hand into my hair and clench until my scalp hurts. *Fuck, fuck, fuck.* I hate every syllable out of his mouth, but I can't deny what he's saying is true.

She did set me up.

Two weeks of gut-twisting anxiety. Sleepless nights filled with hope, then despair. A coolly delivered rejection. Always the same fucking message—no matter how hard I try, I'm not worthy. I stop as the image of how she looked the last time passes through my mind. As beautiful as an angel I can never hope to touch... Her platinum hair flowing behind her, and her eyes flashing a huge warning sign that screams, "Stay away." I bared my soul to her. Told her I loved her...and she called me *toxic*.

The harder I try, the more contemptible I become.

My pathetic fantasy of her being so miserable she'll welcome me back into her life is exactly that—a fantasy. She'll never welcome me back. She'll curl her lip, make it crystal clear I'm unworthy.

That I'm fundamentally, intrinsically too flawed to be redeemed.

Why did I ever harbor such a sad little hope? Haven't I learned better? Shit like that happens in movies, not in real life. If I got hit by a truck, she wouldn't look twice.

Suddenly I'm pissed off.

I did nothing to hurt her. The whole fucking

marriage-for-paintings deal is Dad's doing, and the leak is Wife Number Three's fault. I never treated Ava unfairly, never lied to her.

Why should I feel bad? Why should I grovel?

I'm not some kid desperate for approval and love. That shit's over. I cut ties with my mother for that reason, and I'm not waiting decades before I finally get it through my head that it's over with Ava.

If she hated me, found me so lacking, she should've just said so, instead of playing me the way Mom used to when she wanted to see how far I'd go to earn her love.

"You're right," I say.

Blake nods. "She doesn't deserve you."

"I'm getting the fuck out of here."

"Good call."

"Someplace warm."

"Why don't you try L.A.?" Blake says. "You've been gone for too long. Everyone would love to have you around, and you can stay at my new place. I got a penthouse. Three levels."

"When?"

"A few months ago. Got tired of Boston. Too close to Virginia." *Too close to our despicable father and his vapid new wife,* he means. "I'm only in and out of there, and I wouldn't mind sharing it. It has two giant suites anyway, although the master suite is mine."

I let out a humorless laugh. "Don't worry. I'll take the closet." Knowing Blake's taste, the place is going to be large and expensive.

"Perish the thought. Elizabeth would flay me. The change of scenery will be good for you."

"I know. But before I can go, I need some closure."

"Closure?" Blake raises an eyebrow. "Don't kneel and beg for crumbs. She's not worth it."

My hands clench. Leave it to him to sum everything up with such stark clarity, even if it's something I don't want to hear. There is still part of me that wants to try again with Ava, but fuck it. Everything he said is right. Hope is for the weak, so they can keep digging without realizing they're making the ditch too deep to get out of. A *toxic* drainage ditch. "I'm not begging her for anything, but there's a debt between us, so I need to settle that before I go."

Blake smirks. "Make her pay dearly."

I don't bother to correct him. It would only make him argue with me more.

It's me who owes her. But once my debt is cleared, I'll be free.

6

AVA

By the time I return to the house, my legs are shaking. As soon as I close the door, I let them fold underneath me and bury my face in my hands.

I'm not going to sit around and watch you punish my brother for something he didn't do.

Blake... That bastard.

How *dare* he act like I'm being unfair? I'm not the villain here. I'm a victim of Lucas's deception. And whatever pain Lucas supposedly feels, it can't be greater than mine. After all, he never loved me the way I loved him.

Even now I want to run back and tell him I forgive everything and that we can start fresh, with me helping him get the painting. I don't even care if the marriage is only for a year, so long as we can be together. Surely I can change his mind in those twelve months...

What the hell is the matter with me? I bury my face in my hands. What he's done should be enough to kill my love for him.

Disgusted with myself, I shower quickly, setting the water temp as hot as I can stand. I despise my own weakness. It makes me want to do the very same things that got my mom into trouble.

Too tired to bother with a dryer, I towel my hair and put on some old jeans and a navy-blue sweater. The mirror shows eyes that are dark and unhappy, and I hate it that I'm feeling this way. Why does being rational hurt so bad?

My cell phone jars me out of my misery. It's an email from Robbie at the Sterling Medical Center.

Subject: Offer

Dear Ava,

We loved meeting you, and we would like to offer you a position at our organization.

I blink, uncertain if I'm reading it right. After weeks of disappointment, it seems shocking that something could be going my way.

I scan the rest of the message, which details things like pay and relocation assistance. The salary looks great, although knowing the cost of living in L.A., it's probably not *that* great. Having lived in Osaka, I know how far money goes—or more precisely, doesn't go—in a pricey city.

But L.A. is a new opportunity. And it'll mean being far away from Lucas, since he seems determined to remain in Charlottesville. I hate leaving like this, but staying here just isn't good for me. Driving by Lucas's house, missing him, thinking about him, obsessing about him—all of it's just self-destructive. And until now, I didn't consider the possibility that I'd also run into his family. God. That's the last thing I want. They probably blame me for not falling at his feet and begging him to marry me so they can get their multimillion-dollar paintings. Blake was pretty blatant in his hostility, and the others will be too.

Rich people don't become rich by being nice.

I send a quick note to Robbie, letting him know I'm thrilled to accept the offer and will start as soon as possible. I also text my old college roommate Erin to let her know I'll be joining the medical center. She's the one who put me on Robbie's radar, so I definitely owe her now, even though I know she didn't do it to get a favor in return. I then call the HR contact, Molly Jayden, to let her know my decision and ask for relocation help.

"You sure you don't want to wait until after Thanksgiving?" she says, sounding concerned.

"I'm sure. Besides, after Thanksgiving is Christmas, and then there's New Year's... I'd rather not wait until next year," I say. "I don't have that much stuff to pack anyway. I just moved back from Japan."

"Ah. That's right. I remember hearing about that when you came in for your interview." She *hmmm*s for a moment. "Let me send you our relocation agency's info. We have a contract with them. They'll arrange everything."

It feels amazing to have my life moving forward again. "I'd really appreciate it."

"And it's great you're starting so soon. We needed to fill the position ASAP. Just between you and me, Robbie's been pretty overwhelmed with the opening and all. We want to make sure everything goes without a hitch, you know."

"I'm glad the timing worked out."

"Cool. See you when you're settled in town?"

"Sure. Thanks."

I hang up and sit at the edge of my bed. This is a spectacular opportunity, and the medical center seems to be a great place to work.

A new beginning.

God, I need that after so many disasters. This is going to work out. I can feel it. I'm due for some good luck.

My phone buzzes with a new text. It's Erin. *OMG so exciting! Congrats! We should celebrate when you get to L.A.*

I smile and write back, *YES!* I then Facebook message Bennie. He'll kill me if he doesn't hear the big news from me directly. *You were right. Got the job, and L.A. bound!*

My hair still damp, I go downstairs, phone in the back pocket of my jeans. Darcy and Ray come out from the nursery with Mia in Darcy's arms. Seventeen months old, Mia is a delightful little princess with a bright pink dress with faux-fur trim around the square neckline and a small tiara in her hair.

"Good morning," Darcy says, and Mia squeals with delight at the sight of me, her ice-blue eyes bright.

My foster mother hands me the child, and I hold her slight weight close and smell her sweet toddler smell. Her cheeks are rosy from sleep, and I rub mine against hers as my heart expands with unbearable love.

Darcy runs her fingers through her meticulously cut bob, restoring a bit of order to the messy morning hair. Although her brown locks now have some silver, her sparkling gray eyes and open smile make her look younger than some women half her age. She's in a comfortable sweater, jeans and boots. Darcy was born into old money, but I've never seen her wear anything that looked ostentatious.

His pale blue eyes warm, Ray puts an arm around her, squeezing her shoulders. His hair is bright silver—having gone prematurely gray a while back. Not that the distinguished and professorial effect hurts him any.

"You're up early. Thought you got in late," Ray says.

"I couldn't sleep, so I got up for a short jog around

the neighborhood." I don't want to burden them with my unpleasant encounter with Blake.

"Good for you. Exercise helps clear the head," Darcy says. I know she's worried about me. Both of them were, after I told them what happened between me and Lucas. "How'd the interview go?"

"It went great. I just got an offer...which I have accepted."

A wide grin splits her face. "Good for you! I'm so proud of you."

"Congratulations, hon." Ray hugs me. "When do you start?"

"ASAP. Apparently my boss is swamped."

"Oh." Darcy's eyebrows rise. "Before Thanksgiving, then?"

I nod. "I'll come back to celebrate with you guys, though." Or at least I hope I will. I'll make it happen.

"No, don't," she says. "It's going to be exhausting, flying back and forth like that. Why don't we all celebrate it in L.A.? There's nothing that says we have to do it here."

I blink. "Are you sure?" Holidays are a big deal to Darcy. She spends a huge amount of time and effort decorating and cooking. "My place in L.A is most likely going to be small, and the kitchen won't..."

She pats my hand. "Thanksgiving isn't just about cooking and eating. It's about spending time with your loved ones. It's enough that you're in the States. Besides, it'd be fun to spend some time in California. Isn't that right, Ray?"

"Of course. We'll be delighted to." His smile says he can deny his wife nothing, that he's still deeply in love with her after decades of life together.

Suddenly I see with absolute clarity that I've wanted what Ray and Darcy have, and that Lucas is never going to be the one to give it to me. Our happy moments have been exactly that—moments. Not something we can build anything permanent on, no matter how much I want it to be different.

"Who's ready for some waffles?" Ray rubs his hands together. "We gotta celebrate."

Mia raises both hands and squeals, "Waffos!"

Darcy laughs, and I force a grin. "I'm always up for celebratory waffles."

Ray goes into the kitchen and wraps an apron around his waist. I hold the child that is both mine and not mine, soaking in her small and squirming warmth. I have awesome people around me. I'm going to be okay.

7

———

AVA

I THOUGHT I WOULDN'T HAVE MUCH TO DO FOR THE move—I mean, it's not like I have a lot of stuff—but there's the matter of finding a place and arranging things with the relocation agency. The rep sent me a list of suitable apartments, and I pore over everything with Ray and Darcy. She insists on furniture shopping, since she's a big believer of buying nice things to fill a new home. And every time we leave the house, I see Lucas's pot—how I think about it now—on the porch. Each reminder is like a knot forming in my throat. It's about time I emptied the thing and put it away. What did I promise myself when I started college?

Clean up your own messes. Don't be a burden. Be kind, but firm. Don't let anyone take advantage.

I bend down to pick up the terra cotta, then stop

when my phone rings. I straighten and check it. The call's from an unknown number in Virginia, but I answer anyway. It's probably about my impending move.

"Hello?"

"Is this Ava Huss?" The voice is male, brisk and professional.

"This is she."

"Excellent. My name is Don Peterson. I'm a lawyer representing Mr. Lucas Reed."

My mouth dries as panic flares. *Lucas got a lawyer? Why?*

He knows about Mia...and wants to take her away.

Don Peterson keeps talking, but I can't process anything through the roar in my head. Finally, he stops and says, "Does that make sense to you?"

I want to tell him none of it makes sense. Lucas doesn't want me, and Blake made it clear Lucas doesn't need me to inherit. So what gives?

"I'm sorry," I start, forcing myself to stay calm. "The connection was a little bad, and you got cut off here and there. Do you mind explaining again?" I swallow, then gird my loins and focus.

"Of course. Mr. Reed would like to give you the money he's promised and have you sign a document releasing him from any further liabilities or obligations to you."

My mind goes blank for a moment. *The money?* "I don't understand. What are you talking about?"

"It's my understanding that Mr. Reed promised

you two million dollars when you quit your job and returned to the States with him."

Quit my job. What a joke. Is that what he told his lawyer? I was forced out of my job, thanks to his maneuvering. And the money... What the hell? Does he think throwing some money at me is going to make me forget what he's done? There's nothing that can make me pretend he didn't lie to me. "You can tell *Mr. Reed* it isn't necessary. I don't need his money. I've told him so already."

The lawyer clears his throat. "I'm not sure you understand. The money is yours, free and clear."

"Didn't you say you represent Lucas?"

"Yes."

"So give him my message. This is good for your client, right? He's going to save himself two million bucks."

"Yes, bu—"

"Goodbye, Mr. Peterson. Please don't call back." I hang up, then empty the pot.

But putting it away doesn't make me feel liberated from the hold Lucas has over my heart. Perversely, I feel like I've misplaced something vital.

Come on. Ending things with Lucas is more for my benefit. Do I want to become like my mother, unable to leave a toxic man who used her without any sense of guilt or wrongdoing, just because he could? Do I want to set a poor example for Mia? I'd rather die than to have her look at me with embarrassment or pity.

I've already accepted that Lucas isn't the one to

give me the future I want. I really need to stop feeling so awful. Just...forget it all. Move on.

One day at a time.

I pull my shoulders back and look skyward, opening myself and letting the sunlight fall on my face. I inhale deeply. Eyes closed, I imagine all the negativity and ugly memories fleeing my body like exorcised demons as I expel the air from my lungs. I repeat this a few times, enough to feel more centered and calm.

A loud tire squeal shatters my Zen state. I open my eyes and see a black Mercedes skid to a stop. Lucas jumps out.

I shake my head. This has to be a hallucination. What else could explain his presence? He hasn't shown himself since I told him we were through.

But he doesn't disappear. He walks closer, his gait wide and slightly uneven. The look in his eye is cold enough to freeze nitrogen. A flush tinges his cheeks, and his lips are pressed white.

He's lost weight, I notice with a sudden pang. His pale sweater and dark jeans hang a bit too loosely off his frame, and the angles of his bones are as sharp.

The sight makes my heart ache, then soar, then ache again. I never wanted him to suffer when I made my point. I just wanted to be left alone, so I could rebuild my life. But he's here, and I wonder if he's going to ask me to give him another chance. The most lamentable thing is that I want to, even though I know I'm better off on my own. I'm so weak for him.

He stops a foot away. I can actually feel his body

heat across the distance. Awareness prickles through me, and I curl my hands by my sides and drink him in.

"Why did you say no?" he demands.

"To what?"

"What the hell's wrong with my money?"

Then I understand. "There's no point. You only offered the money to make up for the job I lost, but I found a new one, so..." I shrug. "I can take care of myself again."

"You *will* take the money."

"I will not." It feels too much like a payoff, like he's trying to buy my forgiveness. My dad used to do that, too, with me and my mom, and the memories still leave a bad taste.

His eyes flare. "You think this is about me buying you."

"Now where could I have gotten that idea? Oh, that's right. You offered me two million dollars." I smack my forehead. "Silly me."

"This isn't about any of—"

"What else could it possibly *be* about?"

"Closure." He takes a moment, then breathes out audibly. "I didn't go to Chiang Mai to get you back, Ava. I went there to finish things on my terms. Then I let my hormones derail my plan."

Hearing him say this makes me sick and hurt, because it confirms everything I suspected.

He continues, "Now I'm getting back on track."

"That"—my voice breaks a little in spite of myself—"involves giving me two million dollars?"

"Because that's what I promised. I want nothing left between us."

I swallow and gather myself. "I don't need a payoff to know there's nothing between us."

Something hard flits through his eyes. "I need to clear the debt. To make sure it doesn't come back to bite me in the ass. You understand why a man in my position needs to be careful."

"If I ever come after it, you can say you never promised anything."

"I'm not like you, Ava. I don't lie or lead people on."

"Lucas—"

"Take the fucking money and sign the form. You and I will be strangers."

"You think that will just...erase everything?"

"It will for me, and that's all I care about." He reaches out and cups my jaw. His skin is so warm against mine, and inside I'm crumbling like a pillar of sand at the small connection. "You said I was toxic. So take the money and make me go away."

My throat closes, and I can't speak. If he is poison... there's never been a sweeter one. I'm finally beginning to understand why my mother opted to self-destruct rather than let go of my father...even when he refused to marry her, forgot her birthdays, their anniversaries and Valentine's and holidays. She craved him more than her sanity, more than her self-respect.

And I can't do that.

Letting out a shuddering breath, I nod once. "All right."

His hand drops. I shiver with a sudden cold that has nothing to do with the weather.

"Don is couriering the paperwork today. Sign and notarize it by the end of the week."

With that parting remark, Lucas disappears into his car.

And I watch the man I'm still in love with drive away as my heart breaks again.

8

LUCAS

THE MOVE TO THE WEST COAST TAKES FIVE DAYS
to arrange, even though Blake's place is fully furnished
and I only need to bring some clothes and shoes. It isn't
the actual move that takes the time, but making sure
Gail and the staff will be all right. She and the land-
scapers have been with me for over two years. There's
no way I'm dumping them into the unemployment
office just because I'm leaving Charlottesville.

Then there's the paperwork from Don. Ava
scrawled her signature on the dotted line and the document has been duly notarized. It should've made the
weight on my shoulders ease, but somehow it seems to
have moved to the center of my heart where it sits like a
boulder—hard, uncomfortable and impossible to ignore.

Now I'm on the plane, less than an hour away from

landing in L.A. "So you're not mad, right?" Rachel asks over the phone. We've spent the last forty-five minutes going over items for my arrival.

I gaze at my knuckles and brush them against my pants. "Do you want me to be?"

"No, of course not," she says hurriedly. "It's just I know how much you hate interference."

"I'm not insanely happy that you went to Blake, but I understand why you did."

She sighs. "Thanks, boss. I just didn't know what to do when Gail called. She sounded so worried."

"I know."

"I'll meet you in L.A. next week."

"Don't bother." Rachel doesn't enjoy flying, and I don't ask her to travel on my behalf unless it's unavoidable. "I have something else for you to work on."

"Oh?"

"I'm going to start giving speeches, and maybe taking on a few interesting projects."

"Really?" The single word rises high, almost making me wince. "Are you sure?"

"Yeah. Why do you sound so shocked?"

"Um. Well. I turned down like seven offers without reviewing them less than two hours ago."

"Then tell them there's been an error and review their propositions. Send me the ones that look the most promising." She's been with me a while and knows what I'll find interesting.

"Will do. Anything else?"

"Nope. I trust that you got everything squared away."

"Great. Glad you're back, boss."

"I'm not going to be in Seattle."

"I know, but this is better than you not working and always flying out to that...town."

I pause. Rachel never pretends she doesn't know what's going on in my life. We've been together too long for those kind of games. But her sudden hesitation makes me grit my teeth. She must've sensed that everything went bad in Charlottesville.

Damn it. Am I that transparent?

Of course you are, moron. Why else would Elizabeth have sent the info to get you to go after Ava?

I make a face, suddenly annoyed with myself. Modulating my tone, I say, "I'm finished with that town, now that everything's been resolved." With Ava's signature at the end of a two-page agreement. "Time to find something else, keep myself occupied so I don't die from boredom."

"Perfect. I'll also let Nate Sterling know you'll be in L.A. for the medical center opening tonight. He asked me about it, and I sort of demurred."

"Good. I'm going to do what I can for that center." Even if my initial interest was due to Ava, I'm not going to turn my back on the project. It's a worthy one, something that could really benefit the community.

"I'll send you the latest schedule."

We hang up. Within fifteen minutes, the cabin

attendant serves me another glass of ice wine and informs me that we're ready to land. Finally.

I look out the window. Los Angeles suburbs have begun to appear through wispy desert clouds, grids of streets laid out on a sere and tawny land. Here and there are green patches, where new homeowners have hooked up their sprinklers. I'm as far from Virginia as I can be without fleeing the lower forty-eight.

Fleeing? What the fuck. It's not fleeing. I'm *leaving.*

You're toxic.

My teeth grind together. *So are you, Ava. You with your bullshit test and bullshit words.*

I'm not letting her destroy me, strip me of everything until all I can think about is pleasing her. I've been down that destructive path before. Never again.

Two million bucks is my way of clearing the slate, making sure we have nothing more between us, so I can move on. Scars or no scars, I'm young, rich and smart. I don't need Ava.

I don't need anyone.

The car that's waiting for me is a freshly waxed Bentley SUV. Someone loads my lone suitcase into the back while the driver holds the door open. He's in his late thirties, his hair a pale gold and eyes ice blue... coloration that reminds me of Ava. He has to go.

No, don't. If you do that, you're letting her win.

He can stay. Thoughts of Ava don't necessarily imply desire. They can be contempt...disgust...

I climb into the car and get taken to Blake's penthouse. The traffic in L.A. sucks, cars sitting on roads, burning up gas. But at least here I can be free, away from the ugly memories and hateful indictment of what I am.

Leaning back in my seat, I think about my immediate objectives for the next two months.

One: start working.

Two: find a wife—preferably someone who doesn't find me toxic and gross. Now that I've come this far, I might as well help my siblings get the damned paintings. Fuck my father and his Bitch Number Six.

Three: forget Ava. Purge her as completely as possible from my life, my thoughts...my memory.

My phone buzzes with an email from Rachel. She's already found the five most promising propositions to help me achieve Goal Number One. I take a quick look.

The first is a leadership speech for a Fortune 500 retreat in Vegas. Not bad. The rest are startup-related items. My twin brother Elliot does consulting for tech firms and startups to keep himself out of trouble...not that that's helped. I only do them when I feel like it—which is the case now. The one about online cognitive behavioral therapy seems the most interesting. I make a mental note to look into it more closely.

I glance outside, and there's a platinum blonde on the sidewalk. Something about the way she's walking seems so familiar, my heart stops for a moment. The woman is slender, wearing a simple lavender dress. Her long hair hangs down a trim back, and as the car passes,

I crane my neck to get a better look. She's into something on her phone, a small smile on her lips. A pair of sunglasses hides her eyes.

The traffic picks that moment to finally start moving, and the car speeds up, pulling away. Damn it. My pulse throbs unevenly.

Ava. Ava. Ava.

Damn it. I run a palm roughly down my face. Just what the hell is wrong with me? I left Charlottesville to forget her, and look at me—pitifully hopeful and full of pain in my heart.

Remember the third objective—*forget Ava*. Fuck her. She set me up.

I breathe through my mouth. *Patience.* It's taken years for Ava to dig her claws into me; it's going to take a while to rip them out. One day at a time. And I'm going to get rid of her, even if I have to give up a chunk of myself in the process—the way lizards break their tails off to free themselves.

Suddenly, the engine stops. "We're here, sir," the driver says, opening the door.

I step out, then stretch my left leg. The muscles feel tight and achy. The excessive jogging in Charlottesville didn't help, and the long flight aggravated it further. But I embrace the pain. It's distracting me from thoughts of Ava.

On the other hand... I wince as I walk. Damn, that hurts, and my lower body hates me. Why shouldn't it? I've been pretty nasty to it in the past few days.

Well, my self-abuse phase is over. I'm going to baby

the leg until it feels better, and I'm going to make sure to put myself first. I've cut people out of my life before. I can do it again.

I grasp the handle of my suitcase and walk into the building where Blake's penthouse occupies the top three levels. The lobby is so ostentatious I'm almost embarrassed. Only a person with no sense of proportion would live in a place like this. Everything is done in gold, with shiny brass accents and a smartly dressed concierge in a light caramel uniform. The chandeliers hanging from the high ceiling are contemporary, but no less showy for that. But then Blake compulsively displays his wealth whenever he's around the Pryce side of the family, and most of them live out here. I go to the elevator bank and take the one waiting with its doors wide open.

One side of the car is made of glass—an acrophobe's nightmare. I punch the five-digit PIN to access the penthouse level, and the car starts moving immediately. Everything on the ground grows smaller until I only see dots and small boxes moving. Exactly what I want—to be away from everyone.

When the elevator opens, I'm in a foyer. It's cozy compared to what I've seen of the building so far. A white vase with an Asian arrangement of plum blossoms sits on a dark cherry table. My shoes make sharp sounds on the smooth, spotless dark green and blue marble. I enter the key code Blake gave me, and the double doors unlock with a quiet click.

I step inside. Blake's penthouse is nothing like the

lobby. Airy and open and done predominantly in white and chrome and glass, the place is even bigger than I expected. The staggered lofts on the second and third levels overlook the living and dining area, with a huge kitchen under a high ceiling. The lights are recessed, and a black Steinway baby grand piano takes the place of honor by the floor-to-ceiling window. Blake plays occasionally, although I don't see the point of owning something like a baby grand when he's so rarely in L.A. Out on the deck is a pool, another pointless luxury item, since—unlike Elliot—Blake doesn't swim much. It's probably considered a selling point, though. Californians love their pools.

"Surprise!"

I pause, then blink at the sight of Elizabeth coming toward me with a big grin. She's as beautiful as usual, her artfully curled golden hair bouncing around her slender shoulders, brown eyes warm and friendly. The sleeveless raw silk pink dress she wears is fitted, making her look even slimmer.

Before I can pull back, she envelops me in a hug. "I'm so glad you're here."

"You mean you have more schemes up your—" I don't get to say the rest, as my siblings pour out of their hiding places in the kitchen.

Ryder reaches me first, his bare feet quiet across the marble floor. He is disgustingly good looking—a pure genetic lottery winner. The dark, chiseled looks have women around the world panting and men gnashing their teeth with envy. A white T-shirt and jeans set off the lean physique he's spent countless hours in the gym to create. Once he's within my personal space, he slaps me on the back. I just grunt.

My identical twin Elliot pumps my hand. Unscarred, he's what I'd look like if I hadn't had the accident. He's dressed casually in a fancy black synthetic fiber T-shirt and khaki shorts. From their reactions, you'd think I'd survived a war to reach L.A. Blake, always the reticent one, merely nods in the back. Given his dress shirt and slacks, he probably had a business meeting earlier.

"You've met Paige already, right?" Ryder says, gesturing at his former assistant. She's a big, brown-eyed blonde glowing with pregnancy. Her belly is showing now, but an elegant blue dress makes her look chic rather than awkward.

Paige hugs me, which is a little uncomfortable. If she notices my stiffness, she doesn't show it. "Good to see you in town again, Lucas."

"Likewise," I say for politeness's sake.

I spot a stunning redhead standing by Elliot. She must be the infamous stripper. Contrary to what I've imagined, she doesn't look like a crass, money-grubbing ho. There's softness that says she's a woman of quality. The makeup on her face is light, just enough to accentuate her high cheekbones and pretty lips. Her beige halter-neck dress is cut modestly, the hem almost reaching her knees.

"My wife, Belle," Elliot says, putting an arm around her waist.

"A pleasure." I smile. I'm not a completely hopeless ogre, even if I often feel like one.

Her shoulders relax perceptibly. "I'm thrilled to finally meet you."

"Sorry I missed your introductory reception. I wasn't fit company then."

Blake raises an eyebrow, but nobody's paying attention other than me. "It's good you didn't show," he says. "Thanks to our father's idiot wife, the whole party ended up a clusterfu..."

I'm wondering what on earth could make Blake *not* say what's on his mind when a young girl—fourteen or so—comes out. She's pretty, with wide-set eyes and soft brown hair pulled back into a ponytail. She wears a fitted red shirt that reads *I Love Hollywood* and cropped teal pants with ballet flats. I cock an eyebrow at Blake.

It's Belle who answers my silent question. "That's my sister Nonny." She waves the girl over. "Come say hello to your new brother-in-law."

The title is a bit of a shock. Apparently I've just acquired an impressionable teenage sister. What am I supposed to do with *her*?

The girl raises a hand shyly. "Hi. Nice to meet you."

"You too." I turn my attention to my siblings. "What are you guys all doing here?"

"Welcoming you home, silly," Elizabeth says. "We haven't been together like this in ages."

She has a point. The summons a few months back to our father's new estate in Virginia doesn't count.

"I don't know about you, but I miss that. At least when we were younger, we spent summers and winter vacations together in Europe. In the last few years, we've barely had any quality time." Elizabeth gestures at the dining table. There are a couple of bottles of champagne chilling in a silver ice bucket. "Let's have a toast!"

I go along with it, although I wonder if she's angling for brownie points. If she believes a toast is going to absolve her from meddling in my life, she has another think coming.

Ryder and Elliot expertly uncork the bottles, and everyone gets a flute except Belle, Paige and Nonny, who all opt for ginger ale instead. I look at Belle. "I'm sure people won't mind if you have a little bubbly."

She smiles. "I want to join the non-alcohol girls."

Paige puts a hand on Belle's arm. "Lucas is right. You don't have to."

Elliot wraps an arm around Belle's shoulders. "She doesn't have to, but she wants to. Don't worry, I'll drink two to make up for it."

Laughing, Paige rolls her eyes, while Belle smiles up at Elliot like he just gave her a yacht. I'm not fooled by my twin's little act there. Is Belle a recovering alcoholic? If so, how does she deal with his drinking? Elliot imbibes so much scotch he might as well get it through an IV.

Blake clears his throat to get everyone's attention.

"To us. May our father rue the day he decided to f— interfere in our lives."

Amen. I lift my flute, then sip the champagne. It's good—none of my siblings do bad alcohol.

"So how long are you staying in L.A.?" Paige asks.

"Indefinitely, at this point," I respond.

"Then you're coming to the opening of Nate Sterling's new hospital tonight?" Elizabeth asks. Nate is her cousin's brother-in-law, although she's known him since forever. The Sterlings are important if one of your goals in life is to play Mother Theresa. There aren't many families as wealthy and influential. "It's sort of an opening-plus-fundraiser."

"I'll go if he's invited a lot of unattached women," Blake says.

"They may all flee in terror. You've got a reputation," Ryder says.

Elizabeth shakes her head. "Blake doesn't have a reputation. He just hasn't met the right person yet." She turns to our oldest brother. "And to answer your question, yes, Nate did invite a lot of single women."

Perfect. I could use some gratuitous female company. Besides, I already promised. "I'll be there."

Elliot gives me a look. "Really?"

"It's for a good cause, and I can use the tax deduction." I shrug. "Besides, I'm the one who encouraged Nate to do the hospital project."

"That's great." Elizabeth beams, while Elliot stares at me like I've grown a horn in the center of my forehead.

"It's gonna be boring," he says. "Skip it and come to my place for dinner instead."

"I'll bail early if it is. And take a rain check on the dinner." I meet his eyes squarely and shove both hands into my pants pockets, fingernails digging into my palms. "But you heard what Elizabeth said about the women. It's about time I get to work on fulfilling our father's condition."

Ryder's jaw drops, his eyes almost bugging out. If I weren't so heartsore with what happened with Ava, I'd probably laugh. "I thought you'd rather die," he says.

"Changed my mind." I let my gaze sweep over my siblings. "You guys want the paintings, right?"

Except for Blake, they nod, one by one, their motions a bit uncertain. Not surprising, given how strenuously I protested before.

Abruptly I pull out my hands and let them hang by my sides. "All right, then. Stop complaining."

9

Ava

It takes two days to move and begin settling into L.A. Thank God for the relocation agency. It found me a reasonably priced, furnished apartment about an hour away from the medical center, plus the staff assisted me with used car shopping. I dreaded the prospect, girding my loins to deal with oily salesmen out to rip me off, but I ended up buying from an international student at UCLA who was leaving the country and wanted to get rid of her gently driven Toyota Camry. Only two years old, it's silver and has very few miles on it. The price was quite reasonable as well, since she wanted to be able to sell without having to deal with a middleman.

All in all, I managed everything with the money I saved while working in Osaka and the small signing bonus I received from the medical center. The two million dollars from Lucas sits tight in a separate bank account so I won't even see it. What I wanted from him wasn't monetary, and in the end the sole reason I decided to accept it was Mia. She may never know her father, but she can at least get some financial help from him. Ray and Darcy would never let her suffer, but the world is an uncertain place, and I don't want Mia to be vulnerable and without resources.

The second I'm ensconced in the city, I start working. Robbie turns out to be an absolute slave driver, which is actually nice. Keeping busy makes me too tired to think about Lucas and what happened. I can't believe it's been less than a month since that amazing time at the bed and breakfast...when I thought the world could be mine for the asking.

I should've known better. Stuff like that doesn't happen to people like me. Only in movies and books, where reality doesn't matter.

The medical center opening reception is tonight, it's a big deal, and Robbie is in charge. I close my laptop and rush out to grab a quick bite. Should've brown-bagged it, but I got home late yesterday and didn't want to bother.

The L.A. sun is blinding out on the sidewalks, actually making my eyes water. I put on a pair of sunglasses and walk a couple of blocks, my feet in purple flats that match my lavender dress. There's an eatery near the office that's owned by an immigrant couple from Tijuana. They speak excellent English with only the slightest accent. It's popular in the area because of the low price and tasty food.

"Chicken burrito with guacamole," I order. The sunglasses helped my eyes, but now my mouth is watering with anticipation. As much as I loved the food in Japan, they didn't do Mexican very well.

The owner grins and quickly makes me a burrito that's about the size of the business end of a baseball bat. I'm still not used to the portion sizes in America.

I pay and turn around, about to leave, then bump into a man in a navy suit. "Excuse me," I murmur, although I'm sort of annoyed that he's standing so close to me. *Personal space, hellooooo...*

"Ava?"

I snap my head up and blink at the familiar face. "Oh my gosh. *Jon?*"

Jon Barkley's face splits from ear to ear. "The one and only."

"What are you doing here?" I ask. "Last I heard, you were working for a big audit firm in San Francisco." He graduated a year ahead of me from UVA. Accounting. We were in the same dorm my first year and went out a few times.

"Yeah, I quit that. Work at a bank now, just a couple blocks over. But I thought you moved to Japan. You here on vacation?"

"No. I work at a medical center. Just started."

"Good for you!"

He seems genuinely glad to see me. I stare at the perfect, straight white teeth, then the well-formed, even features topped by neatly cropped sandy brown hair. It's a really nice face, the kind that should get me flushed and attracted. He has a nice body, too, hard and strong. It's obvious he works out and eats right.

"We should have coffee. Catch up," he offers.

That is such a great idea. Jon is perfect. *Normal.* I'm certain he doesn't have a father who's demanding that he marry to inherit some pricey painting.

So what if my pulse isn't racing? Chemistry is overrated.

"Sure. What's your number?" I pull out my phone, and we exchange digits.

"If you want, we could meet after work tonight. Grab something to eat. I know a few nice places around here," Jon says.

"I'd love to, but not tonight. Work function." I flush, suddenly not wanting him to think I'm blowing him off. "The medical center has an official opening reception today, and I'm supposed to be there." Then I remember something Robbie said earlier that morning. He wanted to know if I was going to bring a date, suggesting it'd be good if I did. I said probably not, since I didn't know anyone I could bring...

Before I lose my nerve, I say, "But if you're free... would you like to attend the opening with me? I don't have anyone to go with, and my boss seems to think it'll make him look like less of a slave driver if I bring a plus-one."

"Formal?"

"Yes," I say.

"I can do that. Text me the details, and I'll pick you up."

"Actually, I'm leaving directly from work, so it'll be better if we just meet there."

"Cool. I look forward to it." He gives me another great smile and pretends to shoot me with his thumb and forefinger.

I smile back and leave with my lunch. My mind churns a bit, then starts chiding me. I shouldn't have asked Jon. It's like some kind of rebound...but worse because Jon is actually pretty cool, and I do like him as a friend.

I argue logically, of course. There is no harm in reconnecting with him precisely because he *is* a nice guy and I *do* like him. Who knows? This may grow into something. Back in the day, every one of my friends who met him liked him too.

I text him the event info. His answer is almost instantaneous. *Great. See you there.*

Perfect. Seeing him is exactly what I need. My new beginning isn't just the new job, but a new everything.

I'll be fine. I know I will, I tell myself as I rub the aching spot on my chest.

10

Ava

"So... Final check for the opening reception tonight," Robbie begins, stopping by my cubicle. He's in a pale button-down shirt and khakis, which I've dubbed "Robbie Style." I haven't yet seen him in anything else, and am starting to suspect he doesn't own any other clothes. "Everything good?"

"On target," I say with a smile. "Don't worry."

He huffs. "I'm not used to dealing with nonprofit medical centers like this. Nate barely gave me any warning about this grand opening fundraiser."

I suppress a smile. Apparently Robbie—whose previous positions were in health care management—has never had to do a fundraiser before. He's been a bit frazzled.

"If he's going to invite all those rich people, why not

ask them to chip in?" I ask lightly. Surely they can spare some change for the poor. Stop all those minor illnesses from becoming something major because of money.

"Right." He exhales roughly. "Don't forget you have to be there tonight."

I almost roll my eyes at his tenth reminder. "Don't worry. I'll *be* there."

"Okay. See you tonight then." Robbie hurries toward the elevator. Something else I learned since started working here—Robbie's previous easy and slow manners were for my benefit, so it didn't look like he was rushing me through the tour. Normally he moves so fast it looks like he's practically jogging.

Since the opening reception is a fairly fancy event, I shut down my laptop a little bit early so I can prettify myself and get to the hotel where the reception will be held. I need to change into a more formal dress than the simple lavender one I'm wearing. Thankfully I have a classic black cocktail dress that's right for the occasion —yay for impulsive clearance rack browsing—and I freshen up my makeup. As I squeeze my feet into pointy-toed heels, I sigh. I miss Japan and its love of comfy but stylish shoes. But there's no way I'm wearing flats at a function like this.

The opening of the center is a big deal. One of the main tenets of the medical center is that you deserve to be treated with dignity and respect the moment you walk through the door. Bennie once remarked that rich people probably need to do this to earn a ticket to heaven, but I don't care about the motive. If there'd been more guilt-laden rich people in the town where we grew up, Mom could've gotten the care she needed.

The hotel where Nate Sterling decided to host the event is modern and chic, just like the medical center. Contemporary art and furniture fill the sleek main lobby, and the reception hall is huge, with a smooth marble floor and rectangular chandeliers that look totally space-age. The hotel management is sponsoring the event—thank God—so we're hosting it there for free. I can't imagine how much it would cost otherwise...although from what I can tell, Nate isn't the type to care about money.

Just like Lucas.

Then I mentally smack myself. *You decided not to think about him anymore, remember?* I moved across the entire damn continent to put distance between us, so I wouldn't be tempted to check for women's cars parked in his driveway.

This too shall pass. Bad moments disappear if you stand strong. And I don't care what it costs: I *will* be the last one standing.

I do a final check with the hotel staff to make sure the arrangements are perfect. Thankfully, everyone's professional and on top of things. Nobody seems to notice or care that the event is really to benefit the poor. Their attitude surprises me; the poor always seem to get snubbed or patronized in subtle ways.

Within half an hour, the reception hall starts to fill with people in expensive designer clothes and jewelry. I scan the crowd, then spot Jon stepping inside. He's changed into a fresh suit—this one is dark gray, giving him a little extra gravitas—and I have to admit he looks fantastic. I go over to him.

"You made it."

"Of course." He looks around. "This is awesome."

"It is, isn't it?" I grin. "Come on. I'm supposed to mingle until needed."

"Cool." He snatches two flutes of bubbly from a server and hands me one. "To reconnecting."

I clink my glass against his. "Cheers." I take a sip, let the flavor of crisp alcohol fill my mouth. It's almost as good as what I had on Lucas's plane. And the second the thought enters my mind, I stiffen, unable to help myself.

"What's wrong?" Jon asks.

"Have to be on my best behavior," I fib. "My boss is coming our way."

Robbie reaches us in the next five seconds. He's dashing in a navy suit, and escorting a slim middle-aged Asian woman in a bright red dress that flatters her complexion and vivid coloring.

"Robbie," I say.

"Great job, Ava. You've done well," he says. "This your date?"

"Yes. Meet Jon Barkley. We went to school together." I turn to Jon. "This is my boss, Robbie Choi."

Both men beam, and they shake hands.

"Jay, meet my new assistant Ava. I couldn't have pulled it off without her help. Ava, my wife."

Jay shakes my hand, her grip firm and strong. She

also gives Jon's hand a couple of determined pumps. "Lovely to meet you, Ava. Robbie can't stop singing your praises."

Is it my imagination, or is there a hint of censure in her tone? I blink once and look at her face. She's smiling expectantly, and I realize I should say something. "Oh, I haven't done much except help. This is Robbie's event."

"Nonsense," she says. "Behind every great man is a capable woman."

She seems nice, but my internal alarm is blaring. I force a smile. "He has you."

"And now you as well." She turns to Robbie. "I think I'll go grab something to drink..."

"I'm fine. I have to check on a few things."

"All right, then. I'll leave you to it." She walks away.

Robbie flashes a quick grin, but somehow it looks tight. "I'm hoping you'll mingle and get to meet the people on the list I gave you."

Despite myself, I flinch inwardly. The list contains Elizabeth Pryce-Reed, and the last person I want to see is someone from Lucas's family—the people he never wanted me to meet...people who must've known why he was pretending to care about me.

Robbie continues, "Those are the most likely donors for our cause, and they'll be more receptive if they know you and like you."

Not even my own parents thought I was worth anything, but I can probably fake it for a bit. After all, I won't be spending more than a few minutes with each of them, and I can probably avoid Elizabeth. Let someone else woo her. "Okay."

He nods his approval and introduces me to a few people to start. After that, I'm on my own, along with Jon. "Sorry," I say with a cringe. "I didn't realize he'd ask me to mingle with people neither of us know."

Jon shrugs. "I expected it to be that kind of event. I've had to attend a few for work reasons."

So, Jon's hand at my elbow, I do as instructed. I don't know how Robbie keeps track of all the people. They start to blend together after a while. It's much worse than meeting a class of new students. At least there was a seating chart with names to help me remember. And it doesn't help that my shoes are starting to kill me. I'm not used to being in heels for so long.

Jon runs into a former client, and I quietly excuse myself while they chat. A short break won't be remiss. I'll go out to the lobby, sit in a quiet corner for a few minutes and make notes of the people I got a good reading on for follow-ups.

I start to return to the party, then stop when I see Elizabeth coming in my direction. She's even prettier in person, all delicate bones and gentle curves wrapped in ivory silk. Naturally blond, she looks nothing like Lucas. If I didn't know from my Google searches, I would never suspect they're related.

All the things I read about her flash through my mind. *Angel. Champion of the Poor and the Hungry.*

Charity Queen. No cause for the less fortunate too small to be ignored.

But she's taking part in a scheme to marry some unsuspecting man for financial gain—a painting worth millions. Just because she has a perfect public persona doesn't mean she's the same in private. I should know—all you have to do is look at Dad. Or Mom. They both played the loving, struggling parent to perfection until death did them, and I was the one left hurting.

Not wanting to face Elizabeth, I turn and go to the opposite end of the lobby. There's a door that leads to the restroom, but I also spot a looping staircase to the second level with restaurants and gift shops. I turn and start to climb the steps.

The skin at the nape of my neck prickles, and I look over my shoulder. A dark-haired man has intercepted Elizabeth, and she smiles at him, but her gaze flicks in my direction.

I make a loop and return to the opposite end of the lobby from where she is. I put a hand over my chest. I doubt she wanted to see me for a donation. Most likely she wants to try to persuade me to marry Lucas so the siblings can get their paintings.

I breathe in, but my lungs are tight. *Need some fresh air.* I go toward the main entrance.

A crisply uniformed valet brings out a black limo and hands the keys to a waiting driver. A couple is standing to the side, waiting to get into the car. I shiver as the cool evening air brushes my bare arms.

The woman turns her head, arches an eyebrow as

she notices me and whispers something into the man's ear. My lips part. It's Faye Belbin. The jet-black hair, the pale skin and the dainty face are unmistakable. A low-cut royal-blue dress clings to her stunning body like she had it glued on.

Then the man shifts and I see the unforgettable profile—*Lucas*. His presence slams into me like a sucker punch, and it's all I can do to remain standing.

Faye tilts her head, and her gaze locks with mine. A corner of her mouth quirks up, and she pulls Lucas closer and kisses him, her eyes still on me.

He's still thin, but the black suit fits him like a glove, showing off his wide, strong shoulders. Hot and cold move through me swiftly, and I can barely breathe.

A low moan tears from someplace deep in my throat. The longer they kiss, the more my flesh seems to flay. I bite my lower lip, hoping the physical pain will overwhelm the crippling ache in my heart.

The driver opens the door, and Faye drags Lucas into the car like some mythical siren, their mouths still fused. Lucas palms her waist, and the door shuts.

I clench my shaking hands, then clasp them together. It's not just my hands—my whole body's trembling.

He's moved on. The only person who hasn't is me. My reaction tonight proves that. If I ever meant anything, he couldn't have done what he just did with Faye so soon after the breakup. His "I'm in love with you" was fake, a lie, just like everything else he's ever said to me.

But telling myself that doesn't lessen the hurt. Blinking away tears, I turn back to the hotel. Lucas might've gutted me, but I still have work to do. And I have a date waiting for me inside.

"Oh my God, is that *you*?"

What now? I sniffle, then turn. The air whooshes out of my lungs. It's my half-sister, Elle—my father's real daughter.

It would be impossible for this night to get any worse.

We both have our father's hair, but her eyes are green like her mother's. Elle's in a slinky red dress, her thick blond mane twisted into a fancy updo. "What..." She shakes her head. "What are you doing here? Shouldn't you be back in Hicksville, Virginia?"

"I'm working. What are *you* doing here?" Elle's family was in Northern Virginia last time I checked, and she works for some bank in Boston.

She shifts her weight and straightens. "I'm here to support the poor, of course. My fiancé's family is into stuff like that."

Right. Her Harvard lawyer fiancé, a man who gazes at her like she's the center of his universe. And unlike me, what Elle has is real. A girl like her doesn't get played by slick guys full of empty words.

"I can't believe you're in L.A. working for a hotel."

I shake my head. "I'm not. I work for the Sterling Medical Center."

"You've *got* to be kidding me."

I merely stare at her.

She huffs and looks off into the distance. "Damn it. This is a disaster."

"Why?"

"Why do you *think*? Cedric can't know about a familial blemish like you. And what would his parents think?"

I realize that I don't measure up to anybody's idea of perfection, but being called a *blemish* is a little too much. "Why would they find out about me unless you blab? Do you think I'm proud we're related?"

Her complexion turns red. "Are you serious?" She rests her hands on her waist. "It's your mother who caused all the trouble. She should've left Dad alone. He was *married*."

"And if *your* mother"—I sneer—"had been a better wife, maybe he wouldn't have strayed. It takes two to tango. Don't forget, Elle, men like us crude, crass girls, too." For a cheap, dirty thrill that leaves the woman feeling worthless and used, but Elle doesn't need to know that.

"Are you done?"

I'm not, but I don't want to fight. If her fiancé's family are potential donors, antagonizing them won't go over well with Robbie.

"Oh, there you are!" comes a soft voice.

Damn it. I close my eyes for a moment. *Elizabeth.*

Elle's demeanor instantly changes. "Oh my goodness, Elizabeth! So good to see you again."

"Likewise, Elle. You look beautiful. Engagement must agree with you."

Elle flushes.

"You've made Cedric so happy."

"Thank you."

"Do you mind giving us some privacy?" Elizabeth says, gesturing at me. "There are a few items I need to discuss with Ava."

Elle glances between me and Elizabeth. "Of course. It's always a chore, isn't it, instructing the help?"

My cheeks redden at the snub. She is *just* like her obnoxious mother. I press my lips together and wait for Elizabeth to join the snotty fun.

"I'm afraid you're mistaken, Elle. Ava is a valuable member of the Sterling Medical Center. I'm here to consult, not instruct." The pleasant expression on Elizabeth's face remains the same, and her voice is just as sweet. But a subtle shift in body language makes it clear she's just delivered a rebuke.

Elle looks at me again, this time less certain. "Oh. Well, my mistake. I'll get going now. I hope you have a productive talk."

"We will." Elizabeth smiles warmly. Once we're alone, she extends her hand. "I'm Elizabeth Pryce-Reed."

I ignore her hand. I don't want anything to do with people related to Lucas. "I know."

I wait for her to be upset, maybe deliver a reprimand the way she did to Elle. Instead, she drops her hand back to her side and smiles. "I like you."

"You don't even know me." I wrap my arms around myself. "If you're here to ask me to help Lucas fulfill the conditions so you guys can get the paintings, forget it."

"I would never ask you to do that."

I snort. "Really? Why don't I believe you?"

She regards me quietly for a moment, and there is compassion in her gaze. "I saw you watching him with Faye."

My face heats. Goddamn it. The last thing I want is public humiliation. "You must've enjoyed the show."

"You care about him."

"What do you want me to do about it?"

"Has he told you he loves you?"

I can't hold her eyes anymore. She's seeing too far into me, and I hate that, even though I'm certain Lucas told her everything. "Don't you know?"

"What am I supposed to know?"

"Didn't he tell you how he couldn't act well enough to convince me? 'I'm in love with you.'" I look up and blink as my vision blurs. The memory of it still hurts. The pain is doubly bad after having seen him with Faye. "What a joke."

With horror, I realize I'm crying, and turn away.

"Come on." Elizabeth wraps an arm around me and leads me into an alcove behind a giant planter to give us some privacy. She hands me an embroidered handkerchief from her clutch. "He didn't lie, Ava."

I dab at my eyes furiously. "Sure. That's why he's already moving on to the next candidate—"

"He's with her because you didn't fight for him."

NADIA LEE

My hand fists around the damp handkerchief. "Oh, bullshit."

"I know he loves you. Otherwise he would've never stayed in Charlottesville or gone after you in Asia." A beat of silence. "Where I sent him."

My mouth opens. I wondered why he waited so long before coming after me. To learn that it was Elizabeth's doing—it's the last thing I suspected. "You?"

She nods. "I tracked you down and let him know."

Anger blazes through me. "You must really want those paintings."

"They aren't my main concern. I want Lucas to be happy. I thought you could do that for each other."

"You know what people say about *assuming*."

She sighs. "I'm sorry his love wasn't enough for you."

Bitterness churns inside me. It takes all my control to maintain a somewhat civil tone. "He *never* loved me. It was all about those damn paintings."

"You couldn't be more wrong. He never wanted to marry for them. He told us that loud and clear when our father threw that...ridiculous proposition in our faces." Elizabeth pauses. "Has he ever hinted he wanted to marry you? Or done anything to trap you into marriage?"

"He was working up to it. He forced me to come to the States. Got me fired at my old job."

Elizabeth's mouth thins. "He's used to getting things his way. But did he ever ask you to marry him?"

I shake my head. "He knew I'd never say yes without some serious convincing."

She gazes at me somberly. "You can draw whatever conclusions you like, Ava. But don't blame Lucas for being with another woman if you aren't willing to fight for what you want."

Her words hit me like a backhand. Elizabeth has no right to lecture me like this. She's nobody to me, and I don't trust her motives. She might be a saint, but that doesn't mean she doesn't want the paintings, too. "Maybe a pretty girl from a nice family doesn't understand what it's like for people like me, but wanting and fighting aren't always enough."

Elizabeth moves forward, and I almost take a step back before I catch myself.

"You're awfully prejudiced, aren't you?" she says.

"*Prejudiced?*"

"Dismissing me for my appearance and background."

"And what else do I have to go on? It's presumptuous of you to act like you know me, and I don't believe you're on my side."

"I know you—and your circumstances—far better than you think. Including your daughter."

It's like she's thrown a bucket of iced water over me. Is this a threat—that she'll take my child away? I'd never be able to stop Lucas's family. They're too powerful, too connected. "I don't have a daughter." I manage to force the words out through numb lips.

Elizabeth sighs, letting her shoulders droop for a

second before straightening again. "Because you gave her away. You shouldn't have. We would've taken her in."

"No, you wouldn't." I throw the handkerchief at her.

She lets it drop to the floor, over her stilettos.

"And there's no reason for you to 'take her in'. She's not Lucas's," I say firmly.

I start walking away. Her gaze on my back feels like a knife digging between my shoulder blades. My hands are shaking again, and I make fists so she won't see how badly I'm reacting. *How does Elizabeth know about Mia?*

I stop at the revolving door leading outside—I don't even remember how I got there—and turn around. Elizabeth is gone.

11

LUCAS

I PULL AWAY FROM FAYE AS THE LIMO DOOR CLOSES behind us. "Did you get the reaction you wanted?"

"Oh yes. My snotty little ex is probably drying his tears on his tux sleeves." She smiles. "Thank you."

"My pleasure."

A revenge kiss is the least I can do. She's being a good sport about coming to the opening at the last minute. Contrary to what I've repeatedly told myself, I'm not in the right frame of the mind to be good company to some strange woman at a function I don't really want to attend.

And being at the opening has put more of a damper on my mood than I expected. I kept thinking about what Ava said about her life while growing up. So poor she never went to the hospital unless she felt like she was dying.

That memory is the reason I cut the evening short. I'm not like Ryder, who can fake his way through anything for days if necessary.

"You look tired," Faye says.

"A little."

"Come up to my suite. You can stretch out and have a drink."

I smile wanly at her cheery tone. "Okay."

The limo ride to her hotel doesn't take much time. The hotel doorman rushes over, and we climb out together. Her suite is on the top floor. The living room is sizable and elegantly furnished with ivory leather couches and contemporary tables—exactly the type of interior she prefers. Through the open door I see that a huge four-poster bed with a translucent canopy dominates the bedroom.

I take a seat on the biggest couch and rest my left foot on the ottoman, relieving the tension in the leg. Faye goes to the minibar and brings out two glasses of whiskey. Tucking her feet underneath her, she sits next to me and nestles closer. I let an arm drape around her and absentmindedly caress her bare shoulder as I knock the whiskey back. Her dress is cut low to accentuate her cleavage and show her trim back. She has the kind of body I like—big tits and a nicely curved pelvis and ass. Right now she's pressing her breasts against me, and I wait...

Her hand cups my cheek, and she shifts so she can

place her mouth over mine. Although there's no ex of hers watching, I kiss her back, my fingers tunneling into her inky hair. Her tongue outlines my lips. I wait...

She makes a hum of pleasure, the sound vibrating through our fused mouths. I wait...

And...

Nothing.

Nothing stirs inside me. My body doesn't care what she's doing. It stays inert and cold, my dick totally uninterested.

If I hadn't fucked Ava just a few weeks ago, I'd be more than a little worried. I'm too young for this...deadening.

Faye pulls back, a question in her eyes. "You okay?"

I stand and get another finger of whiskey. "Just a little tired."

She gets up and rubs the tightness in my shoulders. "You'll feel better once you rest a bit."

Her eyes are slumberous, her touch coaxing.

If I put my dirty hands on Faye, will she pull away? If I tell her I love her, will she call me toxic in response?

I'm tempted to try.

"Lucas?" Faye says, her eyebrows pinched. "You sure you're all right?"

"Yes. I'm fine." I rub my forehead. What the hell am I thinking? Tell her "I love you" just to see how she'll react? That's fucked up.

You are fucked up. No better than your mother.

"I should go," I say. "I have an early call tomorrow morning."

"But it's Saturday."

"Yeah, but startups don't do the nine-to-five, Monday-through-Friday thing."

She reaches out and holds my hand. "You don't have to pretend with me. Rebounds can be hard. I know."

I look at her, a little stunned, but don't say anything.

"Oh, come on. We were *lovers*. I *know* you." She tugs and places my hand at the small of her back. "If you're worried about finding someone to marry for the paintings, don't be. I'm happy to help out."

"Faye..." I shake my head. "You saw the interviews and Elliot's tweets, right?"

"Uh-huh. And you know what was funny? Not one of them outright denied it."

Shit. Faye's always been smart. That's how she clawed herself out of poverty and became what she is now.

"We may be exes, but I'm also your friend," she continues. "I don't want to see you lose to that bastard. And yes, your dad is a complete bastard. Don't expect me to apologize for telling the truth."

Despite myself, I smile. I should just say yes. Marrying Faye would be ideal—she's smart, beautiful and we've known each other long enough that we can lie about how we fell in love to maintain the public façade about the deal.

And it'd knock two items off the objectives list.

But somehow I can't. My head urges me to commit,

but my tongue refuses to cooperate. "Let me think about it," I manage.

I leave the suite before she can say anything else. My left leg throbs wildly, as though to remind me about the scars. Will Faye be as tender with them as Ava? The kisses...caresses...

My jaw clenches. None of that meant anything to her. I'm the idiot who gave it a significance that didn't exist.

As the elevator descends to the lobby, I rest the back of my head against the wall. What the hell am I doing?

Rejecting Faye isn't me getting over Ava and moving on. It's me being stupid and evading the issue.

Don't let Ava ruin everything.

When the elevator pings open, I cross the lobby and climb inside the waiting limo.

Tomorrow. I will call Faye tomorrow and say yes.

12

LUCAS

"YOU LOOK LIKE SHIT."

I bury my head under the pillow. Blake's voice sounds like a thousand thunderclaps. Didn't Geraldine teach him how to use his indoor voice?

"...smell like shit, too."

"Go away." I'd rather stay in this lumpy and uncomfortable bed than risk death by getting up.

"Sorry. We have a brunch to attend."

What the hell? "Nobody eats brunch at the crack of dawn."

"It's ten, you idiot."

There's a zipping sound by the windows, and light penetrates my eyeballs like a death laser.

"Are you trying to kill me?" I groan.

"It'd serve you right. You drank all my good stuff."

"Your liquor found it an honor to be drunk."

"Savored, maybe. Not guzzled until you pass out like a lobotomized fool in the middle of the living room. Now get up."

Ugh. I carefully open my eyes into slits and look around. I'm in the living room, and my bed is actually a couch. Four whiskey bottles sit on the table, empty. I don't remember drinking quite that much, but...maybe I did. I was in a bad place last night after returning from Faye's hotel. I don't even know why. I'm usually in a better mood after making a decision, and I decided to marry her for a year. It's completely logical, and will solve a couple of my most immediate problems.

Must've been celebratory drinking...except I obviously took it too far.

"I'll replace the damned whiskey," I rasp. "Go away."

"Can't. We're meeting Elizabeth in less than an hour. I'm giving you a chance to get dressed and pull your shit together."

Damn it. This is why I don't like being around my siblings. They don't know when to stop. "Does it look like I'm in any condition to eat?" The very idea of food makes my stomach roil.

"She won't care. She insisted you come too." Blake hands me a glass of water and a couple of aspirin. I finally sit up with a grunt, take them and down them.

"What happened last night?" he asks.

"Nothing."

"Thought you were gonna get laid."

The last thing I want to think about is how cold my body was—how unresponsive to what Faye offered. "What I'm gonna do is shower."

I stand with an enormous effort and slowly stumble toward the second level, where Blake's stashed my stuff. The suite is large, with a small study attached to it. I kick my shoes off in the giant walk-in closet, which is only about ten percent full. I should probably get Rachel to send my usual wardrobe here. Just ship it. The whole thing.

Leaving a trail of wrinkled clothes, I walk into the glass stall and start the shower. Blake got one thing right with the penthouse—instant hot water all the time.

As it sluices over me, the thick fog around my head starts to clear, and the pounding eases somewhat. The aspirin must be kicking in.

I wash myself gingerly. I really don't want to face anybody today, but I have no choice. Blake won't leave me alone, and if I don't go, Elizabeth may well decide to barge in and cater a bunch of food here because that's just how she rolls. As lovely as she is, she's too used to getting her way. And why not? Men fall to their knees for her, and women can't hate her even if they want to because she's just that nice. Not even her psycho mother bothers her anymore.

I put on a gray V-neck sweater and slacks and stare at myself in the mirror. A hint of green mars my complexion, and the bloodshot eyes and dry mouth do nothing to make me feel better about the upcoming brunch. I brush my teeth, trying to get the nasty taste of stale alcohol out.

"You done?" Blake calls out from downstairs. "You take longer than a woman."

"Fuck you," I mutter, then slip my feet into a pair of sandals and drag myself to the living room.

My brother doesn't look up from his phone. "Seriously. Five minutes longer than my ex."

"Was she hung over and about to be shanghaied to a brunch she didn't want to go to?"

He ignores me. "Come on. We're late."

I keep my eyes closed as he drives us to the restaurant. The motion of the Aston Martin sloshes the alcohol in my belly, and I open a window to draw in some fresh air.

"If you puke, you're buying this car," Blake says.

"Don't worry. It was only four bottles."

"It was five."

Elizabeth has chosen a retro-themed diner. The inside is rather cramped and decorated in some kind of garish, rubbery red plastic. The vinyl-covered chairs match the ugly color scheme. The music coming from the sound system is disgustingly cheery—the Gershwins' "I Got Rhythm." *What have I done to deserve this?*

Blake sees our sister before I do. She's in a corner booth in the back. We walk over, and she gets up to give both of us a hug. A huge pair of sunglasses hides most of her face, and she's wearing a Cubs cap, a fitted white long-sleeve shirt, frayed cropped denim pants and white tennis shoes, like she's about to go to a game. "So good to have you join me." But she says it with a smile.

I take a seat. I *need* to sit down...and cradle my head with my hands before it falls off. "Where's everyone else?"

"What do you mean?"

"Ryder. Elliot."

"They aren't invited."

Huh. "Why not?"

"You want me to call them?" She reaches into her purse.

I start to shake my head, then think better of the idea and wave my hand weakly instead. "No. It's fine."

"Let's order. I'm starving," Blake says, opening the laminated menu.

"I know what I want." Elizabeth lays her hands on the table—slim and beautifully manicured. Sort of how Ava's were after that spa treatment in Osaka. She glowed afterward, and I loved seeing her so relaxed and pam—

Stop thinking about her.

"I'll go with their Man Set." Blake leans back. "You?"

"Whatever. Something." I'm not that interested in eating.

Our waitress comes over. Her huge plastic tits don't even bounce as she moves, although her blond ponytail does. Enhanced lips glisten with too much gloss. Probably an actress or model wannabe. From the way Blake eyes her, she's going to get a fat tip.

Elizabeth orders for all of us, and the server leaves after placing a carafe of hot coffee on the table. I pour myself a steaming cup. Caffeine will be just the thing to get through whatever bullshit lies ahead.

"Guess who I saw yesterday at the opening," Elizabeth says.

"A man with a big—fat—swollen...check," Blake answers, enunciating every syllable with care.

I snort. "If anything would get our sister excited..."

"Don't be a jerk." She gives me a sidelong glance of warning.

Aw, shit. This isn't a good sign. "Okay. Who?"

Elizabeth shifts and sips her coffee. Then with an inordinate care that tests my patience, she places her mug on the table just so. "Ava Huss."

The hammer in my head starts pounding twice as hard. I sit back and glare at her. "Are you *high?*"

"Soberer than you, it looks like."

"You must have been mistaken. Ava doesn't run in circles that get invitations to an opening like that. She isn't rich enough or connected enough. Nate would never invite someone who can't blow tens of thousands without a thought." A couple of events like that, and the two million I gave her will be gone.

"Don't be such a snob. She works for Robbie."

"Who the hell is Robbie?"

"I told you. Her boss."

No way. I'm not letting my sister get away with this. I don't care if Blake is watching. "Right, and I was born last night. *You* did this, didn't you?"

She puts an angelic hand over her chest. "Me?"

"Who else? You were trying to manipulate me—again—into running into her. Well, you failed." I try not to snap at her, since she's my sister and I actually do like her. But she is seriously testing my patience.

"That's completely unfair—"

Her pointless protest is interrupted when our server brings our food. Elizabeth gets French toast topped with fresh berries, powdered sugar and whipped cream, maple syrup on the side, while Blake's Man Set comes with a mountain of bacon, sausages and scrambled eggs fried in butter—a cardiologist's nightmare. The waitress places a platter of pancakes and waffles in front of me with a smile. "Our specialty."

They remind me of the meal I had at Ray and Darcy's house right before I stole Ava away to the bed and breakfast for the happiest weekend of my life... when I thought we both wanted the same thing. I promised to whisk her away to Paris, and she acted like that was exactly what she wanted, too. I bite back a curse.

Fool. Fool. Fool.

"Unfair my ass," I grate out when we're somewhat private again. "You sent me that envelope to push me toward Ava, you interfering little witch."

Blake gestures with his knife. "Language..."

"What? You going to call her an angel when she fucks with your life?"

"Both of you stop." Elizabeth turns to me. "You wanted to go."

"I didn't. Why do you think I never looked her up?"

"But you left as soon as you found out where she was."

My grip on my fork tightens. "Again, proving my point that you're meddling in my life."

"Lucas, just hear me ou—"

"No. You hear me out." I point the fork in her direction, and she shuts up. "Stop interfering. You've done more damage than you can imagine. I'm going to marry and you're going to get your painting."

Blake munches on a strip of bacon. "Who?"

"Faye. She's perfect."

Elizabeth closes her eyes briefly, but Blake remains unperturbed.

"Does she know about..." He waves the half-eaten bacon.

"Who doesn't?"

He grunts. "Not everyone thinks it's true."

"Yeah, well, she's too smart to be fooled."

"Are you sure you want to settle like this?" Elizabeth asks. "Ava is—"

"I'm not going to be with a woman who thinks I'm *toxic*."

"Ava said that to you?"

"Yes." I push my plate to the side and lean closer so she will *really* hear what I'm saying rather than what she wants to hear. Elizabeth is convinced everyone can be saved—a noble enough attitude for someone who's trying to change the world, but totally irritating when she's messing with my life. "I told her I loved her, and she said I was toxic and that we were finished." I spit out the words. "*Toxic. Finished.*" They're like coarse salt into an unhealed wound. "So don't even think about talking to me about settling or any such bullshit. I'd much rather have a little honest greed than a bunch of pretty lies. At least Faye doesn't play games."

"That's crap, and you know it," Elizabeth says. "How can you say she doesn't play games after what she did last night?"

"What are you talking about?"

"She made sure Ava was watching when she kissed you."

I frown. Then it clicks. *Giving Faye's ex a show.* Except it was my ex.

"Ava cried after you left."

My gut tightens at the idea of her in pain. I prayed for it before—wished she would be a tenth as miserable as me so she would take me back—but now it just leaves me hollow.

Still... Nothing's changed. I got my closure when she signed the documents and took my two million. I remind myself that the first time you cut someone off always hurts. It's like the surgery to fix my leg. It left scars, but I was better off for having done it.

Blake shrugs. "She's the one who left. What's she got to cry about?"

"Probably felt robbed she didn't get enough money," I say, grateful for Blake's voice of sanity.

"Lucas! That's so...cynical," Elizabeth says.

"Smart and realistic," Blake corrects. "Besides, I

like Faye. She knows how to stick the knife in when she has to."

The kiss undoubtedly showed Ava I'm over her and no longer the same loser who showed up on her doorstep. But now that I know the truth, I feel vaguely used and dirty, an unwilling participant in Faye's little game.

Why does it matter? If she'd told you Ava was watching, would you not *have kissed her?*

Elizabeth sighs. "You're making a big mistake."

Deliberately, I make my voice cold. "The only mistake I made was going after her." I raise a finger to stall my sister. "Don't interfere again, Elizabeth. I won't forgive you the next time."

"That's totally fine. It's not like there's going to be a next time. And Ava's date showed up to dry her tears anyway."

I pull back while anger and jealousy unfurl in my gut. She's moved on. Why the fuck did she cry then? I was right not to read much into it, wasn't I?

I decide to have the pancakes and waffles after all. And I choke down every damn bite...because *fuck this.* I'm not going to starve pointlessly.

When the waitress brings our check, Blake hands her his plastic. Elizabeth says something, but I'm distracted as my phone starts ringing. I check the number. It's Nate.

"Yes?" I bite out.

"And a cheery good morning to you, too." Nate's voice is dry. "Thanks for coming last night. You finally decided to pull your weight in this venture, huh?"

I drop my forehead into my palm. I'm being a dick, taking my frustration out on people who don't deserve it. "Sorry. Just not in the right frame of mind for...you know." Nate doesn't need to know the details.

"The tabloids haven't been kind to you guys." Nate sounds sympathetic. He's experienced some vulture-fests in his time as well. Can't be helped when he's second in line to take over the Sterling & Wilson fortune. "I was calling to see if you're still serious about contributing to the center."

"Of course," I say without hesitation. It's just the sort of thing I need to keep me from thinking about Ava. I wasted my life doing nothing for two years after she vanished on me. No way am I going for an encore.

"Great. Why don't you come by this afternoon? Take a tour of the place and we can talk. I want to make sure it's really something you want to get involved in long-term."

"I'm sure it will be." I've got nothing better to do with my life, I think and choke back a self-deprecating laugh. "Two o'clock good?"

"Perfect. See you then."

The moment I hang up, Elizabeth asks, "Who was that?"

"Faye," Blake guesses.

"Nate."

"Oh." Elizabeth sits back. "He's finally getting you to help out?"

I nod. "It's a worthy cause." Even if I no longer care about Ava—and I really don't—the medical center is something I want to champion.

"Tax deductible, too," Blake adds.

Elizabeth shoots him a withering look. "There's more to life than tax deductions."

"True, but they help make it more enjoyable." He studies her speculatively. "How come *you* aren't involved? You're a far better candidate than Lucas for fundraising and stuff."

"Hey, I'm not that terrible." But Blake is right about our sister being better. Actually, she's the best.

"I can only take on so many projects," Elizabeth says. "In addition to the international charity work I've committed to in the last twelve months, I'm also managing building and funding shelters for abused women and children. Then there's the No More Childhood Hunger campaign..." Reaching for her coffee, she glances my way. "I don't think I can do a good job with Nate's hospital, so I'm glad you'll be helping out."

God. The expectations keep rising, but I can man up. "I can handle it. Somebody's gotta take on the mantle rather than expecting you to do everything."

"I couldn't agree more."

Blake is watching Elizabeth like he doesn't quite believe her. Something passes between them. "I guess everyone's got their limits," he says, and finishes his bacon.

Somewhere in my head, a small alarm goes off.

13

Lucas

The Sterling Medical Center is much bigger and sleeker than I imagined. The photos and models at the opening showcased the hospital, but I assumed they were designed to idealize it as much as possible.

Nate's office is in the back on the top floor, and I walk past an empty secretary's desk straight into his inner sanctum. It's small—for the moneyman of the whole operation—and modestly furnished with a standard work desk and one of those high-end ergonomic mesh chairs. A miniature painting of a strawberry farm hangs on the wall. Thin white industrial blinds cover the window behind him—which faces the parking deck, unless I'm guessing the building layout incorrectly.

Nate pushes back the chair—it looks like he's being engulfed by some high-tech alien insect—and stands, a big smile splitting his face. "Finally, the mystery man!" He hugs me, slapping my back heartily a couple of times. I'm not a hugger, but it's impossible to pull away when Nate Sterling wants to give you an exuberant greeting.

Although he looks a lot like his older brother—the same dark hair and dark eyes—there's a softer and nicer aspect that Justin doesn't have. It could be a mask, of course. Justin didn't start acting like Justin until he took over Sterling & Wilson.

Nate pulls away. "Honest to God, I haven't seen you in ages."

"A little over two years."

"Right. The crash. How you doing?"

"I'm fine. Did the rehab, got better."

He nods, watching me. "Good to hear. Hey, you want something to drink? The break room has coffee, some tea..."

"You said something about a tour."

"Direct as always." He laughs. "All right, let's go. I can't wait to show you everything." He leads me out and into the hall.

The interior is just as impressive as the outside. Because the medical center will primarily cater to the poor, I assumed it would be utilitarian and low-cost—sort of what you see on those TV shows about harried but dedicated medical professionals in inner-city clinics. But everything's bright and ultramodern. It looks like another hospital the Sterling family built not too long ago—the Ethel Sterling Children's Hospital.

Although I didn't go to that opening, I saw the media coverage. Very high-tech.

"I thought the goal was to stretch our dollar to provide care, not to have the nicest building we can get," I say.

"It was. Still is. Why do you think I had Justin pay for most of this?" Nate gestures around.

"You got Justin involved?"

"He'd been nagging me to do some charity work, so I figured turnabout was fair play. I'm not averse to using the family money if the cause is good. And this *is* a good cause." He smiles at a cute nurse. "Most of the medical staff came from overseas volunteer positions. I thought they'd understand what it's like to serve the needy the best. And since you weren't in the mood to help, I put Elizabeth on the advisory board."

"How many times you want me to say I'm sorry?"

"As many times as I called."

I frown. "Which is...how many?"

"At least ten. Didn't Rachel tell you?"

A shrug. "She might've. I probably wasn't in the mood to listen."

"Because of the crash?" Nate's eyes are exceptionally shrewd as he watches me.

"Rehab. Getting used to my new ugly face. You know, the usual."

He exhales. "Retreating probably made it worse. I don't know why your doctors didn't tell you to go rejoin the living. I mean, you could've been around friends who care rather than staying in the Pacific North-Lost." He shudders.

Nate thinks I'm still in Seattle, and being an outdoors man, he hates the rain and gray skies. I don't bother to correct him. The last thing I want to do is get into why I lingered in Charlottesville.

The main lobby is also a waiting area with tons of chairs. People are filling out paperwork, and a couple of receptionists in pale lavender coats help the ones who come over to their desks. The cheap clothes some of them are wearing remind me of what Ava and I bought in that bed and breakfast town, and I scowl in spite of myself. I would've traded everything I have for a forever with Ava. But she didn't want that.

Toxic.

"Let's talk about what I can do," I say, needing to think about something other than her. *Toxic. Toxic.*

Nate takes me on a circuitous route, showing me the different wings for cancer care, regular pediatrics, maternity and so on. Once we're back to his office, he closes the door. I take an armchair by the desk and stretch my legs out, crossing my ankles.

"I'm thinking about a year-end charity function," he says, sitting across me. "People tend to be more giving in December."

"Okay. So who am I helping?"

"Actually, you'll have to spearhead this one. Robbie's great at managing hospitals, but he's not that great at raising money."

Is this the same guy Elizabeth was talking about? "Who's Robbie?"

"He's the administrator in charge of operations and capital investments. A great guy, just not great at fundraising. He probably never had to do much of it in his previous positions. But he's swamped right now, so most likely he's going to have his assistant do the work with you. I heard she's quite diligent." Nate smiles. "Pretty, too. If she weren't working here, I'd probably ask her out."

I uncross my ankles and sit up straight. Nate is exceptionally partial to blondes. As a matter of fact, to the best of my knowledge he's only ever dated blondes. "What's her name?" I casually ask, even as my heart pushes into my throat.

"Ava Huss. She came highly recommended by a friend who's working here as a nurse, and also by your sister. It was really Elizabeth who sealed the deal for me. I know she'd never refer someone who wasn't good."

Fury explodes in my chest, and it's all I can do not to break something. I stand, my entire body shaking.

"Are you okay?" Nate asks.

"I'm fine. I just remembered I have an appointment. Can we discuss the rest of the fundraiser thing later?"

"I'm actually flying to Chicago tonight, but you're welcome to call or meet Robbie anytime. He knows about your involvement." Nate hands me a card with Robbie's contact info on it.

"Fantastic. Thanks."

I shove the card into my pocket. My gait is uneven as I hurry. If I slow down, I can hide the limp, but I don't bother. If I could wish for any superpower, it would be to instantly appear in front of Elizabeth.

Making my way to my car, I call her. Before she can say a word, I spit out, "How dare you!"

She gasps. "Lucas?"

"I told you to stay *the fuck out of this.*"

"What are you talking about?"

"Ava Huss. You got her a damned job."

"Oh. That."

"*Oh. That.* Yes. *That.*"

"She lost her job—probably because she had to give it up to come home with you. So I thought I'd help."

The way I maneuvered Ava into her unemployment status makes my conscience squirm. *Think of the two million bucks.* "She didn't need your help."

"Lucas, the economy is horrible. It's not like her résumé is stellar. But I figured if she got an interview, she'd be able to impress the guy. And she did."

"She didn't need a job, Elizabeth. I gave her money."

A short pause. "You gave her money."

"Yes."

"How much?"

"Two million. More than enough for her to live the rest of her life in comfort."

She sighs. "There's more to life than money, Lucas. Jobs give people pride, self-esteem."

"You don't get it. I gave her the money so she can be a writer, like she said she wanted. She never needed your help. I certainly never needed your meddling. Now things are worse." I climb into my car and shove a hand into my hair. "If you hadn't interfered, I would never have gone after her. And if I hadn't, she wouldn't have lost her job in Japan. I would've found someone else to marry, and you would've gotten the portrait anyway. It'll almost serve you right if I don't marry anybody after all, and nobody gets them."

"I'm not doing this for Grandpa's painting."

"Then why? Don't tell me it's for my own good. That's bullshit."

"You can believe whatever you want, but know one thing. Women on their own can be vulnerable."

"She has foster parents." *Who are old and have a child of their own to look after. Surely their own flesh and blood come before Ava.*

"I only wanted to make sure she'd be okay." She sighs. "If you don't like how I did it, then undo it."

"A little too late for that."

"No, it's not. Talk to Nate. I'm sure he'll fire her for you." She hangs up.

I smack the steering wheel, hard. How dare she try to turn me into a villain? I did *not* abandon Ava. I did not leave her helpless and vulnerable. *I—did—nothing —wrong.*

I've been trying to put my life together after the accident. Rehab sucked, and trying to prove to myself that part of me didn't die when Ava dumped me the first time...

Being with her the second time proved I'm not dead. So now all I need to do is learn that lesson and move on.

Get Nate to fire her.

My head swivels toward the hospital. He'll probably do it if I ask...although he'll want to know why, and I don't want to discuss my reasons.

I inhale and exhale deeply a few times. There's no need to talk to Nate. I can get her to quit on her own. Surely I'm the last person she wants to be around. After all, I'm *toxic*.

14

AVA

I PASTE ON A BIG SMILE AS I WALK INTO THE medical center on Monday in my pink blouse and forest-green pencil skirt. I chose them because they're my "pick me up" outfit, and I could really use one today.

I stop by the break room to grab a coffee before going to my desk. My laptop boots up in no time, and I review the day's and week's agendas and mark everything that requires my or Robbie's immediate attention.

At least I'm being somewhat productive at work. I was worthless at home. I sat in front of the blank TV and stared at nothing for most of Sunday. None of the items on my long personal to-do list got crossed off. I even begged off meeting Jon for lunch, mostly because I'd have made lousy company, and he deserves better.

I sip the steaming coffee as quickly as possible. My eyes feel like they're packed with sand, and caffeine's the only thing that will get me through this day. Faye and Lucas in each other's arms kept popping up in my dreams, disturbing my sleep. They definitely had it off after going home. You don't kiss like that unless you're planning on more.

She's with him because you didn't fight for him.

Elizabeth's words circle around my head. I imagine them as a halo of vultures waiting for my sanity to draw its last breath. The doubt she's sown wants to feast on my pride, my sense of self-worth. And that's about all I have left.

The first step to fixing a problem is admitting you have one. Well, obviously I have one—my inability to let go of Lucas. If he hadn't shown me what we could have had together, then it wouldn't hurt so much. After all, I survived the first time. But this second time was more... He made me hope for a shared future.

Your future does not have to have Lucas in it, I tell myself forcefully. I can date around, find some other man to love. Who says you can only love once? As a matter of fact, Jon might be the one—the man who could love me, who I could love back openly.

And to that end, it's better that I make sure Lucas and his family don't want anything to do with me. Elizabeth didn't mention Mia just to be chatty. God, my head is a mess of jumbled thoughts and emotions. I *have* to pull myself together...or I'm going to do something to irreparably damage not only myself, but possibly Mia's safety and future as well.

I finish the coffee and stand up to get a second serving before checking in with Robbie. Then I see...

Lucas.

The impact of his presence slices me like a scalpel down the belly. He's stunning—scars or no—and he looks well rested and calm. Blood roars in my head, and my vision feels hazy for a moment. After what I saw at the opening, I'm not prepared to face him.

The expertly tailored button-down shirt and slacks —both in black—emphasize the breadth and leanness of his tall, strong body. Silver cufflinks wink when he checks his watch, and I shake my head, willing the apparition to vanish.

My heart thunders. What the hell is he doing here? Is he here to see me?

Part of me almost sobs in relief and need, even though my head tells me he's probably here for something else. But if he does approach, I can't be weak and crumble. I have to stick to what I told him in Virginia.

He stops two feet away. My mouth dries, bees buzzing in my stomach. I wish I hadn't gulped down that first cup of coffee so fast.

"You're Robbie's assistant?"

This Lucas is nothing like the one I remember. His voice is neutral, and the rigid lines of his body say "hands off." Under his cool, hard scrutiny, something inside me shrivels as though I'm the one who screwed up back in Charlottesville. "Yes."

"Okay. Did he tell you you'll be working with me to organize the year-end fundraiser event?"

"No. I haven't had a chance to talk with him."

Lucas's gaze flicks over me, making me die inside. There's zero warmth, zero recognition. *This is what you wanted.* It's as though I'm a stranger.

"I was under the impression you would be up to speed," he says.

"I just got in."

"Had time to finish coffee." He cocks the eyebrow.

My back stiffens. I'm not going to apologize for having a morning java. "We'll go in together. I need to check a few things with him anyway."

"Ladies first."

He gestures me ahead. I can't decide if this is a way of mocking me or not. I'm pretty sure "lady" isn't the first word he associates with me.

I lead him to my boss's office, all the while praying this is a prank or some kind of huge mistake. There is no way Lucas can be involved with the medical center. Google said he *donates* to causes, not that he gets down in the trenches himself.

Robbie smiles when he sees us walking in. "Thrilled you could join us today, Mr. Reed."

"Glad to be here. And please, call me Lucas." They shake hands.

"Have you met my assistant?" Robbie asks.

"We've met." Lucas gestures at the seats. "Shall we get started?"

I hear the words between the two men, but my

mind barely processes anything. The shock of seeing Lucas is still reverberating through me.

I don't understand what he's doing here. Why do we need him? Surely, there are other people—more famous people—who can draw in the crowds to benefit the medical center.

"That's wonderful." Robbie's voice penetrates my miserable confusion. "I'm sorry I can't be more involved. Operations is taking more of my time and effort than I expected. But I'm sure Ava will do a great job."

I almost drop my pen. "What?"

Robbie frowns, while Lucas studies me like an insect on the other side of a magnifying glass. "Do you have some objection to the new task?" Lucas asks.

My internal sensor screams "trap." I inhale and gather my thoughts before saying, "Not at all. I'm just surprised I'm the one who's being tapped for it. I've never done this kind of work before."

Maybe this will give me an excuse to bow out. I'm certain Lucas doesn't want us to spend time together. He did everything possible to force me to take the money and give him the closure he said he needed to move on. Faye is the one in his life now.

So why does this hurt so much?

"First time for everything." Robbie grins broadly. "I wouldn't have picked you if I didn't feel you were a quick study."

I give him a weak smile in return.

"And whatever help I need, I'm sure my sister can

deliver," Lucas says. "She's world class at this kind of stuff."

"We're grateful for your help," Robbie says. "Both you and your family. I'll make sure to adjust Ava's work schedule so she can assist you and learn exactly what's needed to pull an event like this together."

"Excellent." Lucas stands up. "Then let's get started. I have a lunch meeting."

I have no choice now. The only way I could possibly get out of this is by explaining my history with Lucas to Robbie, but I'd rather die than behave unprofessionally. I can handle this. It's just one job, and the close contact with Lucas will be over soon enough.

Lucas and I move to a small meeting room, and he dictates a huge list of tasks. Not even once during that time does he regard me with anything other than cool detachment.

I've imagined it would be nearly impossible to handle if Lucas came back to me with love in his eyes and told me again that he wanted to be with me. But this coldness is so much worse. It is as though everything I suspected is true...that I don't matter.

Every second fillets a little bit more of my heart. Even though I'm following along on autopilot, my head is full of contradictory thoughts and emotions.

What's wrong with me? This stranger treatment is what I told him I wanted. I even put him through the "test" so he would realize the truth between us. But it still makes my heart ache.

Elizabeth words come back to me, this time with an undertone of accusation.

She's with him because you didn't fight for him.

But how can I fight for nothing?

I'm in love with you.

A last-ditch effort to get me to change my mind. He'd never said those words before. And there were plenty of opportunities.

Gifts. Words. They never mean anything. Just look how easily Dad threw them at me and Mom. And how gullible we were to take them at face value.

Finally, Lucas stops his dictation of tasks. "All that needs to be completed by close of business tomorrow. When you're finished, let me know so we can move on to the next phase."

I place my pen on the yellow legal pad full of scribbled to-do items. "Are you staying in L.A.?"

"For a while. The weather's better, and my family's here."

There goes my hope that he'll return to Charlottesville and we can work long distance.

"Let Robbie know if you can't handle the work. I'm sure he can find me a suitable replacement."

"A replacement... Is that what you want?"

Lucas studies me. "Isn't it what you want?"

"I'm a professional. I can handle it."

He smirks. "That would've been more convincing if you didn't look like you were sucking on a lemon when you said it." He gets up. "Don't forget. COB tomorrow."

The second the meeting room door closes, the charge in the air vanishes, leaving me deflated and drained. I drag a hand through my hair, then look at the mountain of tasks that just got dumped in my lap.

Something about Lucas's demeanor said he expects me to fail...and fail badly. I'd rather drink hemlock. This is just a lark for him, but it's my life.

Firming my jaw, I get up and march toward my desk. I have work to do.

15

LUCAS

CARRYING A COUPLE OF BOTTLES OF EXCELLENT wine—one white and one red—I go to Elliot's home for dinner later on Monday. It's better than eating alone. Blake is out of town, probably trying to figure out which new ventures look the most promising.

But there's more to my visit than just not wanting to eat alone. I'm curious about Elliot's wife—what she's like—plus how marriage is treating my brother. He didn't marry for love, but the few glimpses I had of them at Blake's place made me suspect they have feelings for each other. Whether they've admitted as much to themselves is another matter.

I'd like some evidence that a union entered into with cold-blooded calculation can lead to something other than a lifeless...life. I need at least that much reassurance to marry Faye.

In fact, I have to convince myself of it. And then do what I need to do if I don't want to be the pathetic kid I used to be.

Earlier today Ken Asada came back with the report I requested—social security number, photos, credit check, criminal record and everything else he could dig up on Jon Barkley, Ava's date from the function. The results were incredibly disappointing. The guy is too damn nice. A good, stable job. Normal family. No criminal convictions or arrests. Decent-looking, too, I have to admit. Certainly no scars. He's exactly the kind of guy I wouldn't mind seeing my own sister hook up with.

At first I assumed I was let down because I wanted Ava to date jerks so she would realize how good she'd had it with me. But later I realized it was much simpler and dumber. I was harboring a secret wish—that I'd have a reason to swoop in, save the day, and she'd fall into my arms again.

Such a clichéd setup...it sounds like something from a third-rate romantic comedy. Shit like that doesn't happen in real life, and I should know better.

It's time to get my head screwed on straight and think about what I'm doing.

Elliot's penthouse is still the same—a bachelor pad. The pricey electronics, leather couches and minimalistic interior decoration are just the way I remembered. But the mantel and shelves now have framed photos of him and his wife Belle. Not many—they haven't been together that long—but certainly more than what I have of Ava. The selfies we took while we were at the bed and breakfast are on her phone. She never had a chance to send them to me.

Not that I would've kept them.

Elliot pads over, his bare feet quiet on the floor, and takes my wine. "Finally. Belle thought you might have decided not to join us." His hair is damp, his cheeks slightly flushed. I'd put money on his having used the pool on the upper deck recently. If he could be reborn as anything, it might be a dolphin. He's put on a white T-shirt and loose, long pants instead of his usual shorts. He shouldn't have bothered. Just because I choose to wear slacks in the summer doesn't mean everyone has to.

"Bad traffic, and I'm not that familiar with the roads here."

"No GPS?"

"It's only marginally useful. Doesn't account for the horrible drivers on the road."

Belle comes out from the kitchen with a platter of Chinese food and places it on the dining table. She's dressed in a wintry gray dress with an uneven hemline that flatters her curvy body. A string of pearls circle her elegant neck, and more pearls drip from her ears. Like Elliot, she's barefoot, and I spot a pair of white suede pumps in a small nook between the couch and dining room.

"I hope you don't mind takeout. But we did put it

on real china." She comes over and gives me a quick hug.

I squeeze her back then let go. "Elliot promised me a home-cooked meal."

He jabs me in the ribs. "I promised no such thing."

Belle laughs. "It's really my fault. I came home late from work."

"What do you do?" I'm ninety-nine percent certain she isn't still working at the strip joint where she met my brother.

"OWM. I'm an assistant to one of the fund managers." My shock must be obvious because she chortles. "What did you think I was doing these days?"

"Uh...shopping?" *Oh, good. That's real smooth.* "I had no idea. Sorry."

She shrugs with a small smile. "I did come with a colorful history, so I can't really fault you. Tell you what. Let's toss our assumptions and actually get to know each other."

Elliot wraps his arm around her. "Told you she was awesome."

I smile. "Lucky bastard."

You could've had that...if Ava hadn't found out.

I stop the thought before it can grow into something malignant. I could've never had what they have. Ava never loved me the way Belle clearly loves Elliot. I know my twin. He isn't the easiest man to live with— and has had his share of scandals, several of them having come out since their marriage. She loves him enough to overlook them all. Ava can't tolerate any flaws on my part, and I'll never be perfect enough for her.

Shoving the ugly thoughts aside, I follow my brother and his wife to the table. I don't want to feel sorry for myself or resent the happiness they have. They've earned it. From what I was able to piece together from Blake, she almost died from getting tangled up with Elliot.

"Where's your sister?" I ask once we're seated.

"Nonny's out. She apparently couldn't cancel her evening out with her friends." Belle frowns.

I shrug. "Let her have her fun. We can see each other later."

Belle passes around egg rolls, while Elliot wrestles with the Merlot I brought and serves us. I note he doesn't offer his wife a glass, and the thought comes again: *a recovering alcoholic?*

"Sweet and sour sauce?" Belle offers.

I nod my thanks, drizzle some over my egg rolls and bite into one. It's crisp and perfectly cooked. "Anybody else coming? Ryder?" Ryder and Elliot are tight.

"He's in the Maldives with Paige at the moment."

"The *Maldives*? Isn't she a little too pregnant for that kind of trip?"

"You would think, but he's determined to keep her away from the pressure-cooker media. It's been rough on her."

I shake my head. "He should've thought that before knocking her up."

"They're married, so it's all good. Besides, there's never a perfect time for kids."

"Poor Paige." Belle shakes her head. "I wonder if she knew how it was going to be. People seem to think *I'm* interesting because of my marriage. I can't imagine what it must be like for her."

"Thankfully Paige is smart, and she's seen media circuses while working for Ryder," Elliot says.

"There is a difference between seeing and actually experiencing it yourself." I serve myself some spicy beef and Chinese meatballs. "So. When are you guys going to start a family?"

"Not until I finish college and maybe get settled in my career."

I regard her. "You haven't finished?"

She flushes. "Not yet. I had to take time off, but I'm ready to go back."

"Good for you," I say even as I give Elliot a "what the hell" look.

My brother stares back at me blankly. *Ugh.* Women do not enjoy working. He should've made it clear she could stay home and spend her time pampering herself. It's ridiculous for her to go back to school or get a job... much less a career.

"What field are you thinking of?" I ask, just to be polite.

"Something in financial services, maybe. I want to help people plan for big events in life—buying homes, having kids, college, retirement and so on."

Elliot toys with her unbound hair. "I'm sure you're going to be amazing. I'm so proud of you."

He gazes into her eyes with a naked adoration that seems more intimate than sex. I look away and drain my wine.

After we finish our meal, Belle gets a call she has to take from her boss, so Elliot and I go to the balcony. The November evening breeze is refreshingly cool as it brushes over us, and the traffic below our feet flows like glowing rivers of diamonds and rubies.

"Did you really mean what you said at Blake's place?" Elliot asks.

"About what?"

"Marriage." His brows pull into a deep V. "You and Ava..."

"It's over. I'm marrying Faye."

"Faye? Faye *Belbin*?"

I nod. "Haven't told her yet, but she's the best candidate."

"Huh. From the way you reacted when all that crap came out about Annabelle Underhill, I thought you cared about Ava."

"Yeah, well... It wasn't mutual."

"Ah, jeez. Sorry to hear that."

I shrug with false nonchalance. "It's better this way. No false expectations. I would've wanted everything."

"Well, it's too bad you have to settle like this. I wish you could've found and kept the right woman."

"Didn't you specifically choose her"—I glance inside—"for shits and giggles?"

He nods. "It started out as something to humiliate Dad, but now it's more."

"I can see that."

"If you're going to choose Faye, you guys should date a little first."

"Date? What for?"

"We've been trying to convince the world the article about the deal is fake. I think Ryder did a pretty good job—besides, the shallow types can't believe he would marry a girl like Paige for anything other than love—and I did okay, too. If you marry Faye too abruptly, it'll look like the article had some truth to it."

I sigh. The last thing I want to do is waste my time "dating." Faye already knows what the deal is, and she isn't the type who wants flowers and sweet words.

"A couple of weeks should do it. You two do have history together, after all."

Elliot's advice is sensible, so I nod. I don't want to cause problems, even for Elizabeth. Being pretty and in the spotlight equates to stalkers galore, and as annoying as she is, I don't want her to have issues with a bunch of creeps.

"Here's something I want you to consider, though," Elliot says. "If you have a chance to undo the damage and get Ava back the way you want...then take it. Even if it means no portraits."

I stare at my twin. "The whole point of this is to get the portraits."

"Is it? You were with Ava for a painting?"

I look away. Grandpa's legacy was never a factor.

"Dad's making us dance to his tune because he can. That doesn't mean we should give up a chance for life-long happiness for this bullshit. We don't even know what crap he's going to come up with to renege."

"You really think he'd do that?"

Elliot laughs. "In a heartbeat. Would you put it past him?"

I shake my head. Dad would love to find a loophole to deny us just out of spite. "For all we know, he might've built something sneaky into the deal when he offered it in the first place."

"I know. That's why the least we can do is be happy. He hates that more than anything."

I regard my brother. "When did you figure all this out?"

"When I thought I was going to lose my wife. It's amazing how pure terror can cut through all the bull-shit you've been telling yourself."

I take a longer look toward the penthouse. "Belle must be one of a kind to make you fall so hard."

"I was damn lucky. But there's one for you, too."

I smile. Let Elliot believe that.

16

Ava

"Why are you still up?" Bennie's voice comes loud and clear through the laptop speaker. We're on Facebook, chatting without the video. I don't think he's going to want to see my hideous face with huge, dark circles under my eyes.

"Because I'm working," I say as I type another email to be sent out before I go to bed. Normally I wouldn't be talking with him this late while trying to work, but I need some help staying up. My head feels like it's full of wet, heavy cotton, and my joints ache from hours of hunching over my laptop.

"Isn't it, like, one a.m. there?"

"A quarter after, but thankfully I'm home, so I can work in my PJs." And no bra or shoes. My small dining table is enough space, and I can munch on chips and drink herb tea to my heart's content.

Bennie harrumphs. "For your real boss or That Bastard?"

"It's for Lucas."

"Uh-huh. The Bastard."

I sigh, but don't say anything. If my best friend wants to vent about the way Lucas and my relationship fell apart, I'm not going to get in the way. Nothing can stop him when he's on the warpath anyway, and my brain can barely focus on writing the emails and following the conversation. I don't have the energy for more. Less than five hours of sleep per night for over a week is hell.

"Why don't you tell your manager you're overworked? You've been up until at least one ever since The Bastard started bossing you around."

"There is no way I'm telling Robbie."

"Why the hell not?"

"Because it's payback from Lucas. He wants to see me fail because he thinks I set him up in Charlottesville. And I'm not giving him the satisfaction."

"My God, how stupid *is* he? Does he not understand you were doing it to show him it was hopeless between the two of you?"

I purse my lips for a moment. "Well...I'm sure his pride was hurt."

A loud snort. "Oh, his *pride*. Like he hasn't stomped on yours over and over again. You should tell that fucker you can't slave away to please him because you have a date. With a super-normal, super-nice guy named Jon."

I suppress a second sigh. I told Bennie about Jon, and now my best friend's decided I should marry him. I think Jon's pretty great, too, but my feelings are on the platonic side. I just don't think about him the way I should if I'm going to try for something more than friendship. But that's not what Bennie wants to hear, and I'm too tired to argue. So instead, I say, "It's only for a few weeks. Then I'll be back to my normal schedule with Robbie. At least the work I'm doing is meaningful. I wish you could see the medical center, Bennie. It's awesome, really modern and nice. Nobody's turned away—it's strictly to provide for people in need."

If we'd had a hospital like that when we were growing up, our lives might've turned out differently. Bennie's alcoholic dad could've gotten help for his addiction...and counseling for anger management. My mom could've gotten help to deal with her despair...and maybe she wouldn't have ended up turning to alcohol and drugs to avoid facing the fact that she'd lived a life of lies.

"I'm proud of you for making a difference," Bennie says. "It's exactly the kind of work I imagined you doing after you finished teaching English in Japan."

"Yeah, me too."

My phone pings next to my laptop, and I check the screen. It's a Google alert.

Beauty and the Beast. Budding Romance?

I bite back a pained gasp. I should get used to headlines like this, but I can't. Every new link is like a fresh slice through my heart.

The latest article is about sightings of Lucas and Faye, who are now apparently dating in earnest. The photos include them dining at a fancy restaurant I don't recognize and taking an afternoon walk in a park, their hands linked. Lucas is gorgeous as usual, with his dark air and tailored clothes, and Faye... She looks like his perfect match, beautiful and elegant and absolutely nothing like me. I'll never be that cool and sophisticated, no matter what kind of clothes I put on.

Suddenly I feel inferior and small, like that time when Elle and her mother confronted Mom and me after Dad died. I can't breathe through the hard knot in my chest. I press a hand against the spot and rub, hoping I can massage away the lump.

Bennie can sense something is wrong. "Ava, are you still cyberstalking that woman?"

I put the phone back on the table, facedown. "No."

"Come on. I heard the ping, and you went quiet there..."

"It's not stalking," I say, my voice hoarse. "It's Google."

"You have to stop. Let it go."

"I know, but..." I sigh. "Every time I try to hit the unsubscribe link, I can't."

"Tell me you're hoping for a report of them falling into a ditch and breaking all four legs, and that's why you keep it."

I snort a laugh. Leave it to Bennie to come up with something like that. "No. They're dating." I try to be nonchalant, but my voice breaks at the end. I clear my throat. "I need some water. It's freaking dry in L.A."

"Oh, bullshit. Why torture yourself like this? *You let him go.* You broke it off for your own sanity."

"You're right." I lay a fist on the table and rest my forehead on it. "He's not mine anymore. I know that—I've accepted it. Really. But I can't cut off my feelings and pretend he doesn't exist... It hurts so much to see him happy with another woman."

"Of course it hurts. You want him to mope. Be miserable for the rest of his life. Hopefully he's already impotent."

"Is that what you wanted for Drew when you were going through a rough patch?" Drew is Bennie's British boyfriend. Mr. Perfect.

"What else?" Bennie says. "If he'd screwed around to get over me, I would've never forgiven him. Because I *did* want him back, even though I refused to admit it to myself."

"Well, I don't want Lucas back," I say, even though my mind asks, *Don't you? Really?*

"I know that. But he deserves at least a week of misery for every tear you shed over him, and erectile dysfunction is a good start."

I flip the phone so I can look at the photos again. Faye and Lucas look happy, both of them smiling although dark sunglasses hide their eyes.

Does she know that the deal regarding his inheritance is real? That his siblings lied about it being the tabloids' fevered imagination?

Maybe she does and just doesn't care because she's too sophisticated to care about stuff like that. What do I know about the people in Lucas's circle? Maybe this kind of messed-up deal for an inheritance is par for the course, and only crude, backward plebs like me don't get it.

I hit send on the email I've been typing. That was the last thing on my list. I lean back in my seat, suddenly feeling like the proverbial wet noodle.

"Ava, you there?"

"Yeah. Still here."

"I have to get going, but if you want me to come out this holiday and cheer you up, I'm all for it. L.A. isn't that far from Japan."

"Not as far as Virginia, but still trans-Pacific. Besides, I thought you were going to visit England with Drew."

"*He's* not going through a crisis. And he'll just have to understand if he wants to be with me. I won't abandon a friend in need."

"Thank you, Bennie, but you don't have to. Ray and Darcy are coming out to spend the holidays with me. I won't be alone." *And neither will Lucas...*

"Okay, but if you want me there anyway..."

I force myself to smile, hoping it will put the smile into my voice as well. "I'll let you know. Don't worry."

"Love you, babe."

"Love you too."

17

Ava

I FEEL ATROCIOUS THE NEXT DAY. NOT EVEN A super-hot shower and a latte with extra espresso perk me up. And my throat hurts for some reason. I paste on more foundation and concealer than usual and select a pretty red dress as a pick-me-up because I'm definitely going to need it. I have things to do, and Lucas is coming over tomorrow to discuss progress and our next steps.

While Robbie's in his early morning meeting with the other managers in operations, I go over his agenda for the next few days and answer some emails on his behalf. One in particular catches my attention. It's from a counselor from a private clinic.

Robbie,

You missed yesterday's appointment, and Jay wouldn't talk without you. Is something wrong? Hopefully you can sort out your schedule and get back to me.

The name Jay is familiar...then it strikes me: Robbie's wife. I feel vaguely like a voyeur as my sleep-deprived brain finally registers the name of the clinic: Pacific Family Therapy. I don't ever recall seeing children's photos on Robbie's desk, so it must be for couples counseling.

I forward the email to Robbie and make a mental note to bring it up—delicately—so he doesn't overlook it. Then I go over the replies I received from the catering firm for the fundraising event.

Suddenly there's a commotion. I jerk my attention from my laptop. Jay is marching rapidly toward my desk, her stilettos hitting the floor like bullets. Her fitted camel coat is cinched around the tiny waist, and a loose navy skirt ends mid-shin, showing off toned calves. The floor receptionist is trying to stop her—why, I'm not sure—but Jay won't have it. Meg is no match for the slim Asian woman, who comes to a halt right in front of me.

"You can't come here without an appoint—" Meg says, but Jay raises a hand in her direction, palm out. Meg gives up, and heads off toward the conference rooms.

"Where's Robbie?"

"He's in a meeting at the moment. Is there anything I can help you wi—"

"You're his assistant. So you know his schedule, don't you?"

"Um, sort of." I swallow, my mouth suddenly dry. "Why?"

"What was he doing between five and eight yesterday?"

Is this about the appointment he missed? "I don't know. I'm not in charge of his personal sche—"

"You expect me to believe that? You're *his assistant*."

"Yes, but he doesn't have me handle his personal matters."

"Right." Her dark gaze rakes me.

"Jay." Robbie appears, trotting toward us. "What are you doing here?"

"You didn't come yesterday."

He pinches the bridge of his nose. "I know. It's my fault. I had so many meetings yesterday, and it slipped my mind."

"Sure. That's exactly how it is. You didn't have a party in your hotel room."

I can feel my jaw start to slacken. Robbie is staying at a hotel?

His gaze darts my way for a second. "Can we talk about this in private, Jay?"

"We *were* going to talk about it in private, but you didn't show. Why don't you just sign the damn papers? They're so fair my lawyer's ready to fire me."

"Because that's not what I want."

"Right. Our entire marriage is about what *you* want."

"Come on, Jay." He reaches for her.

She raises both hands and steps back. "You know what? Forget it. Unlike you, I take my commitments seriously, and I have to be in surgery soon anyway. If you don't show on Friday, it's over, Robbie. I'm not wasting any more of my time."

She turns around and stalks away as dramatically as she came in. After she disappears into the elevator, I lower my head, unable to meet my boss's gaze.

"Ava, can I see you for a moment?" Robbie says as he walks past my desk into his office.

I follow him in and close the door.

"Have a seat." He props his hip against the edge of his desk and breathes out heavily, shoving a hand through his hair. "Sorry about the scene."

"No problem." A very awkward silence permeates the room. "Is everything okay? Your...um...therapist emailed your work account last night."

He tilts his head back, his eyes closed. "Damn it. She was supposed to call me on my cell if there's a problem. Well, you're going to hear about it anyway, so I might as well tell you now. Jay and I are going through some rough times."

That would seem to be an understatement. "Um, yeah...I got that impression."

"We're in counseling at the moment—her idea,

because she knows I'm against divorce, but she isn't really interested in reconciliation."

"I'm sorry."

"Eleven years, and it all came down to one thing." His eyes slide toward a recent photo of him with his wife by the laptop. "A kid. Jay can operate on impossible tumors and save countless lives, but not having a child just...put a hole in what we have."

"I'm sorry," I say again, but I don't think he hears.

"She says I make her feel inadequate, that being with me is painful because she feels like she can't be enough for me. I adore her so much."

"Have you considered using the therapy to tell her how you feel about her?"

He shrugs. "She's determined to not hear anything in there. She sits there in silence, and when she does talk, it's to tell me I don't know anything. It's like the therapy is a test to see how far she can push before I break and tell her what she wants to hear." He rubs his face. "Sorry, I don't mean to dump all this on you. God, what am I thinking?" He gives me a tight smile. "I'll make sure she doesn't march back here and put you in an awkward position again. And I'll do my best to ensure my personal life doesn't impact my work here...or yours."

"Hey, it's fine. And I hope everything, you know, works out."

But even as I say it, I know he's not going to be able to give one hundred percent to the job. I'm distracted, letting my feelings for Lucas affect me, and we've known each other for what...maybe eight, nine months total if we add up only the time we've been together? Robbie's been with his wife eleven years, probably longer if you count dating before the marriage.

As I leave, I steal a quick glance at Robbie. His shoulders slope, and he moves like an arthritic man to his work chair.

I feel an intense agony over the dissolution of my relationship with Lucas, and it's got to be a hundred times worse for Robbie, who's built over a decade of life with his wife. I'd probably crawl into a hole and die if Lucas and I broke up after what felt like a lifetime together.

For the first time, I start to understand my mother's obsession with my father because I'm beginning to suspect my depth of feeling for Lucas is the same.

18

Ava

I FEEL EVEN WORSE ON FRIDAY THAN I DID yesterday. I can barely move my head without feeling nauseated. What did I eat to make me feel so awful?

Then I recall I had a Chinese takeout that I like when I'm busy. It's quick and cheap, just what I need. I force myself to sit up, but it only makes me feel worse. Moaning, I crawl to the living room to get my phone. Unfortunately, I left it on the dining table last night after finishing up some memos. I push myself up and grab it, then immediately drop as my head spins until I'm lying flat on my back on the floor.

I dial Robbie's personal number.

"This is Robbie."

"Hi, this is Ava."

"Ava? Are you okay?"

His voice seems far away—crappy reception. I must sound bad if he asks me if I'm okay before I say more. "I hate doing this—I really do—but do you mind if I take today off? I don't feel well, and I'm not sure about driving."

"Not at all. Please take care of yourself. I knew you were working too many hours, and I should've done something earlier."

"It's not your fault. I'm just a bit under the weather. I'll be fine by Monday."

"If you're sure. But if you don't feel okay on Monday, you don't have to come in."

"Thanks, boss." Then I remember something. "Oh, did you get the email I forwarded you from the clinic about...you know...the thing with your wife?"

"Yes." He clears his throat. "You mentioned that already."

"Oh." My mind is like a sieve lately. "Sorry. I won't tell anyone." Then I add impulsively, "I hope it works out for you."

"Thanks, Ava."

He hangs up. I loosen my grip on the phone and lie there, my eyes closed. My brain tells me I should get up and shower—at least—but it's too much bother. It's not like I'm going to see anybody. If I get hungry—doubtful, given how gross my tummy feels—I'll just order something.

I slowly close my eyes and let my consciousness float around, not quite asleep but not awake either—the state I call eighty-five percent sleep...

I notice Faye with Lucas. She's stunning in a skintight silk dress in the most vibrant red I've ever seen. Lucas whispers something in her ear, and she smiles, then says something in return that makes him throw his head back in laughter.

She's with him because you didn't fight for him.

He doesn't love me. Not really.

I'm in love with you.

Because you want the painting.

He—never—needed—you.

Because I was never that special.

Lucas dips me in the big-box store. We kiss like a couple newly in love. Giggle about him kidnapping me to Paris.

Our selfies. We were so happy together. He looks like he cares in those pictures.

If I had the power to go back in time, I'd erase everything that happened since returning from the bed and breakfast. Then at least everything would be fine in my world, and I'd be happy.

Until it all crashes down on me, my house of cards, and I start to cry.

LUCAS

PERHAPS I SHOULD BE GRATEFUL AVA'S APARTMENT

isn't in a war zone, but that's about the best I can say about her shitty neighborhood.

At least it's low crime area—or so my PI Ken assured me—which I find hard to believe. More likely people *assume* it's a low crime area, since there aren't any security cameras and guards around to record unlawful actions for statistics.

I loiter outside her building until somebody goes inside. No one stops me, checks my ID, or looks at me suspiciously. I could be a gang-banger for all they know.

Definitely unsafe.

I go to Ava's unit on the third floor. She and I were supposed to have a short meeting to go over our progress. However, Robbie said she was out sick, and I left the medical center immediately to rush to her side.

But now that I'm here at her door, I hesitate. What the hell am I doing here?

She and I have nothing to do with each other except for the fundraiser. Would I drive over to a coworker's place just because he was sick? Of course not.

On the other hand, I know her work ethic. She never called in sick at work or missed a class when she was in college unless she was half-dead. She wouldn't take a day off unless she was gravely ill.

She has no one in the city, except maybe Jon—my teeth grind involuntarily—and I made sure she wouldn't have any free time to see him. Maybe she needs something to eat. I can just make sure she's stocked up for the weekend and get out. This has nothing to do with my feel—my *previous* feelings for her. It's what any decent human being would do.

I knock, then try the door. *Good God.* She didn't even bother to lock it. Big cities like L.A. are teeming with serial rapists and killers. Just look at the news.

"Ava?" I call out softly, in case she's asleep, then step inside, making sure to close and lock the door behind me.

The place is sparsely furnished with a couch, TV and small dining set big enough for two people. On it is an open laptop. A thin but serviceable beige carpet covers the floor. I look around. Ava hasn't done much to decorate.

I start to walk toward the bedroom, that being the logical place to go if she wasn't feeling well. Instead, I almost trip over her.

She's sprawled on the living room floor. Her long platinum hair lies in tangles, and she's in nothing but a long gray nightshirt with Bugs Bunny in the center holding a carrot.

Fear clutches my heart, coats my mouth with a sharp, unpleasant tang. Horrible possibilities flash through my mind. Seeing her like this sends me back to the winter I found Grandpa passed out on the floor of his rented Spanish cottage. He recovered all right, but half an hour longer and the story would've been very different.

Am I too late for Ava? How long has she been lying here?

Her cell phone is in her hand. Did she try to call nine-one-one before passing out?

I kneel next to her and feel for a pulse. It's steady, if a bit erratic. Her skin feels overly warm, dark circles are like bruises under her eyes, and her lashes are wet.

This isn't Grandpa. She's young and healthy. Don't be melodramatic.

You're here as a concerned coworker. Nothing else.

As I pick her up, she moans softly. God, she hardly weighs anything.

Why did she faint? And don't women usually recover almost instantly after fainting? At least, they seem to in movies.

"I'm taking you to the hospital to get checked."

No "go fuck yourself, you toxic bastard." Not even a moan. Instead she remains limp in my arms.

Panic spikes through me, turning my thoughts sluggish. *For fuck's sake, get a grip.* It's probably nothing. People faint all the time...

I take Ava to Sterling Medical Center. It's close anyway, and they'll surely take care of one of their own. A large and competent-looking nurse bustles over when I arrive. She takes charge, and I have no choice but to hand Ava over even though every cell in my body protests. I watch the staff take her away, her body so small and helpless on the white hospital sheet. I start to say something, start to follow...

I know she's in good hands. Nate doesn't hire incompetent people. But I just...

I want to be by her side when she wakes up.

Don't be idiotic.

I've done my duty. She's with people who can help her. It's not as though she's going to want to see me.

You're toxic.

I haven't forgotten. I can't.

I take a final glimpse of her on the gurney and tell myself to leave.

Walk away.

Walk away.

My legs ignore the command.

19

AVA

WHEN I OPEN MY EYES, I'M LYING ON AN unfamiliar bed in an unfamiliar room. What happened?

The last thing I remember is calling Robbie then sort of drifting away on the living room floor. I probably should've crawled back to bed, but that seemed like too much effort for so little reward.

My mind slowly processes my surroundings. White walls. A narrow bed. A faint odor of disinfectant. A needle in my arm, feeding me some kind of fluid.

A middle-aged nurse walks by, and I call out, "Excuse me."

She stops and turns. Her employee tag reads Leslie Simms, Sterling Medical Center. *I'm at work?* Except I'm not working, I think.

"Oh, you're awake," she says, a kind smile on her round, friendly face. The fluorescent light hits her permed strawberry-blond hair, making it glow like a halo.

"Um. Yeah. What happened? What am I doing here?"

"You don't remember? Your boyfriend brought you. You fainted."

Boyfriend? Fainted? "I don't have a boyfriend."

"Really?" Leslie looks surprised. "I could've sworn he was your boyfriend. He stayed here until the doctor said you'd be okay. Just some dehydration, a lack of sleep and possibly stress. You should take better care of yourself," she chides. "I heard you're Robbie Choi's assistant. We don't want you getting sick, do we?"

"No, ma'am."

She checks a few things, then walks away. My thoughts churn. Who brought me here? I can't think of anybody who can be considered my boyfriend. I went out a couple of times with my coworkers, but the guys at the medical center are all taken. Jon can't be it either, since going to the function together once doesn't make us an item, and he would never presume that.

Now that I think about it... Who the hell came to my apartment in the first place? My coworkers don't know where I live. HR does, but it's most likely against policy to give out my address to—

Lucas.

I dismiss the possibility as soon as it pops in my head. There is no way he came by. He doesn't even like me. In fact, he's probably out with Faye at this very moment.

Suddenly the back of my neck prickles. I tilt my head and see Elizabeth speaking with a nurse.

She's as beautiful as I remember, her golden tresses pulled back in a simple, elegant ponytail. Even her pale lavender wrap dress and the diamond solitaires in her ears exude simple elegance. Every inch of her is carefully groomed, and she easily outshines the basket of yellow and purple tulips she's holding.

I turn away. The last person I want to talk to right now is Lucas's sister. She's probably here to observe or something. Although she's not really hands-on, she is helping Nate Sterling in some kind of an advisory position.

"There you are," Elizabeth says.

I wince, then remind myself she can't see my expression.

"How are you feeling?"

I face her. I hate it that I'm down and she's towering over me. I shrug. "Okay. What are you doing here?"

"I thought I'd bring you some flowers. Everyone deserves some when they aren't feeling their best." She places the basket on the small table by my bed.

"Thank you." The tulips are large and bright, and a small smile tugs at my mouth despite myself.

"And...I wanted to check up on you."

"Why? We're practically strangers."

"Are we?"

"Just because I dated Lucas for a while... We've met only once."

"Still, 'strangers' isn't quite right, is it? And 'acquaintances' sounds a bit clinical. I prefer the term 'Mia's aunt.'"

I hide my shaking hands under the sheet, while she pulls up a chair.

"Aren't you busy?" I rasp.

Her mouth curls into a pleasant smile. "Not particularly."

"I'd like to rest."

"You can listen with your eyes closed. The doctors didn't say your ears were in pain."

Guess she's going to be obtuse. Well, I can be a grownup. "All right." I shift until I'm fully turned toward her. "Go ahead."

Her gaze drops briefly to the needle embedded in my arm. "You should take better care of yourself. This isn't helping anyone."

"I had a lot of work recently."

"The year-end fundraiser."

"Yes. Lucas is helping since you can't." I bite my lower lip, realizing I sound almost accusatory. The last thing I need is to betray my feelings. Elizabeth witnessed me making an idiot of myself over Lucas at the opening. No need to display more of my foolishness.

"I know. Unfortunately, I am truly busy these days." The corners of her mouth turn downward.

"It's okay. I heard."

She sighs. "Why do you make yourselves so miserable? All you have to do is be honest, and you'll know what's in your hearts."

"You don't know anything about it."

"Don't I?" She grows quiet for a moment. "I know you love Lucas."

"You're wrong."

"Then why did you quit your job to come with him?"

"I *didn't* quit. He maneuvered me into it."

"You could've gone elsewhere. Don't tell me you had no choice. People always have choices. You have friends...and foster parents who care deeply about you."

My face heats. Elizabeth's gaze is too direct, too knowing. She's obviously dug into my background. She knows about Mia. She probably knows my shoe size, too.

"When people aren't honest about what they want, it's usually for two reasons. One, they don't think they deserve it. Two, they don't think they'll be able to hold onto the prize. Which is it for you?"

My throat is so dry it feels like there's a wad of sandpaper lodged inside. Finally, I rasp out, "You sound like you have a lot of experience. First hand?"

She merely smiles. "The best defense is a good offense."

"I'm not being defensive."

"Understand something, Ava." She pauses for a dramatic beat. "Lucas is going to marry."

The announcement jerks at my heart with such force, a gasp tears from me before I can control myself. "*Marry?*"

"Marry. Faye Belbin. He's been busy romancing her these days. Unless I'm mistaken, he's going to propose to her this weekend. He booked a suite and"— she makes a few circles with her finger pointed upward —"the works."

The articles and photos. Of course. He isn't just on a rebound. He's... My hand fists over my churning gut. I let Lucas go. I ended it, so I don't know why I'm reacting like this. Have I lied to myself that I was more than ready and happy to let him go to protect myself? But right now the last thing I'm feeling is safe. Elizabeth's news is ripping my heart out, chunk by chunk. "Does she *know?*"

Elizabeth blinks. "Know?"

"About...you know...the thing between all of you and your father."

"Most likely. She's a smart girl."

"And she's okay with it?"

"As far as I know, she doesn't care. She wants Lucas, and everything else is just...so much static." Elizabeth regards me thoughtfully. "To achieve a goal, you need to be brutally honest about what you want and willing to give up everything. *Everything,* including your pride. Faye is more than willing to go the distance."

"And you like it because that will get you the multi-million-dollar painting."

"Money doesn't motivate me. If it did, I wouldn't be involved in charity."

I look away. "Why are you telling me this?"

"So you aren't caught unaware. You were, weren't you, at the opening? I doubt think you want to have a repeat at work or elsewhere." She looks away and sighs. "I'm the one who let Lucas know where you were. I feel responsible for how things turned out."

"We weren't going to work out anyway."

"Lucas brought you here, to the hospital. He still cares about you, but he will never go to you again. His mother made sure to drum into him how unworthy he was from an early age. I've never seen a woman so thoroughly evil, and I'm glad she's not in his life anymore." Elizabeth sighs. "The ball's in your court. Only you can decide if you'll regret not fighting for him and you."

I close my eyes. "It's too late."

I feel her hand grasp mine. "It's *not*. Be honest and fight for what you want. Lucas deserves a woman who'll fight for him." She releases the hand, and the chair creaks. "I hope you feel better soon, Ava."

She walks out before I can gather my wits.

How can Lucas think he doesn't deserve whatever his heart desires? He's rich, handsome and smart. Yeah, so his father's a jerk, and it sounds like his mother is too, but that's just one minor aspect.

On the other hand, I'm a *real* mess. I'm an imposter —a crow tarred with peacock's feathers. It's only a matter of time before people see the truth.

I notice my phone in my peripheral vision and pick

it up from the bedside. My fingers tremble as I navigate to the selfies we took. We're both smiling at the camera, then into each other's eyes—oh so painfully happy in that autumn field in central Virginia.

But there's more—something I've never let myself see. Happiness isn't the only thing on Lucas's face. There is love, adoration. He is looking at me as though I'm everything that matters in his universe. And it isn't just in one shot. Every shot of us... He is gazing at me with love so naked and vulnerable that it guts me.

A sob breaks free of my tight throat, and I shudder as pain wracks me. Hot tears flow freely down my temples and wet my hair.

Could this have been mine if I hadn't pushed him away with the "test"? How do I reconcile the slice of heaven of *that* and the hell of finding out I was just someone he needed to marry to get the inheritance?

I don't want to end up like my mother—broken and dried up. I want to be better than that for myself...and for Mia.

So are you letting Faye have him instead? Give this happiness to her without a fight because you're afraid he's going to use and dump you?

I shift, rolling to my side. My heart aches so much I can barely breathe. It wants to try again. If he won't come for me, I'll go to him. I can tell him I didn't really mean it when I called him toxic. I didn't really want him to go.

What I wanted was to be his number one...and a guarantee of forever.

20

AVA

ONE GOOD THING ABOUT WORKING AT A MEDICAL center is the benefits. I don't have to pay a penny for my treatment. The notion is stunning—a first-rate hospital that doesn't charge? I've always known our mission, what we were doing. But knowing it and actually experiencing it are very different. I feel a swell of pride to be associated with an endeavor like this.

The feeling lasts until I'm out by the exit in my nightshirt and realize that I don't have a car...or money...or even the keys to my apartment. The only thing I do have is my phone. Unfortunately, I don't know anybody in L.A. except Lucas—whom I can't call —Jon and my coworkers. I feel awkward about asking Jon for help when I haven't spoken to him since the opening, so I mentally cross a line through his name.

It's about four o'clock, though. Maybe if I wait another hour, someone going off shift can drop me at my place...

"Ava!"

I turn around to see Robbie trotting toward me. The collar of his white dress shirt is undone. "One of the nurses told me you were here. Why didn't you call?"

"Um..." I pull my lips in, unsure what to say.

"You don't have a ride, do you?"

"Well...no. But I know you're busy—"

"It's no bother. What kind of boss would I be if I let you go like this?" He glances down at my feet, which are in the hospital's slippers.

We walk out to employee parking where his car—a sleek new BMW in dark gray—is waiting. As we pull out of the parking lot, I say, "I hate to bring this up, but don't you have an appointment with your wife right now?"

"She canceled. An emergency surgery."

"Oh, okay."

"She's saving lives." His mouth is tight, but the smile is unmistakable.

"And you're proud of her."

"Very."

We drive quietly, the silence broken only when I tell him to turn one way or another. About halfway home, we stop at an intersection. His fingers drum against the steering wheel, then abruptly stop.

"The nurses said Lucas brought you to the hospital."

"That's what I heard."

He looks at me. "You don't remember letting him in?"

"I don't really recall much after I phoned you."

The light changes, and we start moving again.

"I don't know what's going on between the two of you..." He clears his throat. "But I should've acted on instinct rather than waiting for you to say something."

"What do you mean?"

"Lucas's been driving you way too hard, and you've been working yourself to death without a peep. Does he know how you feel about him?"

The question is so unexpected, I almost splutter. "I'm sorry, what?"

A rueful smile ghosts on his lips. "I saw the way you looked at him...and reacted when you overheard people talking about his affair with his new lady friend."

My belly clenches at the mention of Faye—and what she means to Lucas now. "We...knew each other before, but we aren't... I have no feelings one way or the other now."

"Uh-huh. Well, I think he has feelings for you too. Just an observation."

My mouth dries.

I am in love with you.

"You're mistaken," I say stubbornly.

There's a short stretch of silence. "You know what my therapist told me once?" Robbie looks over at me. "He said people don't always hear what's being said because their mind filters everything through their past experience and bias."

"Oh. Well...I guess that's true."

"Yeah, me too. But I think my therapist missed something. It's not just words that we don't hear. We also don't see what's real because we're too busy filtering that through our experience and bias, too. It's like we're staring at the world through red lenses and wondering why everything is scarlet."

I have nothing to say to that.

"If there's an issue with working with Lucas, I can get Amanda to assist him instead. It's no problem, and I won't hold it against you." He gives me a warm, reassuring smile.

I smile back. "Thanks, but I'm a pro. I can handle it."

"Easy to say, harder to follow through with. Not saying you aren't being truthful, but there's no reason to put yourself in an uncomfortable situation. Feelings drive everything we do."

I tell him to stop the car as we reach my apartment. "Can you get in?" he asks.

"I have the passcode for the lobby door, and if not, I have the super's number."

"Okay. Well, get better and don't come back until you're a hundred percent. I mean it."

He waits until I'm inside the building before driving off. I smile at his thoughtfulness then go up to my apartment, which—thankfully—is both unlocked and un-burgled.

Kicking off the slippers, I flop down on the couch and stare at nothing. The apartment is dead silent, providing a perfect environment for me to sit and let my mind process everything.

Lucas is going to marry Faye. The idea is as painful as an amputation.

I am in love with you.

So am I. I finally, finally admit it to myself in the tiniest internal voice. It's damn scary—terrifying, really —almost as bad as the time I thought I'd lose Mia because she was born too small. My limbs shake, nausea churning in my belly.

You didn't fight for him.

How can I? I swore I would never end up like my mom. And so many things Lucas has done remind me of the way Dad treated us.

Gifts. Emotional unavailability. Smooth talk and excuses about why he couldn't be with us or spend any holidays together.

Of course, he was never available because he had a real home waiting—a three-story brick house with a two-car garage and a yard in one of the nicest and most expensive counties in the country. It's a wonder he spent any time at the roach-infested one-bedroom apartment where Mom and I lived—except for the sex. I didn't understand the moans, the slaps, the filthy things they said to each other until later...but now I wonder if maybe he couldn't get the kind of kicks he wanted from his pricey suburban wife.

I am in love with you.

My hand clenches against my breastbone. *What if he meant it...and you chose not to believe him because of what Dad did to Mom?*

If he meant it, he would've never let me find out about the deal between him and his father that way.

But what if Lucas never found a good time to fess up, the way I never did about Mia? What if I'm the one who's being prejudiced and rejecting him based on past experience? What if I didn't hear what he was really trying to say?

Will I be able to live with myself if I unknowingly throw his love away? I'd crawl across an acre of barbed wire if that would give us the happiness we had at the bed and breakfast. There I felt like the center of his universe, the sole object of his love and regard. And he filled my vision, filled my heart, was only one I wanted to hold in my arms forever.

I bury my face in my hands and let out a soft sob. I'm no longer convinced of anything. I'm looking for a guarantee—that he truly, honest to God loves me and that he won't hurt me...ever.

Except... I should know better. There are no guarantees in life. The only guarantee that we're all going to die one day.

So why not seize what happiness you can while you're alive?

Because it's not that easy. Nothing's that easy.

Crippling fear presses down on me, and I bite my lower lip until it's numb with pain. I've never felt so lost.

21

Lucas

The suite Rachel booked is...nice. I suppose.

It's on the top floor, with large, sumptuously appointed rooms, expensive furniture and silky cotton sheets with stratospheric thread counts. There is also a white grand piano. Why the suite has one, I have no clue. It's not like people book the place to play.

I flick my thumb over my phone, and it comes alive. I go to the photo app and browse the newly downloaded pictures. *Me and Ava. Us at our happiest.* When I thought nothing could tear us apart.

I shouldn't have copied them to my phone, but I couldn't stop myself from rummaging through Ava's mobile. It was laughably easy to access, the passcode being her date of birth. I felt like the cliché creepy ex— checking the previous girlfriend's phone to see who she's been talking to, who she spends time with...who she might be banging, even though I made sure she'd be so overworked she wouldn't have time for such things.

My justification is just as pathetic. I haven't been able to stir myself for any woman. The least she can do is keep her thighs together until I feel my body come to life for someone else.

A tight lump forms in my throat. I want to go back in time.

You're toxic.

I could demand a meeting, make her honor her bargain, try to convince her that...

That what? I'm *not* toxic?

I run a hand over my eyes. She won't buy anything from me. She lies in the hospital because I made sure she had so much work she wouldn't even have time to pee without worrying about finishing all her tasks.

If I thought I could change her mind about the two of us, I'd do anything. But the test and her words made it clear I'm out of options. I grasp the back of a chair and hang my head. I'd give all my money to invent some kind of X-ray that could show Ava what's in my heart.

But...that's just a fantasy. Here in reality, I need to stick to the plan. Marry Faye. That solves several problems. And she'll understand why I'm not banging her if I make up some bullshit story about leg pain or something.

And then you're going to live out the rest of your days only half-alive?

No. In time, whatever hold Ava has over me will weaken. Surely I can't want a woman who has such contempt for me. I have more pride and self-respect than that.

Faye and I had great chemistry before. We can have it again if we're willing to give it a chance. If she's unhappy with our marriage after a year, we can always divorce—amicably and cleanly.

My finger hovers over her number. I should call, ask her to come over, wine and dine her, then propose. The ostentatious diamond and sapphire ring in my pants pocket pricks my leg as though to remind me of the Sunday agenda.

I'm about to hit the green button when there's a knock at the door. Unusual...I haven't ordered anything...

I open the door and freeze.

Ava.

Her complexion is four shades paler than her platinum hair, except for cheeks that are so flushed she looks feverish. For a second I wonder if she's sick, then I tell myself she can't be. The hospital wouldn't have discharged her.

She stares at me, her ice-blue eyes determined. The lines of her throat remain tense, and her hands are clasped together in front of her. Her fitted green jersey dress hangs a bit loosely on her frame. The dark circles under her eyes are still there underneath the careful layers of makeup.

Am I seeing things? I shake my head, but she's still

standing in front of me. I don't get it. She should be resting. It was only Friday that she was at the hospital.

"Can I come in or are you...with someone?" she asks, her voice raspy and low.

For what? What is she doing here?

I drink in her jasmine and vanilla scent, her exquisite presence, and life stirs within me—my broken body a machine only she can fuel.

With sudden clarity, I realize her hold over me hasn't weakened at all. Self-loathing floods through me, and my feeling for her borders on pure hatred. She's done this to me...reduced me to this pathetic state. Or maybe it's like my mother said over and over again. I'm just fucked up all on my own. Either way, I'm screwed.

Ava swallows. "Lucas?"

I should shut the door in her face. Tell her to go fuck herself.

But I can't. My heart tells me to let her in and bask in the delirious sensation of being alive...being truly alive...

I'm an alcoholic who keeps relapsing, each time more painful than the one before. The key to handling it is going cold turkey and staying the hell away.

"Please."

The soft whisper pierces the steel around my heart. I step aside so she can walk in. And the second does, I let go of the door. It shuts, the lock engaging with a click.

22

Ava

My hands are so clammy, I want to wipe them on my dress. But I don't dare. They're too shaky, and I don't want to show him how nervous and unsure I am.

I still don't know what I'd been planning when I called Elizabeth earlier today and asked her where Lucas was. She told me, but she didn't offer any encouragement. Perverse woman. She could've spared a kind word, now that I've decided to follow her advice.

I tried so hard to convince myself I could move on—that I *had* moved on. But that's a lie. My eyes trace the chiseled lines of his face and tall, strong body, my heart galloping like a thoroughbred at a race.

His expression is shuttered. "Why are you here, Ava? Most people avoid toxic waste."

I wince. He'll never forgive me for that...will he?

He's going to throw me out the second I tell him what I'm here to say.

"I didn't give you the five minutes you were entitled to," I blurt out.

If possible, he seems to grow even remoter. "I don't want them anymore."

"But—"

"You can leave." He starts to turn away.

"No! I have to tell you something."

"I think you made your point with the pot."

I ignore him. "I should've told you before, but I was too afraid."

He finally swivels his head my way, genuine surprise in his gaze. "What do you have to fear?"

"When..." I lick my dry lips. "When I learned about the deal...I was devastated. I always felt like what we had was too good to be true."

Something like pain crosses his expression. "It *was* too good to be true," he agrees, his voice soft.

I shake my head. "It's more than that, Lucas."

He waits, neither encouraging nor discouraging me. But his gaze is so cold, I feel like my organs are freezing one by one.

If I don't tell him how I really feel about him, this is over. But if I tell him and he turns away...

The strange nightmare I had in Charlottesville floods my mind. I can't draw in any air—it's as though there's a big fist clenched around my neck. The cityscape behind him, Lucas is as brilliant and radiant as in my dream.

What if he rejects me? What if he knows, with that unerring instinct that well-cultured and moneyed people have, that I'm not worth it? That I'm good enough for some temporary fun, but nothing else?

My heart thunders, and I can't get the words out.

Suddenly he shakes his head. "You should go. I have plans for the day."

He's going to marry Faye. If I let him go like this... Oh my God. My legs are shaking, and cold sweat mists my spine. "I was in love with you."

The words come out in a barely audible whisper, but his entire demeanor hardens. The lines on his face are harsher, colder and more aloof. My mouth is so dry, my lips and tongue feel like dead leaves.

"Then why did you say it was over? Why did you call me toxic?" His voice has no inflection. Just a terrifying calm...and something else I can't process at the moment.

"Because..." I'm jittery all over. I've never been this nervous in my life. "I never wanted to be in love with you. I was afraid."

"Bullshit. I told you I loved you. I said it first."

"I didn't think you meant it."

His hands clench into fists. "Why are you telling me this now?" His jaw flexes. "Is this some kind of game? Didn't I give you enough money?"

"I never wanted your money!"

I'm shaking so hard I can't think or speak. The right words all disappear from my mind when faced with his implacable façade. I blindly reach for something to steady myself and grasp the back of an armchair. My knuckles whiten, and I start to lose the feeling in my hand.

Start at the beginning. It's always easier that way.

"I don't know if I'm doing the right thing by being here. Maybe I'm making a mistake. I've been miserable without you, even though I told myself I was better off on my own. Then I saw you kiss Faye, and it was like somebody took a sledgehammer to my heart. It still feels that way every time I think about it. Then your sister told me I was the one at fault. Because I didn't fight for you." I close my eyes, hoping it'll help me focus. It doesn't work that well, but at least I can block out Lucas's impassive face. "I never fought for what I wanted because I never found anything—or anyone—I wanted badly enough. Then when I found you, I couldn't bring myself to fight because I was certain I'd never be allowed to keep the prize. You're so perfect, so...*everything*. Why would you be with someone like me?"

Silence stretches, and I open my eyes, unable to bear the suspense. Lucas is studying me with the oddest expression on his face.

"Why not? What's wrong with you?" he asks, his voice hushed.

My throat closes. I should've known he wasn't going to let the past go so easily. I should've known I cut him too deeply, that he'd want to see me bleed. "I'll go. Sorry I interrupted your day."

I hardly take a step before his hand closes around

my wrist. "No, you can't leave like this. Answer the question—*what is wrong with you?*"

I yank on my arm, but he holds firm. "What's wrong with me? Isn't it obvious?"

"No."

"I'm a mess!" I fling my free arm. "I'm exactly the kind of girl people like you fuck on the side but don't date, don't introduce to your family, don't think about long-term."

"Why not?"

"Look at me and look at you. I was raised by an uneducated single mom who didn't know any better. She thought she could get my dad to marry her if she had me, but it wasn't enough. He was happy to come by, play daddy when it suited him...and then leave—go back to his perfect upper-middle-class family. Mom and I were just props so he could play at being some rough, blue-collar guy when he was bored with his suburban life."

Realization dawns on his face, but I turn away.

"Let me go, Lucas."

"Why did you come here?"

I shake my head. It's too humiliating.

"I'm not letting you go until you tell me." When I press my lips together, he shakes me. "*Tell me,* damn you. What did you think you could gain by coming here?"

"I don't know." *Liar. Liar.* Every cell in my body begs to leave. I can't stay here anymore and endure the pain or humiliation. I should've accepted I lost. The time to fight was in Charlottesville, not now.

"*Ava, tell me.*"

His visible eye is narrowed, and his nostrils flare. I'm going to have to hit rock bottom, and then bring out a shovel, before he lets me go. "Because Elizabeth told me you're going to marry Faye. Because I thought if I bared myself to you, things might change."

"So you're here to fight...for me?"

"Fight..." I sniffle, then shrug helplessly. "I don't know how to fight. We can't go back in time and erase all the harsh words between us." I drop my gaze. "It was a mistake for me to come, and I'm sorry."

"Is that all you're feeling? Just regret?"

I close my eyes for a moment. I don't want to tell him, but I owe him that much. After all, he bared everything to me before. "No. I feel...defeated. Hollow. You stole my heart twice. I could've survived the first time, but the second..." I swallow. "I'm never going to be whole. I'm in love with you. Always have been. You're an impossible man to fall out of love with." I exhale roughly, my entire being wrung out. "Will you let go now? Please?"

"I can't."

His palms cradle my face, and his mouth crashes down on mine. My thoughts fry, and I let go of everything except the incredible sensation his kiss elicits within me. I part my lips, brush my tongue against his and feel the groan vibrating from his chest. He tastes just like I remember—the sweetest and most amazing homecoming.

I dig my fingers into his hair, hold him tightly to me, afraid if I don't, he's going to slip away...just like in my dream. I'll die if this is just a figment of my imagination.

Now that I have him in my arms, I feel like a starving woman before a banquet table. I breathe in his scent—all male and heat—and feel his body against mine—powerful, sinewy, vibrating with tension.

The edge of my teeth scrape his lip, and a coppery tang laces our kiss. I should be sorry, maybe, but I'm not. He deepens the kiss until all I feel is lush heat blossoming in my belly and spreading throughout.

He pushes my dress up, bunching the skirt around my waist. My leg wraps around his thigh like a vine. His rough fingers dig into my thighs and ass. I whimper, then drag the dress up and up until it's over my head and lost somewhere in the room. My bra gets a similarly unceremonious disposal while Lucas tugs at my thong impatiently. I hear fabric tear and couldn't care less. I'm delirious with the idea of feeling his skin soon.

I devour his mouth while yanking at the buttons on his shirt. My hands are clumsy. They barely manage to get two buttons undone before Lucas rips the shirt apart, buttons flying everywhere, and flings the expensive garment like it's yesterday's garbage. I unbuckle his belt and slacks and push them down along with his boxers. His cock springs out, thick and hard.

He kicks off his shoes and clothes, and we're at each

other. My back presses against the cool, papered wall, and I groan at how amazing his bare skin feels against me. Every nerve in my body is electrified, and a delicious heat courses through me. This...this must be how a desert feels when the first drop of rain hits. My skin's hypersensitive, and even the slightest friction of his chest hair against my torso feels like a rasp.

His fingers dig into my ass, and I spread my legs as widely as I can and cradle his erection within my drenched folds. A harsh groan rumbles in his throat, and I whimper softly at the empty ache that amplifies even more.

"Tell me again," he orders.

"I'm in love with you."

He enters me in a long, powerful stroke. I cry out at the heady sensation of being joined with him. He's huge, so thick, so perfect—my man, my lover, the greatest and most treasured piece of my soul.

He stills. "Again."

"I'm in love with you."

He moves. "Again."

"I'm in love with you. Love with you. Love with you."

He drives into me over and over again as I chant my love for him. My toes curl, and I revel in the rough, uncontrolled coupling, my body winding tighter and tighter.

When the climax rips through me, I scream, my voice breaking as I'm sucked into the maelstrom. But I don't stop the mantra because I know he needs to hear it. He pushes me ruthlessly. The shells around my heart shatter one by one until I'm utterly vulnerable. "I'm in love with you, Lucas." I stare into his dark eyes. "Don't let me fall."

"Never."

The single word is a promise so solid it grounds me, an anchor making sure I'm not lost. He thrusts into me so hard, with such intensity, I orgasm again, my vision almost dimming. Still he doesn't stop. My inner walls are swollen and sensitive, and the wet friction of his cock driving in and out of me pushes me closer to another climax.

His uneven, choppy breathing and frantic pace tell me he's close, and I want us to fall into oblivion together this time.

Tunneling my fingers into his hair, I caress my cheek against his. My mouth almost touches his ear as I whisper, "I'm in love with you, Lucas. Come. Come with me."

He dips a finger into my folds and runs it over my tight rosette. My back arches at the electrifying pleasure, and it catapults me to another height. As I cry out, he pulls out and comes all over my belly. He buries his face in the crook of my neck, his breath hot and moist against my sweat-misted skin. "Ava...Ava..."

I caress his head.

I'm in love with you.

With that declaration, I've made myself as defenseless as a child. I meant it when I begged Lucas to not let me fall. I'm scared witless. I've never let myself be this vulnerable to someone before.

Still, everything around me is clicking into its rightful place. I wouldn't give up this moment for anything.

～

Lucas

As my lungs finally stop heaving and blood circulates back into my brain, I tighten my hold around Ava, not wanting to let her go, ever. If I can have her by supporting her against the wall, I'll happily do it for the rest of my life.

Still, I know I'm crushing her, and the textured wallpaper can't feel good against her delicate skin. I pull back, lowering her gently. She wobbles on her feet, and I allow myself a moment of satisfaction before my gaze hits the sticky mess on her belly.

Why are you so grimy?

Why did I say about making a mess?

Don't touch me with your dirty hands.

Suddenly my throat closes around me, and I take half a step back. "I made a mess."

She smiles, looking down. "I don't mind."

I shake my head. "I shouldn't have."

"Lucas..."

"Let me get a washcloth. Don't move and don't go anywhere."

She regards me, confusion pinching her eyebrows together. She reaches over and takes my wrist. "Lucas, don't."

"I wasn't thinking. Shouldn't have done it when I didn't have a condom on me."

Ava looks at me. "You weren't...planning on sleeping with...her?"

I shake my head. "No. Hold on." I gesture in the direction of the bathroom.

"Lucas, don't. I don't mind. It's part of you, a sign that you enjoyed yourself."

Her words barely register. The only thing hammering in my head is the old memory.

Why would I want to hug you when you're so filthy? my mother would say, pushing me away. *Leave me alone.*

"Lucas." Ava cups my cheek. "Here."

She guides my hand between her legs, lets me feel the slick warmth. My blood heats again, and I can't stop myself from gently rubbing her swollen clit.

A gasp, then a moan. But she doesn't let me continue. She tightens her hold around my wrist. "Does this bother you?"

Helluva silly question. "No. I love it when you're wet for me." I punctuate that by pushing a knuckle into her pussy. I want to see her squirm, then come again, riding my fingers. She's so lovely when she climaxes—

all soft and sweet and pliant. Her pleasure gives me the kind of high nothing else can.

"Mmm." She rubs my cum over her belly. "Then accept that I feel the same way about you coming on me."

"Ava—"

"Lucas, when I said I loved you, I meant it. I don't love some parts of you and reject the rest. I adore everything about you, everything that you are. If you can't accept that, we're going to have a serious problem."

I can't help it. I kiss her, wrapping her hair around my fist. Her words erase the ugliness, each one a precious ablution. She licks all over my mouth, and I feel whole and clean—all the unlovable shit about me washed away.

My eyes prickle, my heart thundering. I finally understand the courtly old love poems I was forced to read in school. If Ava asked me now, I'd gladly climb a jagged mountain barefoot, slay a fire-breathing dragon with my fists, vanquish all those in the way of her happiness and bring her wild flowers to put in her hair.

"I love you, Ava."

"I love you too, Lucas."

I thumb her prominent cheekbones. "I've waited an eternity to hear that."

"It did take me some time to say it, but it took you while, too."

My forehead rests against hers. "Only because you vanished after my accident."

"What do you mean?"

I pull back. She's too thin—the shadows under her ribs are deeper—and I haven't forgotten her fainting spell on Friday. "Time to eat."

"You haven't answered my question."

"I'll answer it. But after we have lunch."

"We don't have to eat right now—"

"Yes, we do." I hand her the room service menu. "Do you know what I hated the most when hearing about your childhood?"

She blinks. "I don't think I told you much."

"No, but you told me how hungry you were, and I hated that." I tilt her chin and give her a quick kiss. "You've lost weight and you fainted on Friday—"

"That was just some stress…"

"—so you'll eat." She still hasn't opened the menu; I do it for her and push it into her hands.

She glances down at the options, then looks at me. "All right, fine. But if I do eat, I want you to talk to me honestly."

I cock an eyebrow. "What if you ask me to tell you something I don't want to talk about?"

"Then just say that rather than pretend like there's nothing to say."

"Will you do the same?" I need to know—that she'll be always brutally honest with me. I can't second-guess or wonder at hidden meanings. I'm not good at that kind of thing.

"Always," she answers, her tone steady.

I believe her. Even if she told me the sky was red, I'd believe her because the alternative would be no more life with her. I'm craven, desperate, but I don't care. I need this. I need her.

"Thank you," I murmur, my gratitude extending not just to her, but whatever cosmic force out there brought her back to me.

23

Ava

I CHOOSE A GRILLED CHICKEN SANDWICH AND lobster bisque combo and decide to clean up while Lucas orders. The bathroom is swanky with a double vanity and huge Jacuzzi tub big enough to party in. Neatly folded white towels sit on an elegant marble pedestal, and I select a small washrag. I might've just left the semi-clear liquid on me—I actually think it's sort of hot—but Lucas seemed really bothered by it.

Even if I'm not super adventurous about sex, I know men don't generally find the sight of ejaculate on a woman they just had sex with a turnoff. Who hurt Lucas to make him feel like he did something wrong?

I wipe my belly clean and put on a robe. When I find out who's been so cruel to him, I'll make them pay. I don't know how, but I'll figure out a way.

Then I go still for a moment. Elizabeth told me his mother was a monster. Was this reaction because of his childhood? I'm tempted to ask, but I loathe bringing up something dark and ugly and marring our time together.

By the time I come out with an extra robe, he's hanging up the phone. "Here," I say.

He shrugs into the robe and gestures at the loveseat. "Sit. Lunch will be here soon."

I curl up on the left side. "So. The answer."

"You have a one-track mind, you know that?"

"You're the one who left me hanging." I haven't forgotten the significance of our prematurely interrupted conversation.

He sits next to me and stretches out his legs. "When I crashed my bike, I felt like I was dying."

The reminder of the horrible accident—how something as random and senseless like that could permanently take him away—chills my blood. I bring his hand to my lips and kiss the knuckles. "I'm glad you didn't."

His gaze softens for a moment before he continues, "And you know how people say when you're about to die, your life flashes before your eyes? Well, that's what happened to me, except everything that passed was about you and our memories together." He takes my hand and kisses it. "I knew then that you were the only thing that mattered."

"And then I disappeared." Because I couldn't stand Blake's cruel words or the possibility that Lucas had used me the way my father used my mom.

"Yeah." He makes a little spreading gesture with the tips of his fingers. "Poof."

"I'm sorry. We wasted so much time. If I hadn't run..."

"Don't. I could've gone after you, but I didn't."

"Why not?"

"I thought you'd come back once you realized what we had together and what you'd given up."

The idea of him waiting for me makes me ache. He doesn't know how hopeless that was because I never told him. "I would've never come back."

Our food arrives. After the server sets up our table, Lucas signs the bill and takes the seat across me. He gestures at an array of beverages. "I ordered one of everything, since I didn't know what you wanted."

I take a Diet Coke and let it fizz into a heavy, square glass over ice. "Want some?"

"No, thanks." He levers the cap off a beer. "So. You were saying..."

I sip my drink and nibble on a fry. It's crispy outside and soft inside. Perfect. "I never told you this. Actually, I never told anyone. The people who know know because they saw it."

"So Bennie knows."

"Yeah." I reach for another fry. Lucas takes a bite of mashed potatoes piled high next to a sizable pork chop. "When I got home after the hospital visit, I looked you up. Until then I'd never bothered because...well, I don't know. I just never did. It hadn't seemed all that important. But there were *tons* of articles about you online.

And when I saw the ones with you and Faye together, I just felt...dirty and gross, and as far as I was concerned, it was over."

"Ava..." He reaches for my hand, and I let him hold it and hang on tight. We need this connection so that no matter what I say, we'll know we're okay.

"I told you about how poor my family was when I was growing up, but I didn't tell you everything. My parents didn't marry...and my mother blamed me. She was certain if I'd been a boy, Dad would've done 'the right thing.'"

Lucas shakes his head. "Completely unfair of her."

"She wasn't rational when it came to my father. She was crazy about him, just obsessed, even though he was hardly ever home. He was..." I pause, debating how to say the rest without sounding pitiful. But what am I thinking? The story is pathetic no matter how I spin it, and just moments ago, I promised to be truthful. "He claimed to be a truck driver, so he was away a lot. Always missed holidays and birthdays, anniversaries... every date that mattered. I can't think of a single time he celebrated a birthday or holiday with us."

Sympathy softens Lucas's expression. "We'll never miss birthdays and holidays. I promise."

I give him an aching smile. When he makes a promise like that in such a solemn voice, it's impossible for me to not to fall even deeper in love with him. "Then there was a car accident. He didn't make it, and Mom and I were devastated. But nothing could've prepared for us for facing his wife and daughter."

I tighten my hand around his until my knuckles pale. Only Bennie and Elle know this humiliating chapter of my life. "They were so beautifully dressed in designer clothes. His wife's skin was so smooth, so well taken care of. She was nothing like my mom, who worked herself ragged to support me. And the daughter... She was the kind of girl who led the popular kids in high school, you know?"

Lucas nods.

"Then we learned Dad wasn't a poor trucker, but a bank manager. He might not have been filthy rich, but he was pretty damn comfortable. He just wanted to play at being a roughneck when he was bored with his white-bread suburban life, go slumming for some kicks with a woman he considered beneath him. I was basically the result of a failed condom. Which explained why he'd never bothered to spend any quality time with us. We didn't matter. We were just a dirty little secret he kept for cheap thrills. He left everything to his real family. It devastated my mom so much that she just...came unhinged and drank herself to death."

"So when you found about me and Faye, you thought I was doing to you when your dad did to your mother."

I nod.

Letting go of his fork, he rubs his face with a hand. "Christ, Ava."

"It's hard for me to take a person's word for something, especially when it comes to relationships. That's why I'd have never come back after leaving the hospital, and why I didn't want to listen to you when the deal between you and your father became public. I was starting to get obsessed with you, and I felt like I was becoming my mother."

"I'm sorry. I never knew…"

"How could you? I didn't tell you, and I'm not famous enough to be Googleable."

A small smile quirks. "Googleable?" The smile disappears. "I'm glad you aren't. I don't want anybody to know about you. I want you to be mine alone."

There's a tiny edge of need in his tone that guts me. I squeeze his hand. "You have me. I'm not going anywhere."

"It's a miracle you came back, given your background."

"I wasn't going to, but weighing my fear and the pain of losing you forever… I had no choice."

"Faye."

I nod, then bite my lip as jealousy unfurls within me. "I know you care a great deal about her."

"We were lovers years before I met you, and I like her. She's older and more experienced than me and doesn't play games. It's…refreshing to be with someone like that."

I drink some Coke to wash away the bitter taste in my mouth. I always thought I wanted to know the whole story about Faye and Lucas, but now that he's talking, I'm not sure if I really want to hear it.

"But she's not you, Ava. Nobody can be you. You're the only woman who's made me yearn."

The quiet intensity of his gaze and voice ripples over me. It soothes the wounds of my soul, and I close my eyes to savor the warm, sweet moment.

"When I saw you for the first time at that restaurant, it was like seeing my fate. My future."

I grin. "You liked my body. I remember you checking me out." An understatement; he'd stripped me bare with his eyes.

"Nice bodies and pretty faces are dime a dozen. You were different." He takes a bite of his lunch and lets the silence stretch for a moment.

"Then why did you act like you didn't want me back? You never wanted to stay the night or take me to meet your family or friends. If they'd seen me before the accident, maybe things would've turned out differently."

He hesitates.

"You don't want to talk about it," I say finally.

His fingers twitch. "It's not that. I'm trying to figure out how to say it so I can avoid looking like an idiot..." He sighs. "Okay, it was my fault. Even as I wanted you, I was fighting it. I felt like I didn't deserve that kind of love."

Then I know. "Your mother."

"What do you mean?"

I shake my head. "Don't do that. We promised to be honest with each other, and you're not. It's not fair."

"You're right, it's not. I'm sorry. No, I don't want to talk about her."

"Okay." He isn't willing to open up yet, so I'm not

going to push it. After all, we can't continue to have mutual respect and honesty if we refuse to let the other person be. I'm afraid to push too hard and ruin what we have. "Then can you tell me about the deal between you and your father? What the tabloids said... It's true, isn't it?"

He nods, his shoulders relaxing a bit. "Basically. What they didn't publish is that the whole thing came about because Dad was furious we missed his Wedding Number Six."

"To some woman who isn't even half his age." I saw that part too on the Internet.

"I'd be surprised if she finished high school. She's so young she could've been our sister."

"He must love her, though."

Lucas snorts a laugh. "He can't stand his wives. His ego was hurt that we didn't show. Blake, Ryder and Elizabeth opted to attend their cousin's wedding—it was his *first* marriage, after all—and Elliot and I chose not to go because after a while, you don't want to be part of your parents' circus. But Dad wanted to make a point, and he knew he could use the portraits to get to us. There were some complications with Grandpa's will, and the paintings went to my father, who thinks we're all a bunch of worthless losers, and that our grandfather was too soft on us."

"That's awful. He's your father."

"A reluctant father. I'm sure he regrets he didn't ask his wives to get abortions."

I gasp.

"We were just bargaining chips in the divorces, although it didn't work out the way he wanted with me and Elliot."

"Why not?"

"Because our mother didn't try to win custody. She preferred a fatter alimony payment."

My image of Lucas as a child, growing up in abundance with everything a person could want, crumbles. Everything online portrayed an enviable life, and I accepted it all without question. "So what's so special about the portraits?" I ask. "Everyone seemed to be focused on how much they're worth, but that's not it, is it?"

"Their monetary value isn't even a consideration for us." He jabs the air with his fork. "I'm not denying they're each worth millions of bucks, but let's face it. We don't need the money. If we get them, none of us will ever sell them. The value—to us—is entirely sentimental. Our grandfather painted them when we turned eighteen, and they show the potential and greatness he saw in us."

"They must be amazing. I wish I could see the one of you."

Lucas shifts his weight, then reaches for his beer. "It's pretty romanticized. Grandpa only saw the best in everyone."

"I don't see the best in everyone, but I think you're incredible." I finish the last of my fries. My mind is made up. "Let's get married."

He stares at me as though I've asked him to climb Everest in the nude. "Ava...we can't."

"What? Why not?"

"I didn't go after you to get the painting."

"I know, and that's fine. I just think that now—"

"I won't marry you. Now yet."

Well, this is unexpected. I cast about for the right argument. "But that means your father's going to win."

He shrugs.

"Don't you want to win?"

"Yes."

I narrow my eyes. "You aren't marrying anyone else, Lucas Reed!"

"Absolutely not. I told you already, you're the only one for me. But I'm not marrying you either, not until the six months is up, because I'm not giving you any cause to doubt my love for you again."

Now it becomes clear. "Lucas...I won't."

But he isn't listening. "My brothers and sister will just have to get over it. I'll find a way to make it up to them."

"But you were going to marry Faye..."

"I didn't love her, Ava. It's not the same thing."

"You're right, it's not. This way, you get both the painting and the woman you really do love. So what's the problem?"

"If anything happens between us because of the damned deal..." He inhales roughly. "I can't go through...everything...again."

"Have you imagined how I'd feel if I cost you something so important to you and your siblings?"

"*You* aren't costing me anything. Even if you were, you're worth a hundred such portraits. My decision is final."

"But—"

"Next week's Thanksgiving. Are you flying to Charlottesville or are you staying in the city?" From the hard set of his jaw, he's not doing to budge.

I sigh. "Staying in L.A."

"Great. Ryder's hosting dinner. Friends and family only. I'm invited, and so are you."

My jaw slackens. "Me? At Ryder Reed's?" Ryder isn't just Lucas's brother but a Hollywood megastar. If I weren't in love with Lucas, I might be in love with Ryder...like millions of other women.

"You're my plus-one."

Shock, excitement and nerves war inside me, each side evenly matched. Then reality intrudes. "Lucas, I'd love to. But I already have plans. Darcy and Ray are flying out to celebrate together, and I can't leave them alone."

"Then they're invited too."

"Lucas! You can't just—"

"Ryder said to bring as many people as I want. And believe me, there's space."

I narrow my eyes. "Did he maybe say that because he was pretty certain you wouldn't bring anyone except Faye?"

He shrugs. "Maybe."

I seize the opening. "When he finds out he's going to lose the painting he married his assistant for, he's going to be furious with me."

"No, he won't. And I'm not talking about this again with you, Ava."

"But—"

"I mean it."

He places his napkin by the plate and gets up. His arms go around me, pulling me up, and I know the discussion is over for now. But if he thinks this is the end of it, he has another think coming. I'm not going to let him lose something that means so much to him because of my insecurities.

His gaze on mine, he slowly lowers his head, giving me a chance to turn away.

There's no way.

The first touch of his lips at the corner of my mouth is tender but sensual. Tingles start and spread in sweet ripples, tightening my nipples and pooling between my legs. Feeling wickedly wanton, I shrug a shoulder, letting the robe slip down, exposing a breast.

He continues to kiss me. If I didn't feel his cock getting harder and thicker against my belly, I might've never known that he noticed. I do the same with the other shoulder so I'm standing topless. His unhurried seduction of my mouth leaves me breathless, my limbs weak. The only thing that's keeping me up is Lucas's hands wrapped around my waist.

"You're so beautiful. So sweet," he whispers. "I could live on nothing but you." A deep groan vibrates in his chest, and I feel it through my nipples all the way to my clit. I whimper, needy and wanting this moment to go on forever.

He picks me up and carries me to bed. Without breaking the kiss, he lays me down in the center of the mattress and unties the robe. I push his out of the way, annoyed there's anything between us. I clutch his wide shoulders, marveling at his strength, grateful that he's mine.

I came so close to losing him because of fear.

"I feel like an idiot, wasting so much of our time together. If I'd just given you five minutes, we could've had this all along," I murmur.

"Don't blame yourself. You weren't ready to listen and believe what I had to say."

He's right. But that doesn't make it any better.

"Now stop thinking," he whispers. "And just feel."

His clever mouth travels along my jaw line and the sensitive skin of my neck. He slowly traces the underside of my breast, his fingertips barely touching. I arch my back for more concrete contact and get rewarded when his big hand closes firmly around my breast. My nipple pulses as he drags his thumb slowly across it, up and down. Lust pulses through me, and I am indecently wet. "Lucas. Don't tease me."

"I want to learn your body again. I want to take my time and relearn everything there is to know."

He lets his mouth travel slowly down my torso, all along my curves. He breathes against the small mounds of my breasts, and I spread my legs wider, heat thrumming in my veins.

"Not yet."

He takes the tip of my breast into his mouth, sucking hard. The sensation is so sharp, so electrifying, that my back arches of its own volition. The emptiness between my legs aches so badly, I cry out, undulating my pelvis.

With deliberate care, he thumbs my clit and hisses. "You're so damn wet."

"I want you."

"You have me. You'll *always* have me."

Two thick fingers plunge inside, gliding in smoothly. I groan at the sensation, but it isn't over. He licks the glistening fingers, then switches position, getting under me with my legs on each side of his chest.

"Sit on my face, Ava."

My cheeks heat.

"Come on. Straddle my head and let me tongue-fuck you, taste your orgasm."

The image that comes to my mind is so wicked and hot, I can't breathe. But I don't want to come alone. I want him with me.

I reach behind and wrap my hand around his erection. His engorged shaft pulses, the tip wet with precum. *Oh, that's right...he doesn't have a condom.* I smile wickedly.

"You can tongue-fuck me all you want. But I'm turning around."

His cheeks flush, and heat darkens his eyes until they're pure black.

"Deal?"

He nods.

I clamber around and position myself so we can pleasure each other at the same time. His fingers dig into my pelvis as he runs the flat of his tongue along my folds. Sanity quickly departs as his hot breaths fan against the most sensitive tissues in my body, and he devours me as though I'm the best dessert in the universe. Lust sears through me, and I feel like my blood is boiling. I pull him into my mouth, wanting him to share the moment.

He groans harshly, the vibration rippling through me. I use my tongue and lips and cheeks and hands to stimulate him, give him the pleasure he's giving me.

We drive each other to greater and greater heights. I grind my hips against his face. Our love frees me, leaves me shamelessly honest with him.

He grows thicker and harder in my mouth, and I know my uninhibited response is driving him insane. I'm going crazy too, but I hold on, wanting to prolong the most basic connection a man and woman can share.

"Come for me," he growls against my clit.

Instead of letting go, I pull him harder and deeper into me. He moans, and I say, "Not without you."

He thrusts two fingers inside me, filling me, stretching me. He bumps against my g-spot, and I shatter, helpless to hold back anymore.

His pelvis moves once, twice, mouth fucking me,

then he groans, spurting in a hot, salty froth. I drink him in greedily, loving it that I'm the one responsible for that tortured sound he makes as he comes.

He pulls me up and kisses me. The taste of us mingles, and I lose myself in him, trusting he'll keep me safe, he'll put my shattered self back together.

"That was...pretty amazing." I can feel myself blushing.

"First time in the congress of the crow?"

"The what?"

"Sixty-nine. That's what it's called in the Kama Sutra. No idea why."

"Oh. Yeah, first time. Alas, I'm not that, uh, adventurous."

He grins wickedly. "We should rectify that."

"We should."

He brushes his lips over the tip of my mouth, then my mouth. "To new memories."

"To new memories."

Ava

AFTER BUYING A BOX OF CONDOMS, LUCAS AND I spend the rest of Sunday afternoon and evening in bed. I can't bear to be away from him...but at ten o'clock, I finally extricate myself from his embrace.

"I should get going."

He takes my wrist. "Don't."

"I have to go to work tomorrow. I have no change of clothes here."

"We can get the concierge to get you a new outfit. Stay."

I smile at his near-petulant tone. "Lucas, it's okay. I'll be back tomorrow." When he keeps pouting—rather adorably so—I can't help but tease. "Unless I have to work. My boss is a slave driver who gives me so much work I'm up late."

He winces. "That asshat was probably jealous you might go out with Jon."

"Seriously? Is that why you gave me so much to do?"

"Yeah. Sorry."

"I think it's cute that you were jealous. Too bad I couldn't do that to you so you had to stay home working instead of..." I trail off, suddenly feeling like I'm on the wrong track.

"I'm a moron, and I don't deserve you."

I glare at him. "Don't say that."

He continues as though he hasn't heard me: "But I want you to know. Nothing happened between me and Faye. You've wrecked me, Ava. I don't want anyone but you, and if I can't have you, I want no one at all."

"But..."

"I 'dated' Faye because it would look more convincing if I did that before marrying her. Most people believed Elliot and Ryder's show, but not everyone. If I'd married her out of the blue, people would start talking again."

"You care about what they say?" The idea is unfamiliar. Lucas is always so steady and clear on what he's trying to do.

"I *don't* care...but Elizabeth probably does. She's beautiful and wealthy, and has her share of stalkers and creeps. If they knew she had to marry soon, they might think it'd be their chance."

My mouth forms an O. I never thought about that.

"And just to let you know, I'm going to have to see Faye again tomorrow."

"Why?"

"To break things off cleanly. We may not be...intimate anymore, but she's always been a good friend."

"Do you regret she's going to feel used?"

He runs his hand through his tousled hair. "I don't know. The marriage was her idea, and even though we were seen in public, I never told her I would marry her." He scowls. "I know you were watching when we kissed at the medical center opening."

So he did that on purpose, to hurt me... I push away the ugly feeling it elicits. We were estranged then, angry and in pain.

He holds up a forestalling hand. "Elizabeth told me. I had no idea until then." His visible eye narrows. "Faye said an ex-boyfriend was watching, and she wanted to show him they were through. So I figured, why not? It was an easy enough request, and I was still messed up from our separation. But I didn't like being manipulated into hurting you."

"Thank you for that."

"So...stay the night?"

I laugh softly. "All right. I have a feeling if I say no, you're going to move into my place."

"It's a distinct possibility. But that apartment is small, and I don't like that it doesn't have any security."

"It's a safe enough neighborhood."

He snorts. "I'm not leaving anything to chance. Rachel's going to look for an acceptable property, and we're moving in together ASAP."

"Can't we just move into your current place? It's not like I need a separate bedroom."

"Not the best idea. I'm crashing with Blake at the moment."

My happiness dims a little at the mention of his oldest brother. "You are?"

"We're on two separate floors, but still."

I'm quiet for a moment. "I see." I clear my throat. "Okay, that's fine. I won't pretend I'd be okay living with him, but I do need to work things out with Blake. He's your brother, and I don't want awkward feelings between us."

"Well, he's going to have to deal or I'm cutting him out of my life."

I gasp. "You can't do that!"

"Watch me."

"He's your family."

"My family is *you*. And anyone who tries to make

you feel unwelcome or unwanted can go straight to hell."

He pulls me down for another kiss. Even as I slowly submerge into the heady pleasure, I make a mental note: I *have* to mend things with Blake.

24

———

Lucas

I wish Ava would call in sick. It'd be perfectly acceptable, since everyone at the hospital knows she fainted on Friday. But then if she did, she wouldn't be the woman I fell in love with.

She only has a cup of coffee—no time for a full breakfast, since we spent way too much time savoring each other in the morning—and that makes me frown. I should've budgeted our time better.

"Don't," she says, knowing exactly why I'm unhappy. "I'm perfectly fine with coffee. I'll grab an energy bar on the way in, and if I'm still hungry, I'll have early lunch. I promise."

She kisses me lightly on the mouth, but it's the promise to eat that mollifies me. I hate the idea of her being hungry. She grew up that way, and she should never have to re-experience it.

Ava puts on the gorgeous red Dior dress and matching pumps I had the concierge buy. The silk skims her body just so, and I can't help but lick my lips as my cock swells.

"No," she says at my undoubtedly lustful expression. "We've had enough the past twenty-four hours, and I've got the soreness to prove it."

I smirk.

"We can hang out after work, but you are not going to make me late." She kisses me again and walks out before I can pull her down in my lap.

At least we had hot shower sex. My blood heats at the memory of her cries echoing around the bathroom.

I check out around ten thirty and try to call Faye, but she doesn't pick up. I text her to meet with me for lunch at an elegant Italian bistro she likes. Normally I won't go to these lengths to break things off, but Faye is a friend, and I feel slightly guilty for having to end things like this.

If she's your true friend, she'll be happy for you.

Except...friends don't use friends, even if they volunteered.

My phone vibrates. *Got it*, Faye's text says.

I text Rachel to find a suitable place for me to move into ASAP. Something spacious with great security. At least two full baths, with a tub big enough for two adults. Three bedrooms, but only one with a bed, preferably with strong, sturdy boards. The other two should be converted to home offices. Just in case Ava brings work home. She'll look totally sexy typing away on her laptop. How long will her focus last if I sit between her knees? That'll be a fun experiment to try.

After giving Rachel instructions, I head to the bistro. Faye took me to the place about six years ago when we were together. She thought it her duty to introduce me to all the great things in the world, including L.A.'s finer dining options.

Faye is already waiting when I get there. Our table is by the window and intimately small. Thick, white cloth covers the top, a pretty pink and yellow rose centerpiece adding to the romantic mood.

She's dressed in a shimmery golden wrap-dress that flows over her like liquid metal. Her black hair frames her delicate, smiling face in waves, and from the way her amber eyes shine with expectation, she believes the lunch will go very differently from what I've planned.

Damn it.

Just then a love aria, "Che gelida manina," soars from the sound system, wrapping around me like the proverbial wet blanket. I curse myself for choosing this particular venue. I should've picked a casual café with no romantic vibe.

"Hey," she says softly.

"Hi." I take my seat, smoothing down my black V-neck shirt. "Have you ordered?"

"Not yet. I just got here."

A crisply dressed waiter comes by. Faye decides on

grilled halibut with basil and pine nut sauce and a sparkling pink lemonade. I ask for whatever the special is—I'm not in the mood to be finicky about lunch—and a dry Riesling. Something stronger would be better, but it really is too early for hard liquor.

Our drinks appear almost instantly after the waiter goes away. Faye sips her lemonade and looks at me through her lashes. "I was surprised to get your text. I thought we were going to spend some time together yesterday."

That was the plan...until Ava. "Something came up."

"Get cold feet?"

"What?"

"I saw you go to a jeweler on Wednesday when I was out shopping. I didn't say anything, but..."

I scowl, but she's correct. I went to get a ring, something large and flashy enough to suit her. But there's no way I'm telling her that now. "I was shopping for a gift. For my mother."

"Oh? You have a sudden attack of filial piety?" I haven't told her much, but Faye is smart enough to read between the lines.

"Yeah, I know. But she's still my mother." Who I stopped buying anything for when I cut ties with her. This, Faye doesn't know.

The arrival of our lunch interrupts our conversation. I push the angel hair pasta around, and Faye takes a small bite of her fish, then stops.

"What is it?" she asks.

I pause. I assumed this would be easy, but it's not. Maybe if I didn't like her, it would be simpler, but I do, and I don't want to hurt her feelings.

"Lucas, you can tell me anything. You know I prefer straight shooters."

I nod. "Okay. I wanted to let you know it's not going to work out."

"What isn't?"

"What you said at the hotel. I don't think we can marry or...pretend to have romantic feelings."

She blinks a few times, then looks down at her fish. "What happened?"

"I'm just not interested in you that way anymore."

"You mean I don't turn you on anymore."

Damn it. "Faye."

"I'm not stupid, Lucas. I can tell when a guy wants me. You don't."

"It's not *you*..."

"Then what? You're way too young for physical issues."

I run a hand across my lips. "No, it's nothing like that. It's just that...I can't do it with anyone but Ava."

Faye pulls back. "She *left* you."

"She came back."

An awkward "I knew it" smile crosses her face, then she shakes her head. "So it's that simple, huh?"

"You're still my friend, Faye. I'll always be your friend, but sometimes friendship isn't enough."

"She'll never love you the way I do."

I grow quiet. Faye is right. Ava's love is hard won and hard to keep. But it's worth it because she doesn't love easily, and when she does, it's absolute. And now that I have it, I can't give it up, not even for my friendship with Faye. "No, but I love her, Faye. I want to grow old with her, have family with her and give her the world."

Her eyes shine with tears. "What about me? Have you felt anything about me?"

"I love you too, but as a friend. The more time we spent together, the more I realized that." I reach over and hold her hand. "This doesn't change our friendship. I'm still going ahead and invest in the venture you wanted to talk about. I'll always support you and be there for you. But I can't go beyond that. It wouldn't be fair. You deserve a man who can't keep his hands off you and thinks the sun rises and sets with you."

Her chin trembles, and she presses her lips hard until she can control her emotions again. "How can you say such pretty things when you're dumping me?"

"Don't think of it that way. Think of it as creating a relationship that works for both of us."

She manages a smile. "You're right. Forcing anything when you feel this way would only ruin our friendship. Thank you for telling me in person."

A knot eases in my gut, and I smile back. "Thanks for understanding. Really."

We finish our meal, chitchatting about immediate plans and the gossip we've heard about people in our circle. Faye's a bit subdued, but she tries hard to be a good sport, and I know we'll be all right. And I meant everything I said about being her friend.

After lunch, I pick up the tab. "You don't have to," she chides.

"Hey, I asked you out." I pay and hug her.

Turning her head, she brushes a kiss on my cheek. "You're the best."

She walks away to her car, head high and stride elegant. After making sure she gets inside her Mercedes, I climb into mine and text Elliot.

You're inviting me and Ava to dinner at your place tonight.

A second later, his responds hits my phone. *Ava?*

Yes.

What happened?

We got back together. Now invite us.

Don't you want to spend some private time with her?

I do, but I also remember her story from the weekend. I'm never going to do anything that'll give her the impression I'm not proud of her or that I'm treating her the way her douchebag dad treated her mother. The bastard is lucky he's dead, or else I would've made him wish he were. *Of course. And I don't want to see your ugly mug, but she wants to get to know you and other members of the family better, so just invite us already. Or I'm gonna show up anyway and embarrass the shit out of you. In front of Belle.*

That's low, and FYI if my mug's ugly, so is yours, oh thoughtless twin of mine. You guys can come by, but we're doing Thai takeout because it's Monday.

Thanks. I'll be there after our appointment with the realtor.

Moving in together?

ASAP.

That done, I text Ryder to know I'm bringing Ava for Thanksgiving. Within a minute, I get a call from him.

"I thought you two broke up," Ryder says, no hello or how are you.

I'm feeling too good to be annoyed with his shock. "We made up."

"Since when?"

"Yesterday."

He laughs. "Dude. Did you beg or did she?"

"There was no begging. A mutual decision." I'll always treasure the memory of her choosing us over her fears and insecurities, even when I probed her to see how real it all was.

"Okay. That's fine with me."

"Oh, I forgot, she's going to bring her foster parents and their kid, too. A toddler."

Ryder grunts.

"Don't worry. They're great people." Ray and Darcy treated me with skepticism, but they're the ones who nurtured her, making sure she grew up to be the strong woman that she is. For that alone, they have my eternal gratitude. I'm sure her biological parents didn't do shit.

"Cool. You going to bring them, or should I send a car?"

"I'll deal with everything on my end. You just worry about making the holiday awesome. Just wanted to give you a heads-up."

"Okay, 'preciate it." He hesitates for a moment. "So. What's gonna happen between you and Faye?"

"I talked with her, and we ended it. Friendly and no drama."

"She didn't try to stab your face?"

I snort. "Life isn't one of your movies, Ryder."

Ryder's quiet for a moment. "Watch your back."

"What? Why?"

"Faye really wanted to marry you, and now you're going to toss her aside for Ava. No woman's just gonna be okay with that."

"She doesn't feel that way about me."

He sighs. "For a smart guy... Have you seen the way she looks at you?"

"Yeah...and trust me, it's not the way you're thinking."

"Oh my God. You're so blind it hurts. Mark my words, Lucas. 'Better safe than sorry' was coined for situations like this." Ryder hangs up.

I shake my head. Maybe in my brother's experience, every woman who hangs around wants to marry him, but not in mine. Besides, Faye has never been dishonest with me.

Except that one time at the opening...

Whatever. She probably thought she was protecting me.

I check and see a text from Rachel. She's already found a realtor who can help.

Whistling, I drive to the agent's office.

25

Ava

WHEN I FLOAT INTO THE OFFICE ON MONDAY, everyone asks me how I'm feeling. I answer honestly—fantastic—because nothing can possibly mar my day. The sun is brighter, the air's cleaner and even the industrial carpet on the floor somehow looks luxurious. My new and pricey Dior feels like a billion bucks, but even if I were in a potato sack I'd feel like at least a million.

I place my purse on my seat, boot my laptop, grab a legal pad and pen and walk down to Robbie's office. He's already in, seated behind his desk. He drops his phone on it as I close the door behind me.

It's hard not to gasp at how awful he looks. His eyes have sunk—a pair of dark craters on a sallow face. His hair seems thinner, and the lines that run from the sides of his nose to the corners of his mouth have deepened into valleys. His shirt collar is undone, and his slacks are wrinkled enough that I wonder if he slept in them.

"Are you all right?" I ask.

"Yeah." He digs the heels of his hands into his eyes. "What's going on?"

"I wanted to brief you on the week's agenda."

"Can you just leave it on the desk or email it to me?"

"Sure." I bite my lower lip. "Is it Jay?"

He doesn't answer.

"Anything I can do?"

"Just your job, Ava." He swallows, then smiles wanly. "That's all."

"Okay." Whatever happened over the weekend must've been hell for him.

I keep my head down and get caught up on stuff from Friday. I have an email from Darcy with the details of their flight to L.A. She, Ray and Mia are landing on Wednesday because that was the only thing they could grab on short notice.

I can't wait to see you, Ava.

I smile and respond, *Likewise! I have so many things to tell you. Give Ray and Mia my love.* I could've told her about me and Lucas in the email, but I'd rather do that in person, with Ray present as well.

After I send the week's agenda to Robbie, I get a text from Lucas.

Started condo searching. Found a few promising candidates. Photos attached. What do you think?

I scroll down and study them. They all look lovely —large and airy and expensive. I click on one of the links leading me to the listing page, and my jaw drops at the rental price. It's more than what people on my floor make in months!

The frugal part of me wants to tell Lucas we can live where he is, but there's no way I can be comfortable with Blake around. He can deny his cruel comments all he wants, but I haven't forgotten. Besides, he's too cold and nasty.

I reply: *They all look great, but should we spend so much on a place? And do we need so much space?*

They aren't that expensive, he responds. *I wanted something closer to the medical center but also relatively central and convenient.*

I shake my head. I suppose to a guy with over billion dollars in his bank account it's all par for the course, but I can't be that casual about it.

A moment later, another text comes. *If you don't like any of them, say so. I don't mind making the agent work for her commission.*

I snort a laugh. I can imagine him ordering the poor realtor around. It's not her fault that I grew up poor and became a cheapskate. *I like them all, just not the price.*

I won't ask you to chip in for rent, although I insist we share a bed. Does that take care of your objection?

This time I let myself giggle. *Okay. You made me an offer I can't refuse.*

Perfect. We can see the one you like the most after

work if you can get away a little early. And then we're having dinner with my brother Elliot. He invited us.

Elliot. The twin. My only encounter with him was at the hospital two years ago when he looked at me speculatively—Blake was the one who handled the opportunistic gold-digger stuff—and I hesitate. Do I want to spend that much time with Elliot?

On the other hand, I was upset when Lucas kept me away from his family like a dirty secret. He's trying to show to the world we're together, and I can meet him halfway. If Elliot turns out to be a jerk, well, we don't have to hang out with him again. *Sure. 4 good?* I type.

I'll pick you up at work.

I have my car here.

Still picking you up. I'll take care of your car.

During lunch break—I take mine early, since I'm starving after a sad, one-granola-bar breakfast—I grab a sandwich and a bottle of pink lemonade from the cafeteria and eat at my desk while checking Facebook for a private message from Bennie. We try to keep in touch as much as we can, even though we're on separate continents. No matter the distance, he is my best friend.

A message is waiting: *I have no idea what to wear in England.*

I thought the trip wasn't until later.

Within a minute, he responds. *You don't get it, Ava. It's his parents. They're like aristocrats! I have to make a good impression.*

I smile. I can't remember the last time Bennie cared

about stuff like this. And I love it, because it means he isn't thinking short-term with Drew...and a guy like Drew is a keeper. *You're one of the best-dressed men in Osaka. I'm sure you'll be fine. Just be yourself. They'll see you're smart, funny and loyal and awesome for Drew.*

I dunno. Ugh. I hate this. This is why I don't date seriously.

I chuckle as a bite into the sandwich, which isn't too bad for hospital cafeteria food. *Ha. You never dated seriously because that was BD.*

What the hell is BD?

Before Drew.

There's a pause, then he writes, *WTF. Jon's in a relationship, and the chick isn't you. That cheating fucker. How can he do this publicly on Facebook? What the hell's going on?*

Are you stalking him?

No. I friended him after you said you were dating.

We weren't really dating. And he probably gave up because I stopped seeing him after that one time. Too busy.

Can we send anthrax to The Bastard?

No. I sigh. *I need to tell him. We're back together.*

WHAT?

It's a long story, but... I type him a super-condensed version.

You went to him?

Yes.

That was a bad move.

But he came to my place first.

Probably to drag your prone and lifeless body to work.

Come on, Bennie. Be fair.

Fine. He MIGHT have wanted to check up on you. Still...I don't like it.

Why do you hate him so much?

Don't hate him. Well, maybe a little. I think he's pretty fucked up, and rich people are extra fucked up because money gives them a certain immunity. They get away with shit we can't.

I sigh. Bennie used to get into fights with some of the kids in the neighborhood, and since their parents had more money and actually gave a damn, unlike his drunk dad, they always made sure Bennie paid with heaps of humiliation and insults hurled his way. *I know, but it's different,* I type back.

You going to tell him about Mia?

I'm going to have to.

I wish you'd ended up with a guy who's not going to complicate your life.

He's worth every complication.

Then do it. The longer you wait, the harder it's gonna be.

Don't I know it. I've already lost chances to tell Lucas. Honestly, the best time to tell him was back in Charlottesville, when he first saw Mia. Still, better late than never. I just have to find a good opening to tell him without damaging our relationship. I believe in our love, but I also know it's still fragile because of our past and personalities.

When Ray and Darcy visit with Mia...I'll tell him. He can hold her if he wants to, but I also want him to understand Ray and Darcy are fabulous parents to Mia, and we can have other children of our own. And we can always see her. Unlike most adoption cases, it's not like Darcy and Ray are strangers.

Gotta go. It's after three AM, and I'm not as young as I used to be.

I smile.

Love ya.

I type, *Love you*, and hit send.

The time passes by quickly after my talk with Bennie, mostly me working on my own, since Robbie hasn't given me any tasks since the morning. I stop by his office to see if there's anything, but he waves me off, telling me I can leave whenever I want.

At about ten till four, I go to the restroom to freshen up my makeup. I'm glad Lucas got me this gorgeous dress...but at the same time, I wonder if Elliot will see it as a sign that I'm only interested in Lucas's money.

I inhale deeply. *It's just dinner.* I shouldn't hold any preconceived ideas about him. I don't want Lucas to give up his family to be with me. That would be completely unfair.

At precisely four, Lucas arrives in front of the medical center in a shiny black Bentley SUV. A uniformed driver gets out and holds the rear door open for me. I climb inside, absorbing the luxuriously smooth leather and expensive-looking wood trim. Before the chauffeur shuts the door, Lucas pulls me toward him and gives me a thorough kiss. I melt into it, loving the way his mouth devours mine. The air in my lungs thickens, and my breathing grows shallow. His big hands cradle my face, while my fingers dig into his warm, silky hair. Moments like this, I feel like there's no barrier between us. Surely we deserve this happiness after the hell we've been through.

Lucas pulls back. His pupils are dark and dilated as he gazes at me. "Hi."

I grin like an idiot. "Hi." I tilt my head, parting my lips in invitation.

His forehead touches mine. "As much as I'd love to, we're only two blocks away from the place."

"Already?" We haven't been kissing *that* long, have we? I squirm, my panties damp.

"Yeah. I wanted someplace nice and not too far from your work."

"What about you?"

"Doesn't matter. I can work from home."

Our car stops. The chauffeur opens the door. As Lucas and I emerge from the car, a sharply dressed brunette comes forward. Her carmine skirt suit is expensive and carefully fitted to show off a gym-toned body. Swinging her big leather bag out of the way, she extends a hand. "I'm so glad you were able to make the appointment," she says as she pumps hands with Lucas and then me.

I look at her and Lucas questioningly. He shrugs. "I

said we might not be able to make it if you had to work late."

"I'm Jennifer Brown," the realtor says, handing each of us a business card. "It's only four ten, and you're my last appointment. So we can spend plenty of time looking around and discuss any concerns or questions you might have."

I let my gaze climb along the tall, gleaming building. It looks ridiculously pricey. Jennifer leads us inside the lobby, which is all marble and glass, something I might see on a TV show about how rich people live. We take a large elevator to the top floor.

"There's only one unit on this level," Jennifer explains. "So it's completely private. Every unit in this building is soundproofed, and perfect for a busy and discerning couple looking for peace and quiet in the middle of Los Angeles."

She punches a six-digit code into a security pad, and the door unlocks. As we walk inside, I can't help but gasp. The penthouse makes the lobby look like a homeless shelter. The ceiling absolutely *soars*, multiple fancy chandeliers and fans hanging from it. The hardwood floor sparkles, and the place smells like fresh wax. The view of L.A. is breathtaking. I feel like the whole city is at my feet.

Jennifer gestures around, pointing out the features and highlights, and I start to wonder if she has the entire sales brochure memorized. "The floors are all hardwood —refinished oak—except for the bathrooms, which have heated tiles. All the windows are floor to ceiling, but you don't have to worry about privacy. With the centralized control, you can shade the panes, and nobody can see inside. You can also make the glass totally opaque if you want to sleep in, and it's treated to block out all the harmful UV rays, so you can enjoy as much natural light as you want during the day without worrying about sun damage." She leads us to the kitchen. "Every appliance is stainless steel and less than a year old."

I tap my fingertips against the stainless steel countertop. It's solid and totally smooth. The realtor smiles. "Do you like baking?"

"A little. I don't bake all that much."

"Perhaps with this kitchen you will." She runs her hand along the smooth metal like she's displaying a game show prize. "This countertop was designed for a baker. But you also see that the breakfast bar counter and the island have marble tops, giving you that elegant feel you're looking for when you dine at home or entertain."

I just nod. She continues to point out features as she takes us to the huge master bedroom suite, three other bedrooms and four bathrooms. Except for the powder room, all the rooms are bigger than my apartment. Seriously, do we *really* need this much space?

"Do you mind giving us some privacy?" Lucas asks Jennifer.

She smiles. "Of course. Take your time." She walks away, leaving us in the master bathroom. It has a tub big enough to host a party, and I perch my butt on the edge.

"You don't like it," Lucas states.

"What makes you think that?"

"You're smiling in that vague way that says you're not really comfortable. But we don't have to get this one. There are plenty of other places."

I clear my throat. "I don't have anything against this particular penthouse."

"Then what's the problem?"

I bite my lower lip, wondering how to word my discomfiture. I don't want to sound like I'm whining about stuff that most would be thrilled to have, but...

As my hesitation stretches out, Lucas's frown becomes deeper. "Is it Jennifer? If you want, I can get a male realtor."

I chuckle. "As I much as I appreciate the offer, it's not her. She seems nice enough. It's me debating if we really need this kind of space. When we talked about it, it seemed all right. But I'm just wondering if this can be a home where both of us can be comfortable."

His gaze softens as he squats before me. He reaches out and holds my hands, his palms warm. "Listen. Don't think about the cost or the size. None of that stuff matters. What matters is that we're together. What matters is that we love each other. I've lived in a big mansion, and I've lived in a small cottage. Home is being with someone you love. All this"—he sweeps the multimillion-dollar penthouse with an arm—"it's just a...prop. A disposable prop."

My heart swells with emotion, and I can't speak through the hot knot in my throat. This man just slays me with his honesty. So I do the only thing that I can. I nod and kiss him softly.

"Is that a yes?" he whispers against my lips.

I nod again. "Yes. This place is perfect because I have you."

26

Ava

After telling Jennifer to contact Rachel to go ahead with the lease, Lucas takes me to Elliot's place. He also gives me Rachel's contact info in case I needed anything from her, which I doubt. She's *his* assistant, not mine, and I don't feel comfortable using her for my personal tasks.

I cuddle next to Lucas in the car, enjoying the closeness. The driver can see us in the rearview mirror, and maybe I shouldn't be so obvious, but I don't care. I can't bear to be away from him any more than I have to.

To be honest, I'm a bit nervous about meeting Elliot and his wife. I only know what I've read on Google, and he seems unpredictable and sort of out of control.

My nerves get even more frazzled when I sense

Lucas starting to stiffen as we get closer to Elliot's home. "You all right?"

"Why?"

"You seem tense."

He waggles his eyebrow. "Because I'm horny."

I laugh, but I know he's not telling me the full truth. Before I can probe, his phone buzzes.

Lucas takes it out of his pocket and checks something, a frown appearing. "Do you just want to skip it?" he asks suddenly.

"What?"

"You're going to meet everyone when we go to Ryder's Thanksgiving dinner. We don't have to meet Elliot today."

I straighten and push the hair out of his face. He doesn't flinch when my fingers brush his scar—a huge change that shows how much he trusts and feels secure in my love. "What's wrong?" I ask.

"Just..." He shrugs, then clears his throat. "Nothing."

"Lucas. We promised to be honest with each other, remember?"

He nods, inhales deeply. "His wife's younger sister's going to join us. She's a teenager, and teenagers are bipolar at best."

I laugh. "Oh, come on. I'm sure she's fine."

"I don't think you'll like Elliot, and I don't want to waste our time with people you may not like that much."

My lips part. "Why would you think that?" Then I

tilt my head. "Are you worried that Elliot might not like me?"

He snorts. "He *will* like you because I chose you and I love you. There won't be any other option for him."

I grin. "So by that logic, I have to like him too."

"No. That's not how it works with you. You already don't like Blake." He laughs harshly. "Who am I kidding? You probably can't stand the guy, not that I blame you. He can be...insensitive." His expression turns serious. "You chose me despite all the odds, but I'm aware that my relationship with you can be made difficult if none of my family manages to endear themselves to you. I just thought...it'd be nice to have someone who everyone likes there to smooth things a bit."

"You mean Elizabeth."

"Yes.

I can't help but fall a little bit more in love with this man, which is insane because I thought there was no way I could love him more. I can't believe he's worried about how I'm going to feel about his family. "Just like they'll have to like me, I'll do my best to like them because they're your family and I know they matter to you."

He shakes his head. "You aren't going to do anything you don't want to. You're my priority, Ava, not anyone else."

I press a kiss on each of his cheeks, then his mouth. Does he have any idea how much his regard means to me, how sweetly he wrecks me? I'm more determined than ever to get along with his siblings. Unless I misunderstood Elizabeth at the hospital, he already doesn't talk or otherwise communicate with his parents. Losing contact with his brothers and sister would be too cruel.

The car stops in front of a high-rise, and we make our way inside. The building is astonishingly swanky—more luxurious than the one that houses the condo Lucas and I saw earlier. Not that the place we're moving into is shabby. It's just that Elliot's building is like a palace, except constructed with modern sensibilities.

When we step out of the elevator, Lucas squeezes my hand. "Are you ready?"

"Yes." I smile even though nerves are jittering through me. I'm sure that Elliot will probably behave—I can't imagine anybody being more appalling than Blake—but I really want him to like me...just a little bit...and hopefully be nothing like their oldest brother.

Elliot's penthouse is breathtaking—ultramodern and ultra-expensive. A view of nighttime L.A. glitters on the other side of floor-to-ceiling windows, and a beautiful, contemporary staircase leads to a second level. The furnishings are opulent and quite masculine in taste. It's obvious that his wife hasn't had a chance to change the décor at all.

"Finally! You made it." A man who looks just like Lucas comes out. Unlike the love of my life, his hair is short, cropped to show off his unscarred and handsome face. But even so, I feel no spark, no stirring. What I feel for Lucas isn't about his appearance. It's about his soul, what's in his heart.

Elliot is dressed somewhat casually in a well-fitted V-neck shirt in sleet gray, and slacks as black as ink. His ebony leather shoes are shiny, looking like they've been freshly polished.

"Perfect timing," comes a soft, feminine voice. Heels clicking, a pretty redhead walks toward us, her designer yellow dress showing off her lovely curves.

Lucas makes introductions. I shake hands with Elliot and his wife Belle. Their smiles seem genuine, and I start to unbend. "And Nonny is Belle's sister, but I'm not sure where she is," Lucas says.

Elliot cocks an eyebrow at Belle. "Finishing up her homework, I think," she says.

"Are you sure? She's not obsessively checking her messages again to see if that boy texted her back?"

Belle rolls her eyes. "Let her be. It's her first real crush."

"Ugh." Elliot makes a face. "I'm going to have to find out who this boy is and have a firm conversation with him about treating women right. Well...one of them, anyway."

"That's rich, coming from you," Lucas says, putting an arm around me and pulling me closer. "So is the food here yet?"

"We ordered about ten minutes ago." Belle gestures to the open space behind her. "I prepared some cheese and crackers and decanted a bottle of wine. Why don't we have a drink before the food arrives?"

Ever the gracious hostess, she leads us to the low coffee table in the living room. I'm surprised at how much I like her. Given what the tabloids said, I thought she'd be slightly...mercenary or something. I don't think she's soft the way Elizabeth is, having grown up in the lap of luxury, but Belle is definitely the kind of woman I would love to befriend.

"By the way, *love* your dress." Belle smiles. "I wish I could wear red, but it's really hard with, you know, the hair."

"Well, who needs a red outfit when they have hair as stunning as yours?"

Belle flushes, and I know then we've taken the first step toward forming a friendship, and that more than anything else helps me relax—because she's my second ally in Lucas's family.

"Did you find anything you like?" Elliot asks as we sit around the table.

"I'm sorry?"

"You guys are looking to move in together, right?" He studies me and Lucas until I feel like squirming.

"We are." I smile. "Lucas's realtor found a very nice place."

"It's a little small, but it'll do." Lucas pulls me tight and presses a soft kiss on top of my head. "Once we're moved in, I just need to buy her a ring so everyone knows she's taken."

I quirk an eyebrow, bemused but glad that he's changed his mind about the wedding.

"Congratulations. When's the date?" Belle asks.

"Not for several months. I'm going to give her the kind of wedding all women dream of. She deserves the best." Lucas looks at his twin and his wife with something that seems halfway between envy and admiration.

Then I finally realize something. Lucas isn't trying to get the beautiful penthouse and give me nice things like this pretty dress to control me the way my dad did my mother. Lucas is doing this because he has a need to provide for me, to prove I matter to him. I'm not blind. I see the huge diamond on Belle's finger, and beautiful pearls dangling from her ears. But she doesn't merely look like a woman who's expensively kept. People glancing at her will know with certainty that she has a loving and indulgent husband who she loves to death. It's in the way she glows, the soft gleam she gets every time she glances at her husband. Then there's Elliot. He grins at her affectionately, and occasionally feeds her the cheese and crackers.

Lucas wants that for us. He wants it so bad, it's almost palpable. My heart twists at the cruel words I said to him in Charlottesville. Even though we're back together, he'll never forget—and the wounds they left probably still hurt underneath.

I've got to find a way to make it up to him—show him I was a scared little girl back then, but I'm braver and wiser now.

Elliot puts his free arm on the back of the couch and twists away from us. "Nonny, if you don't come out soon, we're going to eat all the brie!"

The door remains closed.

"My brother and his wife are here. I'm about to tell them about that boy in your algebra class."

Before he can straighten back to us, the door opens, and a teenager with brown hair marches out, the hem of her black maxi dress almost skimming the floor. She's probably thirteen or fourteen, and she's skinny without any curves yet, although her facial resemblance to Belle is striking.

"*Must* you share details of my life?" Nonny says.

Elliot shrugs. "You wouldn't come out."

"Totally unfair. I was about to."

"Hey, whatever means are necessary." Elliot turns to us. "I'm thinking about hacking into his account."

"Just hire a PI and see what he's up to," Lucas suggests.

She flushes as she takes us in. "Hi."

I smile at her. "Hi."

"Sorry about the outburst. And just so you know"—she glances at Lucas—"that idea is terrible."

He merely laughs.

She rolls her eyes in the way only a teenager can, until I'm afraid they'll spill out of her eye sockets. "Elliot can be overprotective. And drive me in*sane*." She sits down on the floor near the table and takes a cracker.

"I think it's nice," I say. "It means he cares about you."

"I really want to figure this out on my own. What do old people know about love anyway?"

I can't help it. I burst out laughing at her serious expression. Elliot, Belle and Lucas join in my hilarity. Elliot pats Belle affectionately and hands her a thick slice of brie.

In that moment, I learn two things.

One: Elliot is cool. He's protective and he cares deeply about not only his wife but her younger sister. An asshole like Blake would never be as indulgent or patient.

Two: I'm glad we're having dinner together. Because I know that Elliot can be my ally in convincing Lucas that we really should get married ASAP.

27

Ava

I'M BACK IN THE OFFICE ON TUESDAY, BLEARY-EYED but with a huge cup of coffee in hand. We stayed at Elliot's until almost eleven, then Lucas and I went to my place to get me some fresh clothes. I'd rather not spend the night at a hotel again and have to get another emergency outfit...even if it would be a Dior or some other fancy label. And of course, instead of sleeping like responsible adults with jobs, we spent a big chunk of the night rolling around in bed. It's no wonder I'm exhausted.

Lucas got me a car service in the morning to take me to work. "I'd drive you, but I have an early call with some inventor in Korea."

I kissed him on the mouth. "Have fun. Love you." I

smiled as I left, leaving my ridiculously handsome billionaire boyfriend in the small and incredibly ordinary apartment. It felt good to see him at my place in the morning. He never stayed when we were together in Charlottesville two years ago. Not like this anyway. This time it feels more permanent, and I can see us staying together no matter what happens.

Today's the last day I'm coming in for the week. Unlike the medical staff, most of the people on my floor are on vacation starting at two p.m. Since it's not quite a full day, everyone's dressed casually. I'm no exception in my long-sleeve UVA shirt, faded blue jeans and flats. Erin, my nurse friend, is working tomorrow, but she gets to take Thanksgiving off, for which she's grateful.

Wanna get lunch? she texts me.

Sorry! I have a date.

Woohoo! Do tell...

Later. ;)

I grab my purse and take off at eleven thirty to make it to a small mom-and-pop sandwich shop about ten minutes away on foot. I get a BLT special and take my seat. Soon I see Elliot walk in. I wave.

He spots me and gives me a quick grin, then grabs a sandwich and joins me. He's in a crisp pale blue button-down shirt sans tie and black slacks. Seeing him like this, I can't help but think that the online articles about his reputation have to be wrong. He seems so...normal.

"Thanks for meeting me," I say.

"No problem. I was in the area anyway." He smiles,

all gracious and sweet, then takes a sip of his soda. "I was surprised to get a call from you. Figured it must be important."

"I got your number from Rachel. I hope you don't mind," I explain, then flush. Is that going to get her into trouble? Probably not. Lucas told me to contact her if I needed anything, and he was unavailable this morning, or so I tell myself. "And yes, it is important. It's about marriage."

One dark eyebrow creeps upward, slowly and deliberately. "Oh?"

"You heard him say he doesn't plan to marry me soon, but you know what that means, don't you?"

He raises, then drops a massive shoulder. "What does it mean?"

"Come on." I lean across the table and lower my voice. "You know the stipulation from your father."

"Don't you want a big wedding?"

I resist the urge to roll my eyes at his nonsensical question and instead shake my head. "I want Lucas to have what he wants." I exhale roughly. "I don't want to cost him—or you—the paintings."

"Did you tell him that?"

"Yes, but he's being stubborn. Says he won't do anything to make me wonder if he married me for love or the inheritance."

Elliot makes a sort of moue of understanding. "A fair point."

I blink, unsure if I heard him right.

He grins. "If you're here to ask me to intervene on

your behalf, sorry. I'm not going to. I've already done enough damage to both of you when I failed to anticipate and counter Wife Number Three's moves."

He must be referring to the tabloid article that exposed the whole ugly deal surrounding his father and his siblings. "That's why you owe us one."

"Uh-uh. I want Lucas happy. He's not like the Grim Reaper when you're around."

"And I'm not going anywhere." Why is Elliot being obtuse? I thought he was supposed to be smart. A genius, actually.

He gives me a warm smile. "You have no idea how possessive and protective he is of you, do you?"

"I know he loves me. And I love him back. That's why I'm trying to help him get what he wants."

"He already has what he wants—you. I don't blame him for not wanting to jeopardize that. I didn't know how irrational and territorial I could be until I met Belle."

"So you're saying you didn't marry her for the paintings?" The question slips out before I can stop myself. I cringe inwardly. It's none of my business why and how they ended up together.

"At first I did, but my feelings changed. Lucas never even wanted to marry, not even to inherit. If you push, it'll make things worse. Have faith. We are not going to hate you because of Lucas's decision."

I flush. "How did you know?"

He chuckles. "I'm actually a pretty smart guy.

Look, we are all very happy for him. Well, maybe not Blake—yet—but he'll come around."

"I don't know. I think he hates me."

"I know he said some things to you."

"You do?"

"When you showed up at the hospital, he said he would take care of you. I wish I'd stopped him. Then maybe things would've worked out better."

If you only knew. I would've had Lucas with me while I was pregnant.

Elliot continues, "So this is my way of making things right, giving both of you my full support regardless of what you decide to do. The paintings mean a lot to us, but Grandfather didn't create them so that we'd do something that went against our morals and happiness. And hurting the women we love? Definitely not something that would make our grandfather proud."

A small lump forms in my throat, and I can't speak. I don't know how I could've misjudged Lucas's family so badly. I purposely chose Elliot, assuming that he'd jump all over any idea that would net him his painting. But...he's not.

Maybe I just thought everyone would be like Blake. But from Elizabeth to Elliot, these people genuinely want Lucas and me to be as happy as possible, even if it means losing a multimillion-dollar inheritance.

"Thank you," I murmur. "It means a lot to me that you feel that way."

"My pleasure. Look, I know the men in this family can be a pain in the ass. And Lucas can certainly be difficult, but it would mean a lot if you could be a little bit patient with us."

I smile. "Of course."

Elliot gets up and walks around the table until he reaches me and gives me a tight hug. "I know he hasn't married you yet, but still, welcome to the family, Ava."

28

Ava

My workday ends at two, so I stop by the store to stock up on some ingredients for homemade baby food. Darcy's probably going to bring a bunch with her, but I want to feed Mia something I've made with my own hands. My slim purse is full of printouts of recipes I found online.

As I carry the groceries to my apartment, I think about what Bennie told me while we were in Osaka. Mia's real identity simply cannot be kept secret forever, especially if Lucas and I are going to be together. He has the right to know, and to keep him in the dark when he's going to see her—and my foster parents—would be completely unfair.

The problem is how to tell him. There's no manual on how to drop a secret baby bombshell on your boyfriend. I think he'll understand why I had to do what I did, but it's not something you just blurt out over dinner or after sex... Or at least I don't think so.

Not to mention I have no idea how Lucas feels about children in general. He seemed nice and sweet enough with Mia, but does he actually want a child? Is he going to be resentful that I gave her away or relieved that he won't have to be a father? The only thing I'm pretty sure of is that even though he called children "interesting" that one time at the bed and breakfast, "interesting" isn't really what he thinks about them.

When I open the door and step inside, I almost halt at the sight of Lucas sprawled on my couch, a tablet resting in one big palm. He's in a white T-shirt and a pair of long, loose lounging pants, his feet bare. I tilt my head. He looks entirely at home and ridiculously comfortable.

"Welcome home." He gets up and takes the groceries from me. "I thought work ended at two," he says, as his lips brush over mine. "I was literally dying waiting for you to return." He sighs dramatically, the back of one hand at his forehead.

I laugh. "It did, but I had to get some stuff for tomorrow. Ray and Darcy are arriving."

"That's right. I forgot." He places the bags on the counter in the kitchen. "You know...we're sort of stuck for Thanksgiving, but do you want to go someplace more fun for Christmas?" He hands me the beef and chicken.

I blink, taking the meat and putting it in the fridge. "Like where?"

"I believe I mentioned Paris at one time..."

"You were supposed to kidnap me," I say with a smile, even though I'm wondering about his use of the word "stuck." "Are you uncomfortable seeing Ray and Darcy again?"

He shrugs. "I don't think they like me. They probably prefer that I stay away from you."

"No, they don't." I put a hand on his bicep. "The only thing they care about is that I'm happy, and I'm very happy with you."

A small smile lightens his face. "I can't possibly make you half as happy as you make me. But my real worry is for them to tell you to ditch me and you doing exactly that."

"Lucas. I'm an adult now, and I make my own decisions. Really."

"Okay." He hands me the last perishable item from the grocery bags. "So, Christmas...?"

"Can we spend it with our families? Please? We can leave immediately after and go wherever you want for New Year's."

Lucas's gaze sharpens. "Anywhere?"

"Yes. Even a racy lingerie factory."

His head tilts back and he bursts out laughing. "Don't remind me of the trauma. I never want to see white cotton underwear again."

"I thought you looked pretty hot in them."

"Ha! You never saw me in any of them. You kept me naked...and busy."

I giggle. "I believe our decision on the activity was mutual, and you never once complained."

"I'm a man of silent perseverance. And an endless hunger for you." He pulls me closer, his hand at the small of my back. A thick erection presses against me.

All humor leaves me. My senses are replete with him. Need throbs through me, a persistent aching emptiness only he can fill.

My hands clutch his broad shoulders as I raise myself and kiss him. He slants his head, devours me as though he's starving. It's like we've been apart for months.

Hunger drives us as we pull at each other's clothes. Lucas's shirt comes off first, immediately followed by mine. Smooth skin stretches over his well-muscled chest, dark hair springy under my palms. His nipple ring glints in the light, and I can't resist toying with it. He inhales sharply, and I give him a wicked grin. "I love that thing. It's so fun." I flick my thumb over it. "But most of all, I love it that I'm the only one who can touch it."

"You're the only one who owns this body. Owns me."

My bra drops to the floor at my feet. "I know. And you're the only one who owns my body...and all that I am." My voice is almost shy. I've never thought I was much of anything, but this man... He makes me feel like I'm the center of the world, the axis of his universe.

When he looks at me, I feel powerful, beautiful and fulfilled.

"Ava..." He groans. "You slay me."

I tug at his waistband, and he strips out of his pants and underwear at the same time. I kick off my flats and ditch mine, too.

Fully nude, we look at each other. I don't try to cover myself—the stark admiration in his gaze says I shouldn't. And in return, he doesn't try to cover his scars, for which I'm grateful. Some might see them as flaws, but to me, they're just part of him and as precious as the smooth skin on his torso and tight butt.

His big cock juts out, the tip glistening. I lick my lips, wanting a taste.

"Don't," he warns, his voice raspy.

"Why not?" I say. "I love it when I have you in my mouth and you groan deep like you're going to die if I stop sucking."

He almost chokes. "You dirty, dirty girl. Yes, I would like that, but not right now." He places me on the edge of the breakfast table. "I've been thinking about this..."

"This...?"

"Yes." He slips his hand gently between my legs. I'm indecently soaked, but I keep my thighs relaxed and watch him touching me, my breath shallow.

"Feel how wet you are." He licks my juices off his fingers. "Do you get wet thinking of what I do to you?"

"Yes."

"All I have to do is think of your name, and I'm

hard." He reaches into his pants and pulls out a condom from the pocket. "I smell your shampoo, and I feel like I can build a whole damn house with just my dick and some nails."

My heart pounds unbearably, my breathing so shallow I feel like I'm going to hyperventilate. This man kills me because when he talks like this, it's like he has no barriers or protection. He's so raw and naked that I'm humbled by his trust, his love.

"But most of all, when I think of you, I want to find a way to make you happy. I crave your happiness, and I want to be the one to give it to you."

"You do," I murmur. "You're everything."

I gasp as he glides smoothly into me, the stroke long and unhurried. His eyes are on mine, his hair pulled away. I caress his cheeks, loving how he leaves himself so vulnerable.

"When we were apart, I had a dream about you," I whisper.

"Was I being a jerk?" He pulls almost all the way out, then slowly re-enters me.

"No. I was kneeling in front of you because your very presence was as vital to me as the sun is to flowers. And at that moment I knew I'd never get my heart back. Even if you were to give it back, I'd never be whole because my heart was meant to be yours."

"God, Ava," he groans as he drives into me so deep I feel like he's reaching for my soul.

His big hands grip my hips as I hold on to his shoulders. Our gazes are locked as he thrusts over and over again, uniting us in the most intimate way possible. Sweat mists over our hot skin. Liquid pleasure pulses through me, and I dig my fingers into him. A climax shatters me, leaving me breathless. I tighten and spasm around him as another orgasm peaks.

His breathing grows choppy, and the muscles in his jaw bunch. I brush my fingers over them. "Now, now, now..." A low groan tears from his throat, and he flicks my clit as he shoves into me, hard and thick and relentless.

We come apart together. He kisses me on the mouth, swallowing my sharp cry.

Arms around each other, we stay there against the table until our breathing is somewhat calmer. We're both sweaty, sticky, but I don't care. I run my mouth along the lean, strong line of his shoulder, grateful I didn't give up and that he's all mine.

"I never knew it could be like this until you, Ava," he whispers and presses a soft kiss on my forehead.

"Me either," I whisper back, tightening my arms around him.

Lucas is my rock, the foundation of my world. I'm never, ever letting go.

29

AVA

"YOU SURE YOU DON'T WANT ME TO COME WITH you?" Lucas asks for the fifth time since lunch.

"I'm fine. Honest." I check my purse to make sure I have my phone.

He regards me, his eye a skeptical slit. I don't know what's going through his mind, but I'm not leaving him stewing.

"What's really bothering you?" I ask.

"You spending time alone with your parents."

I sigh. His doubts and feelings about Darcy and Ray are completely understandable, and normally I wouldn't object to having him come with me. But this is different. I need a private moment with Darcy and Ray to let them know I'm going to tell Lucas everything. They deserve that much after all they've done.

"I told you already," I say. "I'm not giving you up for anything. Can't you believe that...especially after last night?"

The skepticism darkens with sexual heat. "Yes, but I still have a bad feeling about it."

"I know. But it's going to be okay." I kiss him on the cheek. "Trust me. Once I explain everything, they'll love you."

He sighs. "I wish we had more time. That way we'd already be moved into the new place, and they might like me better."

I smile warmly, touched by this hint of vulnerability. "They'll love you because you make me happy, not because you can keep me in a swanky penthouse. Darcy's a trust fund baby, and believe me, she isn't impressed by money."

Blowing a kiss, I step out of the apartment, leaving Lucas behind.

I feel pretty good about the conversation to come. Darcy is totally cool, and Ray will be supportive. After all, hiding it from Lucas now that he's back in my life would be cruel, and I'm convinced Lucas will be okay with leaving Mia with them. It isn't like we'll never see her. We'll be able to watch her grow up, be in her life. And we can always have another baby. I'm young, and although my first pregnancy was tough, the difficulty came mostly from stress, heartache and me not knowing what the hell I was doing.

LAX is a total mess, people swarming around the arrival area like bees around a hive. I look around and finally spot Ray after about ten minutes. I fight my way through the crowd to reach him.

"Ray!" I hug him tightly, and he hugs me back.

"Ava! You look fantastic!"

"Thank you."

"L.A. must agree with you."

"It does. Where're Darcy and Mia?"

"Mia soiled her diaper just as our bags started to come out on the belt, so Darcy took her to the bathroom." He sighs. "I'm sure it's a mess in there too."

"I imagine. Hope the flight wasn't too terrible."

"Nah. Mia's a champion traveler."

I laugh. "That's great."

He studies my face. "You meet somebody new?"

"Huh?"

"You have that soft look women get when they're in love."

My cheeks heat. "Am I that obvious?"

"Yep. So who's the lucky fella?"

I bite my lower lip. "Lucas."

Ray comes to a complete standstill and stares at me.

"You know," I say. "Lucas. We're back together."

Ray frowns. "I...see."

"You don't approve."

"Kind of tough when he's already broken your heart twice."

"It was all my decision, Ray. He and I did a lot of talking and soul searching."

"So this time's going to be more permanent?"

"Yes."

"Have you told him about Mia?"

"No, not yet—"

"Do you intend to tell him about Mia?" His voice takes the tone of a professor grilling a PhD candidate on her thesis.

"*Yes.* I totally plan to. There just wasn't a good chance last ti—"

"*Don't.*"

Even in the buzzing of the crowd, Ray's voice is like a gunshot. "What?"

"Lucas doesn't need to know."

"But Ray... Mia is—"

"I know, but we can't afford to lose her. Darcy...she can't go through it again."

I tilt my head. *Darcy and Ray tried for adoption...?*

"This is going to be so much worse. At least when you miscarry, you never get a chance to hold the baby. Darcy couldn't love Mia more if she were her very own flesh and blood. You can't do this to her, Ava. I won't stand and watch her suffer."

"I'm sorry, Ray, but I'm not doing anything to her. I just thought Lucas should know. It'd be wrong to be around Lucas and have him play with Mia and so on without letting him know she's really his."

"If that's the problem, we just won't spend much time together." Ray runs his fingers through his gray hair. "You and Lucas are young, Ava. You can have more babies. We can't. It'll devastate us, and I don't know what it'll do to Darcy. She lost five babies, and our last adoption came to nothing because the mother changed her mind at the last minute. Does she have to lose the sixth, too?"

I gasp. I knew she'd miscarried, but *five* babies? Poor Darcy. No wonder she was so eager when I offered to let her adopt Mia.

Ray's argument that Lucas and I can have another child is the same one I made to myself. But it would be wrong to withhold the information from Lucas. He *is* the father.

"You put down 'father unknown' on Mia's birth certificate," Ray continues. "If you say Lucas is the father now and you knew all along, he might say that his parental rights were never properly terminated and try to take Mia away from us. As long as there's even a tiny chance of losing our daughter, you can't." Ray grabs my hand, his grip desperate. "Please."

I'm torn, but his fear is so genuine I can't do anything but nod. "I understand, Ray."

"So you won't tell him?"

As I study his tight expression, I can't help but recall Bennie's prediction that if Lucas and I got back together, it would have a profound effect on my foster parents and Mia. He was right about everything.

I shake my head. "Not...for now," I say. "I hope you make an effort to get to know him. Then you'll realize he won't tear you and Mia apart. All he wants is to love me and make me happy, Ray. He knows hurting you will hurt me."

"I'm glad you have that conviction, but I don't. At least not yet. I just want to protect my family, Ava."

"I know." I squeeze his hand. "I'm not upset with you or anything."

He nods. "Okay."

"There you are!" Darcy's bright voice makes me jerk like a dog guilty of gulping down a steak that was laid out on a counter.

Making sure to paste on a big smile, I turn around and hug her. "So good to see you, Darcy!"

She hugs me back. "Ava! You look wonderful."

"Thanks," I say. "I'm thrilled you're here." I squat down and kiss Mia on the soft cheek. "Welcome to L.A., little one."

She smiles sweetly.

"She was a champ on the flight," Darcy says, beaming. "Such a perfect child."

My chest tightens with love. "That's wonderful. Let's get going. I'm sure you're exhausted...and I have a lot to tell you."

LUCAS

I PACE BACK AND FORTH IN AVA'S TINY APARTMENT, waiting for her to return with her foster parents. Despite her reassurances, I'm anything but sanguine. I need time to cement the bond between us—time without interference from friends and family who disapprove of me. I appreciate that they're genuinely worried about her. But it will be impossible for her to trust me if the people she loves keep sowing doubts—about me, about us.

Normally, I wouldn't care what anyone outside the relationship thought. But these people are important to Ava, so I want them to at least find me acceptable.

Finally, the door opens, and Ava enters with Darcy and Ray and little Mia. I hurry over to help with the luggage.

"Hello, Lucas," Darcy says with a small smile.

Relieved, I smile back. Behind her, Ray is looking rather reserved. The man doesn't totally trust me. *Smart.* Much as I hate to admit it, if the situation were reversed, I wouldn't trust me either.

"Sorry I couldn't meet you at the airport. I had some business."

"It must've been very important, the day before Thanksgiving and all." Although Ray's expression is neutral, his tone is definitely cool.

"It was. The other party happens to be overseas, so unfortunately they don't have much respect for American holidays."

"So, this is my place," Ava interjects brightly. "It's small, but I think you'll be comfortable enough. I'll use the sofa bed, and you guys can take the one in the bedroom along with Mia." She clasps her hands. "Do you want to do anything tonight? My schedule's wide open..."

Darcy shrugs. "We're pretty flexible."

"Yeah, because we couldn't get the reservation we wanted," Ray grouses.

I arch an eyebrow. "Reservation?"

"A restaurant called Éternité. Supposed to be an amazing experience. We heard so much about it we wanted to go while we were out here, but they said they're booked full until next year!" Darcy shakes her head. "Can you believe it?"

Ray's annoyance is palpable. Oddly, it makes him appear more human. "I knew it was popular, but a year's wait to get in..."

Darcy pats his hand. "We can go next time. You know we'll be back to visit again."

"Have you ever been there?" Ava asks me.

"No." The place is owned by one of my half-siblings' cousins on the Pryce side of the family. And for that reason, I didn't rush to the grand opening or bother to dine there. I absolutely *loathe* running into Geraldine Pryce—Blake, Ryder and Elizabeth's mother. She's an exceptionally difficult person to like to begin with, plus she hates my guts because she despises my mother. Never mind that I'm not too crazy about my mother myself.

At the same time, booked full or not, I'm pretty certain I can wrangle a reservation. Elizabeth is very close to her Pryce cousins, and she can probably get a table. And it will be a small way to endear myself to Ava's family.

"But let me make a few calls and see if I can arrange for something interesting to do," I say.

I go out to the tiny balcony and close the door behind me. I don't want to get anybody's hopes up in case I can't deliver. I call Elizabeth. She picks up fast, as though she's been waiting.

"If you're calling me to tell me you've finally reconciled with the love of your life, don't. I already heard. Congratulations," she says happily.

"Of course you heard." My lips twitch. "Everybody talks to you."

"Well. People like me. What can I say?"

"Perhaps you can help me then, using your super likability."

"What is it?" I can almost hear her lean closer to the phone. "I can't remember the last time you asked anyone for a favor."

"This is actually for Ava's parents. They really want to dine at Éternité tonight, and didn't think to make reservations a year in advance. I know it's owned by your cousin Mark... You think you can get us a table?"

"Sure. He always keeps an empty table for family. How many people?"

"Four adults and one small child. A toddler, really. Is that gonna be a problem?"

"Don't think so," she says. "Assuming the child is well behaved."

"I think she is," I say slowly. She seems happy and well behaved enough.

"Hmm." Elizabeth muses for a moment. "Maybe

you should get a nanny for the evening. Vanessa knows a few good ones. I'll text you the info."

"Thanks. I owe you one."

"No, you don't. I'm just happy to see you happy. You deserve this."

"Even if I don't plan to marry Ava until after...you know...the deadline?"

"Lucas, I support whatever decision you want to make. That's what Grandpa would've liked."

"Thanks." I force the word through a tight ball lodged in my chest. Suddenly, I feel like an idiot for having avoided my siblings after the accident. It's obvious they love and care for me deeply. I should never have assumed otherwise.

A few minutes pass before I get a text from Elizabeth.

Done. Reservation's at seven. Hope you like it there. The food is amazing. André is a true artiste. As for nannies: here's the info. Vanessa says they're all excellent and thoroughly vetted. Knowing how she and Justin are, I'm a hundred percent certain they're all saints.

Thank you, I text back.

Elizabeth sends me a bunch of hearts. I grin and go back inside.

"So, what are we doing?" Ava looks at me.

"Going to Éternité, for one."

Darcy and Ray gape at me. "How did you manage that?" he asks.

"Eh, I know someone who knows someone..."

Ava tilts her head, studying my face. "Let me guess. Ryder or Elizabeth?"

"Elizabeth. She's tight with her cousin Mark...who owns the restaurant. So she hooked us up."

Ava claps her hands. "That's wonderful! Thank you."

"I told her we have Mia, so she also sent a list of nannies. That should allow us to have a relaxing dinner," I say.

Ray begins, "That's un—"

"That sounds wonderful!" Darcy interrupts. "We haven't had an adult dinner in a long time."

Ray almost looks pained, which is surprising. You'd think he'd like an opportunity to dine in a fine restaurant without a baby in the way. On the other hand, maybe he's anxious about leaving Mia behind. "The nannies are very well qualified. Mia will be fine," I say.

He gives me an oddly tight smile. It's almost like he thinks I'd harm Mia or something.

"Of course," Ray says finally. "Thank you."

30

AVA

ÉTERNITÉ IS NO ORDINARY RESTAURANT. I CAN SEE
why Ray and Darcy wanted to try it, and why dining
here is on some people's bucket list. And I understand
why Ray finally decided to leave Mia with the nanny,
even though I could tell he'd rather not. Despite my
promise to keep my silence a little longer, he seems to
harbor an instinctive wariness toward Lucas. I remind
myself that once he has a chance to get to know Lucas,
he'll change his attitude.

The place is stunning, with the aesthetics of east
and west merging together to form a harmonious and
lovely atmosphere. The music is lively yet quiet. The
wait staff is outfitted in crisp black-and-white uniforms,
and the diners are dressed to impress in priceless
designer silk, chiffon and leather. I'm glad that Lucas

had Rachel get me and Darcy new dresses and matching shoes. It sounds shallow, but I don't want to do anything that would reflect badly on Lucas or embarrass him among his social peers.

Every table has expensive wine and food almost too beautiful to be eaten. The maître d' takes us to a table in the loft that overlooks the floor below. Screens and hangings create the illusion of a private balcony. After browsing the leather-bound menu, I order the waiter's recommendation—a surf-and-turf seven-course dinner. Everyone else also orders it, and Lucas adds a bottle of red and one of white, his voice a quiet murmur.

Despite the crowd, service is quick. The wines come first, and after Lucas approves them, the waiter serves everybody. We clink glasses. "To a new beginning," Darcy says. "I'm glad that you two were able to work everything out. It's obvious you love each other."

Lucas inclines his head. "Thank you."

"So what the tabloids said about your inheritance..." Ray takes a small sip of wine and places his glass on the table. "Was it true?"

My cheeks heat. "Ray—"

"No," Lucas answers. "All true, unfortunately. But before you doubt my sincerity, I want you to know that I will not marry Ava until my father's deadline has passed."

Ray squints. "But...your siblings will lose out as well, won't they?"

"Yes, but certain sacrifices have to be made. And I choose Ava."

"I see." Ray leans back in his seat, his shoulders slightly slumped.

I give him a quick look, hoping it communicates what I've told him before. Lucas loves me too much to hurt them through Mia. A man who can walk away from an inheritance worth millions for love is a man worth trusting and keeping.

"That couldn't have been an easy decision," Darcy says. "I'm glad Ava found a man who puts her first."

"Actually, it *was* an easy decision. When Ava came back and gave me another chance, I knew this was the only way. I don't regret it."

Just then, the server brings out the first course—vegetables and thinly sliced lamb cooked in a dark chocolate sauce. I stare at it, somewhat skeptical. To me, chocolate equals dessert. On the other hand, I'm not going to turn it down just because it happens to start the dinner.

It's surprisingly good, the texture and flavors blending perfectly. Contrary to expectation, it's not at all sweet. Rather it's slightly bitter with just a dash of mint at the end.

"This is incredible," Rays says as he polishes off his portion. "Wow."

"Wow indeed. Thank you for bringing us here, Lucas," Darcy says.

"It's nothing. You don't understand how much I owe you for all that you've done for Ava." Lucas brushes a hand along my shoulder. "Otherwise I would've never met her."

"She's always been resilient and bright," Ray says softly. "We didn't do that much."

"With or without us, you would've met if it was meant to be. And it looks like it was." Darcy looks at me and Lucas. "I'm so happy for you both. May you always be together."

"Thank you," I say. It is a huge relief to know my foster parents accept Lucas, even though Ray is still a bit hesitant. But I can sense he's gradually seeing that Lucas isn't the enemy—and that he's actually a good guy.

The waiter clears our plates and brings out the second course—a creamy bisque with huge chunks of succulent lobster piled high in the center of the bowl. "I know you're looking forward to spending some time with Ava," Lucas says, "and I'm more than happy to give you that time, but in case you don't know, you're invited to my brother's Thanksgiving party."

"Elliot?" Rays asks.

"Ryder."

Darcy's hand goes to her chest, reaching for the silver pendant. "My goodness. Who would've thought we'd get to have Thanksgiving with a *Hollywood movie star*!"

I grin. It's sort of fun to see Darcy's stunned reaction. Now I'm beginning to understand why Lucas wants to spoil me. He's probably anticipating something like this from me. And it's surprisingly fun to treat the people I love.

Lucas smiles as he pours more white wine for her.

"Don't do that when he's around. He's already insufferably arrogant."

"As bad as the media says?" Ray asks.

"Oh, worse. Although he's pretty tame now, what with being married and having a child on the way."

"That's right. He married his assistant not too long ago."

"And it was a love match," Lucas says. "Nobody makes Ryder do anything he doesn't want to."

The conversation turns to plans for Christmas and what Darcy and Ray want to see and do while they're in L.A. Lucas is attentive and charming throughout, and I'm relieved to see Darcy's beaming smile of approval.

Although we've all eaten together like this before, this time it's different. It's not the venue, but the dynamics. Lucas is more relaxed, and he's openly possessive and affectionate with me. My foster parents are also starting to relax around Lucas.

Although each course is only a few bites, I'm starting to get full by the time the sixth one is done. Everything's perfect—a sublime indulgence in taste and smell—and the wines Lucas chose complement everything.

"So..." Darcy licks her lips. "I've heard great things about the desserts here."

Ray looks at her fondly, and I laugh have to at her enthusiasm even as I stand up. "Excuse me. I need to visit the ladies' room."

A server lets me know that the restrooms are on the

first level. I hurry down. Maybe I shouldn't have had so much wine, but it was impossible to turn down such great vintages. The bathroom stalls are individually done with those fancy Japanese bidets. The warmed seats feel like heaven.

After I'm finished, I wash my hands, freshen my makeup and exit. I walk down the long corridor and into the main dining area, where I almost bump into a woman coming the other way. "Sorry."

"Excuse m— Wait. What is this? Why are *you* here?"

I stiffen at the tone. "Hello, Elle. Fancy running into you again."

Her gaze rakes me up and down. "Do you...*work* here now?"

"Actually, I'm here to have dinner." I note with catty satisfaction that my dress is made of finer material than hers. Last time we ran into each other, she acted as though I was the hired help, beneath notice. "In the loft."

"Are you now? Well, I see you're playing this game far better than your mother. Did you snag someone who spends money on you? I hope he's not secretly married..."

I inhale sharply. The way my father treated Mom will always be a source of raw pain.

"You should've never been born," Elle continues. "People like you absolutely ruin it for the quality folk. If it weren't for you, Dad would've never stayed so long with your pathetic mother."

"Don't you dare talk about my mother that way."

"Why? Does the truth hurt?" Elle smirks. "And it is *all* true. My mother told me everything. God, how stupid was your mom to think Dad could be a blue-collar worker? I mean, really. He had a banker's hands."

"Why are you so hateful, Elle? What did I ever do to you?"

"You keep running into me, for one. *So* embarrassing it is to have someone like you in my past. Do us both a favor and take your cut-rate boyfriend and get out of L.A., Ava. Please."

Fury and humiliation choke me, and I can't think of a clever comeback. All I can do is clench my hands so Elle doesn't see how badly they're shaking.

"There you are, Ava."

Lucas. He slips an arm around my waist and pulls me closer. He turns to my half-sister, his face a hard mask. Apparently he heard her last line. "You are...?"

"Elle," she says, cataloguing his clothes. Lucas's outfit is simple, but impeccably tailored in superb material. Her gaze takes in the Rolex on his wrist, the two-thousand-dollar shoes.

"You're the reason a word like *cunt* exists."

She gasps, and so do I. I've never heard him speak so brutally before.

"Who do you think you are?" she says.

Before Lucas can answer, a man comes over. It's her fiancé, whose picture I saw when I got the Google alert about her engagement. "Sweetheart, you were gone for so long **I thought you**'d gone on safar— Lucas! Good to see you."

"Hello, Cedric." Lucas's voice is ice smooth. "Do you know this woman?"

"I do, in fact. She's my fiancée."

"I see." Lucas smiles. "Normally I'd offer congratulations, but in this case I'm sorry to hear you're marrying a vicious, ill-mannered shrew who sees nothing wrong with harassing another woman."

Cedric pulls back, his eyebrows almost hitting his hairline. "Excuse me?"

"I had to intervene when I noticed your fiancée was verbally abusing Ava here." Lucas pulls my hand up and kisses the back of it with his eyes on both Cedric and Elle. "Perhaps you should ask her who gave her the right to behave so abominably to the woman I intend to marry...so we all can be enlightened."

"Cedric, how can you let him talk to me like th—"

"Not a word." He raises a hand to stop her.

Her face is scarlet, a small vein in her forehead ticking visibly, but she shuts up. Cedric turns to me and Lucas. "I'm terribly sorry for the offense. I'm sure Elle didn't mean anything by it."

I pat Lucas's forearm. "Of course. Everyone makes mistakes. It'd probably be better, though, if we didn't run into each other so much."

She stiffens, but Cedric smiles, all decorous and proper. "It does seem as though that would be for the best. We'll try to avoid such encounters in the future."

"Excellent. You'll hear from Rachel later this month," Lucas says, then leads me away.

After a couple of steps, I can't help but look back. Elle and Cedric are arguing. Well, "arguing" isn't quite the right word. It's more like him leaning in, clearly furious at her, and Elle looking like she's about to cry.

I feel slightly bad about the whole thing, but glad that it'll mean an end to our unpleasant confrontations, especially if we're going to be in the same city and move around in the same social circles.

"Seen enough?" Lucas says.

Flushing, I turn away. "Yes." I clear my throat. "How did you know?"

"I could see both of you from our table. I knew something was up from the way you were holding yourself."

"I'm that transparent, huh?"

He squeezes my hand. "Nobody has the right to upset you—no one. You're mine, Ava, my top priority. You're up here"—he stretches his arm way above his head—"and everyone else is here." He drops his arm.

Suddenly, I can't help myself. I've never been anybody's most important priority or felt like I truly belonged to someone the way I do with Lucas. I give him a tight hug. "But why did Cedric back off like that? It was amazing...like you had a string tied to his tongue or something."

"More like his wallet." He presses his lips to the top of my head. "Cedric's a lawyer, and Elliot and I are responsible for a big chunk of his firm's billables."

"Thank you," I whisper.

LUCAS

I HAVE THE LIMO TAKE AVA, HER PARENTS AND MIA to the apartment, and then I return to Blake's penthouse. My oldest brother hasn't been around since our brunch with Elizabeth. If I could be certain he wasn't coming back for a while, I'd move Ava in here.

Although her parents are fantastic cock-blockers, I am glad that Ray seems to be softening a bit. He was pretty hostile—without being overtly rude—at Ava's apartment at first. Not that I blame the guy. If some shithead made my daughter cry the way I did Ava, I'd hire a hit man.

My belly full of good food, I lie on the couch and put the phone on my stomach. I'm hoping she'll text me once her parents are settled in. I offered to put them up in a hotel—which would be more comfortable than Ava's small apartment—but they categorically refused. The only reason I managed to pay for dinner was by slipping my credit card to the server before anybody noticed.

My phone buzzes, and I grab it instantly. But the message isn't from Ava.

Got a small problem, Ryder writes.

I frown. *Don't tell me you're canceling.* Darcy's

dying to meet Ryder. Every woman in the world loves a movie star, and Ryder's one of the hottest leading men at the moment.

No. Lemme call you.

A second later, my phone rings. "What's going on?"

"My idiot assistant screwed up," Ryder says.

"I thought Paige quit."

"Not her! She would've never messed up like this."

"Okay, so what did she do?"

"*He.*"

"You got a guy?"

There's a slight pause. "Thought it'd be better that way. Tabloids can't make shit up about how I'm having an affair with the new assistant. Anyw—"

"They'll start saying you're secretly gay."

He snorts. "Like anyone's gonna believe that. *Anyway*, the moron sent out invitations to all the plus-ones."

"Okay. So?"

"He invited Faye last week. And she accepted."

"Ah, jeez..."

"Yeah. To make things worse, he made it sound like I *want* her to come, like it was a special separate invitation."

"So she's going to show."

"Well, you said the breakup wasn't awkward. And people do have this thing about hanging out with celebrities."

"This isn't good." I run a hand over my face. Ava isn't exactly crazy about Faye, and I'm sure her foster parents aren't either. How the hell do I explain Faye's presence at a holiday dinner that's supposedly family only? "Can you rescind?"

"Kinda tough to do. The dinner's tomorrow, and it's already after ten. I just found out." He sighs heavily. "That idiot's totally fired. Let's just hope Faye doesn't show. She might not, 'cause you guys are broken up... and she knows you're back with Ava, right? Plus, I'll text her tomorrow, make sure she knows you're bringing Ava. Maybe Faye'll get the hint that it won't be comfortable if she comes."

I purse my mouth. I don't like it, but Ryder has a point. Faye made it clear she wants to be my friend, and doesn't wish me anything but best. Although Ryder— jaded bastard that he is—believes she can't possibly mean that, I do. She's never done anything to make me doubt her friendship.

But as I hang up, a nasty feeling starts forming in my gut.

31

Ava

Darcy and Ray sneak out of the bedroom at seven. "You're up early," I say. Both of them are in flannel pajamas, Darcy's pink and Ray's dark burgundy.

She winces. "Sorry, we were trying to be quiet so you could keep sleeping."

"It's okay." I sit up on the couch. "Jet-lagged?"

"A little. We were up around five and read for a while. But I'm getting hungry now."

Uh oh. Breakfast. "I only have some bread...and a few eggs."

"Got any syrup?"

"Maybe a few packets from takeout places."

Ray tut-tuts. "You ever cook?"

"I've been really busy at work."

"That man isn't bringing home-cooked meals to you?"

I chuckle at his disgruntled expression.

Darcy sits by me, her legs tucked under her. "How did the reconciliation come about? I was shocked, but we haven't had a chance to really talk."

"It's...sort of a long story." I tell them about how Lucas and I ran into each other in L.A. and the things I've learned about him—and myself—since, while Ray putters around my humble kitchen, putting together breakfast and coffee and listening with one ear.

"And you haven't said anything about Mia yet?" Darcy says when I'm finished.

I shake my head.

"You should."

Behind her, the corners of Ray's mouth turn downward, but he manages a smile as he hands coffee to Darcy and me, gesturing toward the table, where he's served up some simple French toast.

Pretending not to see his reaction, I take my mug and join them. Badly stocked kitchen or not, Ray has somehow whipped up excellent French toast and fried eggs.

"Are you sure about telling Lucas?" I ask Darcy after a few bites. "You aren't worried that he might... want to take Mia back?"

"You know... I'm grateful for Mia. I always wanted a child, and frankly, I'd given up hope since we just didn't have any luck no matter what we tried." Darcy puts a hand on my arm. "But as much as I like telling myself that I'll be around until I'm old enough to see her have children of her own, I'm fifty-five. And so is Ray. Life can be uncertain." She squeezes me. "My mother passed away when she was only sixty-one. Aneurysm. Nothing to be done about it."

"I'm so sorry, Darcy."

"But there's one consolation, which is that if something does happen to us, Mia won't be alone. She'll have you. And it eases my mind to know that she'll have her father as well."

My breath hitches as an unspeakable fear slithers through me. "Are you...?"

She smiles. "I'm fine. No cancer or anything. Same for Ray. But it's something to think about. You just never know." Her gaze turns to the bedroom where Mia is still sleeping. "And I don't want her to be alone."

"She won't be. She'll be loved and taken care of. I didn't mention this to you, but Lucas gave me two million dollars back in Virginia."

Ray and Darcy both stop eating. "Two—! What on earth for?" Ray asks.

"When we came back to the States, he made some promises, and the money happened to be one of them. I didn't think much of it at the time, but he was serious."

"My goodness." Darcy blinks. "That's a fortune."

"I'm not touching a penny of it."

"You going to give it back?" Ray grows thoughtful. "Guess that makes sense if you plan to be together."

Darcy is shaking her head. "A woman needs to have her own money."

I laugh. "I've set it aside for Mia. *She* deserves the money."

Darcy grows quiet. "I see. But are you sure? We plan on leaving Mia plenty, so you shouldn't..."

"She's mine too, and I can always make my own money. Please don't worry."

Darcy and Ray nod. "So...when are you going to tell him?" Ray asks.

"Before tonight's dinner. I'm going to call him and set a time so we can talk face to face."

~

Ava

Finding a time to talk to with Lucas is easier said than done. Sadly, he's unavailable all day long. "If it's really important, I can swing by," he offers.

"No, it's okay," I say, not wanting to disrupt his schedule. He's been working with people in Asia, and like he told Ray yesterday, they don't care that it's Thanksgiving where we are. Koreans work straight through until a few days after Christmas.

"I'll pick you and your family up around four," he says. "We can talk in the car, or at Ryder's. His place has lots of space."

"Okay."

I hang up. Normally I'd be jumping up and down at the idea of meeting a big movie star like Ryder Reed, but I'm too nervous. Lucas will be in for a shock, but I'm sure he'll also understand why I couldn't tell him about Mia before. I want him to be happy and proud of our daughter, even if she's being raised by foster parents. He's met Ray and Darcy and knows them a little now. Hopefully he realizes they're good people who want the best for Mia.

Come on. Lucas is a reasonable man. Besides, he may not even really want to be a father yet. Remember how he called children "interesting"?

I know all that, but I also know that what people *assume* their reaction will be in a given situation and how they *actually* react are two different things. I never knew if I wanted a child of my own. I never longed for a family, since my childhood and early teens were such painful chapters of my life. But when I saw the sonogram of Mia...heard her heart beat for the first time and felt her kick against my belly... I knew that not only did I want her, I was prepared to do anything to give her the best chance in life, which is why I gave her up for adoption to Darcy and Ray.

I get ready and go into the living room around three thirty. My foster parents are already dressed in stylish outfits—a simple light gray sweater and dark slacks for Ray and a long spring-green dress for Darcy. Mia is in a pink dress with a fluttery, tutu-like skirt and a small tiara, looking like the pampered princess she is.

Ray raises an eyebrow. "Are you sure you want to go like that?"

"What?" I glance down at myself, wondering if I

overlooked a stain or something. No. It's far worse. I'm in a fuzzy black and orange dress with small stars. I might as well scrawl "Halloween Reject" on my face.

Darcy rises. "Let me help." She puts a hand between my shoulders and marches me back to my closet. "I'm sure you have something more suitable."

"I do, but..." I groan. "Sorry. I don't know what I was thinking."

"Don't stress about the dinner. Or telling Lucas about Mia."

I sigh. "That obvious, huh?"

"Of course it's obvious. It's big news, and I'd be just as jumpy. But Ava, I've seen the way he looks at you, and his feelings won't change over this. He knows what your circumstances were like." She picks out a blue cocktail dress and holds it out for me. "What about this? Stylishly cut...and it'll bring out your eyes."

Instead of taking the garment, I lower my voice and whisper, "What if he wants Mia?" When Ray mentioned the possibility yesterday it seemed really far-fetched, but now it feels not so improbable after all. Even if Lucas doesn't mind letting Darcy and Ray raise her, his family may object, especially that bastard Blake. He seems like the type who'd stomp on a bunny just because he can.

Her chin quivers slightly, but she smiles. "Well. That's his right as her father."

"Darcy..."

"I'll be devastated, but it's not like we can't ever see her. We can still be in her life, perhaps as honorary grandparents or godparents. I'll always think of her as my own, but I want you to be happy." She exhales softly. "It'd be easier for me to ask to keep Mia a secret. But secrets never remain hidden. They always come out, and when they do, they destroy everything. If he hears it from you, now, he'll have a chance to digest the news and he'll appreciate your honesty. If he hears it from someone else, the only thing he'll think is that you lied to him." Darcy holds my eyes, making sure I get the point. "Ava, you've fought so hard for this relationship. I've seen how miserable you were without Lucas, and how you glow when you're with him. I don't want to take that away."

The skin around my eyes grows hot with unshed tears. She's so perfect and so loving, and I can't help but wonder for the hundredth time why someone like her couldn't be a mother when my own mom could.

I put on the dress. As soon as she pulls the zipper up, the intercom buzzes. "That'll be Lucas," I say.

"Perfect timing." She squeezes my hand. "You look fabulous, dear. Let's have a great time! I've never been invited to a movie star's mansion before. If I were still young and single, I'd throw myself at that man, propriety be damned."

We both laugh as we leave. Ray smiles at our good humor, and Mia chortles as though she's in on the joke.

Lucas arrives with a warm grin, kisses me and then greets everyone. He is gorgeous, this man of mine. The brown V-neck shirt deepens his eye color to dark chocolate and stretches over his big, muscular chest, revealing the outline of the nipple ring. His slacks are two shades lighter, and fit his narrow pelvis and tight butt perfectly. If we were alone, I might run my hands all over his body just because.

Mia watches him with fascination, then points at her tiara. "Pwincess."

"And very pretty, too." He bows to Mia, his motion as fluid and elegant as any medieval knight's. Then he lowers himself on one knee, bringing the two of them to somewhat the same height. "Princess Mia."

She laughs, clapping. Her eyes are fantastically bright and curious as she studies him, then pushes the hair out of the way and touches his scar. He stills, and my heart stops. He's so sensitive about the crash...

"Wha dat?" she asks.

"It's called a 'scar,'" he answers solemnly. "This is what happens when someone gets hurt."

"Did you figh'?"

"No."

She shakes her head. "No figh'. Be fwiens."

He nods. "That's the best way."

The smile he gives her is so pure and loving, my heart aches until tears cloud my vision. I'm tempted to just blurt out, "That's our daughter," but my tongue feels huge and clumsy in my mouth. Still, wouldn't this be the perfect moment for him to learn who Mia is, when he's feeling this connection and affection for the child...?

Ray picks her up, laughing, and the tableau is

broken. I bite my lower lip, then look away. Suddenly there's a hand on my arm. "You all right?" Lucas asks.

"I'm fine."

"If you're nervous about Blake, don't be. Everyone's on your side."

"Really?" I blink up at him.

He nods, sidling closer. "It's just dinner. I promise they won't try to have you as an appetizer."

I laugh despite myself, and we go out together. The Bentley SUV is waiting for us outside, sans driver. I give Lucas a look, and he shrugs. "It's Thanksgiving. I gave the man the day off."

"I need to grab Mia's child seat from Ava's car," Ray says.

"It's okay. I already had one installed for her."

"Thank you. That's very thoughtful of you," Darcy says.

"My pleasure, ma'am."

Lucas waits until everyone's settled before starting the car. Of course I'm seated next to him, since there's no place I'd rather be.

I don't say much during the drive, thinking of a good time and place to tell Lucas everything. Darcy and Ray chat about what they'd like to do while in L.A. and Lucas throws out a few suggestions. He even offers to set them up with a concierge, but they decline.

"You're awfully quiet," Lucas says, giving me a quick glance.

"Just imaging if Ryder's mansion is as grand as people say."

He snorts. "It's more like a fortress. The only things missing are a moat and some catapults."

I bite back a laugh. "Seriously?"

"That's the word. Ryder takes security *very* seriously."

"Is it because of his wife?" Ray asks. "I saw some articles about her. Nasty stuff."

"That probably cemented his hatred of the media, but it was already pretty full-blown. Some crazy fans were stalking him for a while...one actually tried to run him over, screaming that if she couldn't have him, nobody could."

Three gasps rise. Mia merely laughs as though she finds our shock hilarious.

"Wow," I say.

Lucas gives me a look. "Yeah. Since then he's been stricter with security, although I think it makes him unhappy that he's lost his privacy."

"The price of fame," Ray says.

"Unfortunately, yes. Although Ryder would prefer that people didn't bother him so much. He enjoys acting more than all the trappings that come with being a star. Since his wife has been targeted a few times, he's doubly upset about that."

"It's a shame."

"Par for the course in Hollywood. But Paige is very understanding. She knew what was going to happen, since she worked with him before as his assistant."

Soon we reach Ryder's place. Lucas hasn't exaggerated at all. The wall surrounding the estate looks forbidding, and the security cameras mounted everywhere don't appear to be just for show. Lucas pushes a button at the gates and says, "It's me."

"Welcome, Mr. Reed," comes a growly male voice, and the gates open automatically.

I gape as our SUV follows a winding road through an immaculate garden and past a huge pool. The place is practically a resort. The mansion is exceptionally large, with three stories, and Lucas kills the engine in front of the entrance. I spot a few other fancy cars.

"Paige's family's here too, I think," Lucas says. "Her sister and husband are in L.A. and her parents are from Ohio, if I remember correctly."

"Super," Darcy says. An extrovert to the core, she loves to meet new people.

Lucas leads the way into the mansion. The foyer is stunning, with beautifully framed paintings that look gracing the walls. I stare at them like a wide-eyed fool—all of them look like originals—but Lucas barely seems to notice. I hear the clacking of heels on the marble floor.

"Oh my gosh, you made it!"

It's Elizabeth, a mimosa in her hand. She's as well put together as usual in a pink dress and nude pumps. Her makeup is flawless, maybe done professionally, and her golden hair is pulled back, revealing dangly pearl and diamond earrings.

Lucas makes quick introductions, and Elizabeth greets everyone warmly. Then her gaze falls on Mia. "Hello, little princess. Aren't you gorgeous?" She gives her drink to Lucas, opens her arms, then looks at Darcy. "Do you mind if I hold her?"

"Not at all." Darcy hands her off.

Elizabeth takes Mia with care. "She's so *precious!*" she coos. "Oh my gosh. I think I just ovulated."

"I...did not need to know that," Lucas remarks.

"Oh hush. Let's go to the living room." She walks with us. "Everyone's here except Blake. I don't know when he's coming, or even *if* he's coming. He isn't answering his phone, and Paige says he didn't bother to RSVP." She rolls her eyes. "I swear we were taught better than that."

"That's a shame," I say, although secretly I'm hoping he doesn't show at all. I know I have to make peace with the man eventually. He's the sibling who showed up in Charlottesville when Lucas and I broke up and gave him support. But I can't forget what Blake said to me, and I'm not going to pretend that it was okay, even though I'm willing to be friendly with him for Lucas's sake. However, with the confession I need to make, I'd rather not deal with him today if possible.

"Look who's here!" Elizabeth announces as we spill into the sizable living room. I notice it has a view of the garden and the pool.

Ryder Reed, in the flesh, gets up from the loveseat he's sharing with a pregnant blond woman and welcomes us. He's famous for his chiseled, impossibly handsome movie-star looks, and if anything he's even better in person. Darcy is quite taken with him, naturally, and even Ray looks a bit shocked. It's a little surreal having a face you've seen hundreds of times in movies smile at you in real life.

Lucas clears his throat and squints at me in mock displeasure. I look up at him, then grin. "Jealous?"

"Depends on what you're thinking about."

"I was wondering what genius surgeon gave him that face."

"Sadly, it's all natural."

"Really?" I gape at Ryder, who I think knows what we're talking about and has the chutzpah to wink at me. I turn back to Lucas. "You're the most perfect man for me though."

"Even with the scar?" he asks, but there's no pain or darkness in his gaze.

"I'm rather fond of it. Plus, now all you need is an eye patch and you can be a pirate." I kiss him, then notice Elizabeth and Ryder over Lucas's shoulder, watching us with huge grins.

Soon the two of them introduce us to Paige and her family, including her mother, stepfather, stepsister and her husband. All the women fawn over Mia, who preens shamelessly with a wide smile and bright eyes. Paige rests a hand over her belly and says, "I hope I have a baby just as precious as Mia. She's adorable."

"So do I," Belle says. "Which is bad because I really want to finish college first."

"We can do both," Elliot calls out, while serving scotch to Ryder, Lucas and Ray.

"Easy for you to say," Belle shoots back. "You won't be the one with morning sickness and cankles."

Elizabeth rolls her eyes. "Ignore him. What do men know about pregnancy anyway?" She caresses Mia's cheeks.

"Exactly. Men...know nothin' 'bout women. Thass the problem."

My jaw drops at the sight of Blake, who sways as he walks in. His shirt and pants are wrinkled like he's slept in them, and he reeks of stale alcohol. Red rims his eyes, and he hasn't shaved recently. I can't believe it's the same self-possessed, supercilious bastard I met before.

I glance at Lucas, unsure what to do. But I suppose my plan to make friends with Blake is going to have to wait, just like my confession.

32

LUCAS

GODDAMN IT. I FEEL AVA AND HER PARENTS' GAZES boring into me. Ryder swears under his breath. I grab Blake before he stumbles and embarrasses himself further.

"What the hell's going on?" I hiss under my breath.

"Had some problems. So what?" It comes out "sho wha'".

I grit my teeth. "Come on. Let's get you cleaned up before dinner."

"Jus' came by to wish erryone a happy Thanksgiving…"

This is worrying. Blake is generally detached and unemotional. I can't imagine what could've made him show up in this condition at Thanksgiving, especially knowing people outside the family are present.

I drag him upstairs to one of the guest bedrooms. Ryder's place has plenty—all large, opulently appointed and stocked with everything anyone could want. Hopefully the one I picked hasn't been used for orgies. With Ryder, you never know.

I lay Blake down on the bed. He resists, but not very well, and I take a vicious pleasure in pulling the clothes off him and shoving him between the sheets. "Sleep it off. Jesus, I hope you didn't drive here."

"Course not. I Lyfted. Coss a lot of money. You know those lazy assholes don' wanna work today? 'S only Thursday."

"Uh-huh. Thanksgiving Thursday." I'm surprised he was able to find someone at all.

"The world would be better...if we were 'maphrodites."

"What? *Hermaphrodites?*"

"Yeah. That. Wouldn' need women."

"I...guess that's true."

"They're vile. Pretty...feel nice...but vile. Impossible. Evil. Untrih...untruh...untrus'worthy. Always lying. Commission, omission... All the fuckin' mind games. But you know what's wors'?"

I wait a beat, wondering, *What's brought this on?* Blake has never lost his head over a woman.

"Can' live without 'em." Blake shakes his head sorrowfully. "Jus' can'."

"What the hell did you snort?"

"Nothin'. I'm perfelly fine."

I lay a hand on his shoulder. "Okay. Why don't you

have a nap before dinner?" *And before you do something to embarrass yourself further.* "Remember, we have a lot of female guests, so they probably don't want to hear how you feel about women right now."

Blake groans, throwing a forearm over his forehead. "Did I say that in fron' of them?"

"No, thanks to my heroically quick action. Now stay put. I'll have the housekeeper bring you some aspirin and water and you can get some sleep."

He doesn't respond as I leave. I need to have a conversation with Ava's foster parents. She probably told them about Blake, and I don't want them to think he's going to cause problems for us.

Damn it. He was supposed to show up, be his usual cool, urbane self, charm Darcy and Ray and put their minds at ease that he wouldn't be an asshole to Ava ever again. *But no. He had to ruin it.*

Now all I can hope—rather fervently—is that Faye doesn't show. Because her popping up now? That would ruin everything for sure, and I can't think of a good excuse to explain her presence.

When I reach the living room, Paige is announcing that the dinner's ready, and my ex is nowhere to be seen. The tension in my shoulders eases as Ava puts an arm around my waist. I hug her back, relishing our closeness.

"Is he okay?" she whispers as we move to the formal dining room.

"He's fine. Just...drunk for some reason. Sorry about that."

"It's okay. Does he do this a lot?"

"No. A business deal probably went bad or something." I wince inwardly. *Lame.*

The long table has been set up with a perfectly roasted turkey and honey-glazed ham. All the usual fixings are laid out—mashed potatoes, salad, buttered corn and peas, and moist stuffing, gravy and cranberry sauce. There's a card for every seat, and I end up with Ava to my left and her family, including Mia, taking the chairs to my right. Elliot, Belle and Nonny are at one end of the table, and Ryder, Paige and her family occupy the other, with Elizabeth immediately across from me. A lone chair stays empty since Blake is in no condition to join us. I want to confirm if Ryder was able to get Faye not to show, but I can't talk about it in front of Ava and her parents.

"We're going to have candied yam and pie later," Paige announces.

"I generally like the yam *with* my food," Elliot says.

"No can do," Ryder says. "Gotta eat 'em in the kitchen afterward."

"*What!*"

"Hey, I only had them made because you like them so much. Candied yam makes Paige nauseated."

"Seriously?" Elliot stares at her.

"Told you. Men know nothing about pregnancy," Elizabeth says.

"Yeah?" Elliot says. "Well, I'll put money that Belle's going to eat everything."

"Keep on saying that. She's going to tolerate everything except the food you love, dude," Ryder says.

Elliot makes a face, then winks at his wife.

The food is served, Ryder carving the turkey and ham with surprising expertise. If I didn't know better, I'd think he did it all the time.

Ava leans closer. "Did he cook all this?"

"I hope not. None of us want to die." She gives my arm a light slap even as she laughs. "If there's anything you don't like, you don't have to eat it. Ryder and Paige won't mind."

"Okay."

The dinner is surprisingly low-key, all things considered. I can't remember the last time we all got together just to eat and relax, and I realize with a bit of guilt that it's my fault—after the accident, I cut myself from my siblings' lives out of some misplaced sense of loss and pride.

And at the same time, the family never had holiday dinners together like this. This whole event is most likely Paige's idea because Ryder certainly wouldn't bother to host one. Here at the table he makes sure she's comfortable, handing her whatever strikes her fancy. He's totally smitten, but happily so. And the same can be said for Elliot...which is kind of surreal. I was certain he'd never fall for anyone.

Elizabeth is serene as usual, chatting with everyone. The smile never leaves her face, and she directs the various conversations with courtesy and grace. People have said she has to be faking it—supposedly no one can be that sweet all the time—but as her brother, I know she's the genuine article.

Suddenly there's a small commotion at the door, and a familiar voice drifts into the dining room. "Terribly sorry I'm late. I took a wrong turn off Rodeo Drive."

Ava freezes, and I stiffen. *Shit. Faye.*

Ryder's gaze darts toward me, then to Faye, and even Elizabeth's smile falters for a fraction of a second. Faye is dolled up in a designer red dress with a short hem that fits perfectly. Diamonds sparkle on her ears and throat, and I immediately wish I hadn't eaten anything because the turkey's suddenly threatening to come back up.

It's Paige who finally says, "Hello, Faye."

My sister recovers as well. "We thought you weren't going to be able to make it after all. Sorry we started without you." She gets up and gives Faye a light hug and an air kiss. "Why don't you take that seat?" She gestures at the empty chair, removing the card set in front of the empty plates.

"What about Blake?"

"Probably won't be joining us," Elliot says.

"Well, then." She takes the seat directly across from Ava.

I feel the weight of Darcy and Ray's gazes like a mountain on my shoulder. Now I wish I'd declined the invitation like I normally do.

"You look very nice, Ava," Faye purrs.

"Thank you." Ava gives a brittle smile. "So do you. Beautiful dress."

"Well, you know...red's always been my color."

Before Faye can say more, Elizabeth says, "By the way, I love the work you've done planning the charity event, Ava. Nate sent me the latest draft, and I couldn't find a single fault."

Ava flushes. "Thank you."

"If he weren't such a good friend, I'd poach you."

"Get in line," Ryder says. "I need a new assistant, and Ava would be perfect."

Elizabeth blinks. "How so?"

"You just said she was great at her job. I know what it takes to organize something like that, and anyone who's that on top of things will know exactly how to juggle all the crazy stuff in my life."

"You should just steal Gavin Lloyd's assistant," Elliot says. "What's her name? Mallory? She's supposed to be good."

"Hilary. And no, I don't want Gavin coming after me with a sniper rifle," Ryder says. "Besides, she's married to Mark, and I don't hire family. Can't fire 'em later."

I reach for some wine. My siblings continue to talk pointedly about assistants, without giving anyone an opening to butt in. I need to find an excuse to get the hell out of this dinner. Or pray that Faye's called away for some reason. *Please, God... I'll be good. I'll forgo drinking and swearing for the rest of my life...even donate half my money to the charity of your choice.*

Mia waves her fork, and a gob of cranberry sauce lands on her shirt. Darcy jumps into action. "Goodness. Can you tell me where the bathroom is?"

"Over there, down the hall, third door to your left," Paige says. "Do you want me to show you?"

"No, it's all right. I've got it." Darcy grabs the child and takes her away to wash up.

"That's Mia, right?" Faye says casually as she takes a slice of ham.

My eyebrow twitches, pulling at the scar. *How does she know?*

Before I can ask, she glances at Ava and says, "I guess this means you told Lucas about her."

Ava stiffens next to me, so fast I'm afraid she might pull something.

"Told him about what?" Elliot asks.

Faye gives him a *you don't know?* look. "That she's his daughter."

Silence crashes through the dining room, and all the air seems to have suddenly been sucked out of the house. I can barely breathe. My lungs ache, but the thoughts in my head...they spin like a tornado, gathering speed as the seconds tick by. Extreme emotion wells inside me, and I struggle to hold it back. Faye is obviously confused. She has to be...

Because for Ava to hide our child from me all this time...

I take in Ava's bloodless face...Ray's tight-lipped expression...

It's true.

It's true.

It's true.

Faye is right.

Why didn't Ava tell me? Why did she hide this?

"You didn't know? But I thought..." Faye blinks.

"You most likely thought wrong." Elizabeth's tone isn't cold, but hard with authority.

Suddenly, everyone's all moving and talking at the same time.

"...should take this elsewhere..."

"...must be a mistake..."

Elliot turns to Ava. "Can you say something here? Tell her she's wrong? This is stupid."

I stare at her, and she drops her gaze. "Faye's... right," she says. "What she said... It's true."

"Why didn't you say something?" My question is barely audible, but she hears it.

"For the same reason I left. Your family thought I was a gold digger...or worse."

"And afterwards...?"

"There wasn't a right time."

"No right time." I jump to my feet, my hands digging into my hair. "No *right time*? Everyone out except Ava."

"Lucas—"

"Not now, Elizabeth!" Then I finally turn and take in the openly incredulous expressions on everyone's faces. Well...not totally incredulous. There's pity as well.

Fuck this. I won't be pitied.

"Better yet, stay and enjoy the damned food!" I snarl. I grab Ava's wrist and start to drag her away.

Ray gets up, looking like he's going to do something.

"*Don't* get in my way," I say.

"Ray, it's fine," Ava says. "Just give us time to talk. Please." She turns to me. "Let's go."

I haul her upstairs.

Should've known better than to think I could avoid something like this. Happiness never lasts.

As much as I despise my mother, I can't help but wonder if she saw something that nobody else did when she called me "unworthy." What else could explain...this absolute *clusterfuck* that my life has become?

I find an empty room on the second floor, pull her inside and slam the door closed. Ava's hands are shaking, and I squash an instinctive need to comfort her.

"Tell me. *Everything.*"

"Faye's right. Mia is yours."

"Then *why didn't you say something?*"

"Lucas, I was going to. The day you were rushed to the hospital...I'd just found out and I was going to tell you that night. But then I met your family...which was a shock. One, you'd kept them hidden from me, and two, Blake accused me of being a parasite and swore he'd destroy me if I didn't stay away from you."

I smack an open palm against my chest. "But you were carrying *my* baby! *Mine!*"

"Yes. Exactly. Mia is the daughter of a fantastically wealthy man from a fantastically wealthy family. And do you know what I learned about rich people growing up? It's that they can get away with anything. Things that would get a normal person in a heap of trouble... You guys get away with it because you have money and influence. When I got home and looked you up, I knew I'd never win against your family."

"I'd never have let anything happen to you."

"Yes, but we didn't know each other as well back then. We'd never talked about our families. And I didn't know about Faye until I googled you."

The reminder of Faye makes me hesitate. "But later, when we reconnected...you could've told me."

"I could have, but I didn't know how you'd react. Not to mention, I couldn't seem to figure out a good time to bring it up."

"There were plenty of times."

"Lucas...all I can say is, I'm sorry." She hugs herself. "So what's the decision?" Her throat works. "Is this... Is this it?"

It? My head keeps churning. I can't let her go like this, but I don't know what the hell kind of conclusion I'm supposed to reach. People can call me genius all they want, but this is a fucking bombshell, and my mind's reeling, trying to process what it all means.

I'm a father.

To a girl who belongs to somebody else now...

"I think it's better I give you a little time," Ava whispers.

It barely registers.

She starts to walk out, and I follow on autopilot. All

my life I've been told I needed to see my date home. It's just good manners. And I wonder deep inside what the fuck I'm doing—really—and why the hell it matters if I'm polite or not or if Ava even cares.

Darcy and Ray are preparing to leave. Ray is holding the child.

I reach for the girl, unsure how something this perfect and precious could be mine, but her expression is no longer bright with happiness. Her face has crumpled, as though she's aware of everything that's happened while she was in the bathroom, and is clutching Ray's shirt. He tightens his hold, turning away with a motion so subtle that I doubt anybody else notices.

Dirty.

Don't touch.

Don't you know better?

I drop my hand, my jaw tight. It's as though the old man can hear my mother's damn words in my head.

Ava watches us, her expression torn. I'm not sure what's gotten her so conflicted. Either she's on my side or she's not. It's that simple.

The hostility pouring off Ray is palpable as he escorts his wife out. If he thought he could get away with it, he'd stab me with the carving knife.

Ava looks at me, opens her mouth, then shakes her head before following her foster parents out. As the door closes behind them, my entire body feels hollow.

Just like that. *Gone.*

Ryder places a hand on my shoulder. "I'm having a

driver take them home. Darcy thought it'd be best if they left."

"Of course," I say automatically.

I turn and look at Faye. She's watching me, her porcelain-like face set in innocent curiosity.

Except I know better.

If she were really worried about me...or cared about me at all...or meant what she said at the bistro, she wouldn't have blurted that out about Mia in front of everyone.

"You hypocritical *bitch*," I hiss.

She draws back. "Lucas..."

"You never wanted the best for me, did you? You lied to me."

"If you're upset that I told you—"

"You didn't tell *me*," I say. "You announced it in front of everyone."

She hesitates. "She's your daughter, Lucas. I wanted to make sure you had a chance to be in her life."

"No. You wanted to drive a wedge between me and Ava, and you dug around until you found something. I'm not sure why, because now you've lost me forever."

She gasps. "Lucas!"

"I didn't make a big deal about it when you lied to me at the hospital opening. But *this*... We're finished, Faye. Get the fuck out!"

Her eyes fill with tears. I generally hate it when women cry, but I feel absolutely nothing in this moment.

Sniffling, she grabs her purse and leaves.

I drag in air. "Sorry about that, everyone. I shouldn't have come." I ruin everything. It's like I'm fucking cursed. Actually, I *am* cursed.

"Don't be ridiculous!" Elizabeth puts an arm around my shoulders. "Come on, Lucas. Get some food in you, and we'll figure this out. We've survived worse."

Elliot and Ryder murmur agreement. "This is a shock, but nothing, you know, nuclear," Ryder says.

He's wrong. Mia is a fucking hydrogen bomb.

33

AVA

THE INTERIOR OF THE LUXURIOUS SUV IS oppressive. I feel like I'm confined to a windowless cell barely big enough for me to stretch my legs. The windows are tinted, the chauffeur doesn't speak and Ray and Darcy are as tense as statues. Even Mia is quiet, observing us, her eyes solemn.

The car is only a few blocks from my apartment when I can't stand it anymore. "Can you pull over?"

"Certainly, ma'am." The driver's voice is professionally pleasant, as though driving unwanted guests back home on Thanksgiving is an everyday occurrence.

I hand my keys to Darcy. "Here. Take these and go to my place. I need to clear my head. I'll be back soon."

"Ava..." Ray begins.

"Not now. I need to..." I don't know what I need at the moment. "I need to think."

I shut the door before my foster parents can stop me, and watch the car go. After that, it's mostly aimless walking. The city seems deserted—but then I'm sure people are where they're supposed to be—eating with loved ones or at stores grabbing bargains.

I, on the other hand...

I can't stop seeing Lucas's face as I left. He wasn't devastated or desperate like in Charlottesville. It was mostly anger that drove him back at Ryder's home. The silent accusation and questions in Lucas's eyes scored me like a whip, and it was all I could do just to stay upright.

Why did you lie to me?

Why did you hide it?

What about our promise to be honest with each other?

How could you?

I trusted you.

Is this what love is to you?

I cover my eyes, but it's no use; my hands can't stop the tears from flowing. I've failed. I just couldn't...

My phone beeps loudly. I jump at the sound, then my heart starts hammering. Maybe it's Lucas. He might've decided we need to talk... Or at least that I need to explain—

But it's a Skype call coming from Bennie. I sniff then clear my throat. I don't want him to know I've been crying. "Hello?"

"Oh my God. I'm going to kill Drew!"

"What happened?" I ask in a voice I hope is normal. I don't think Bennie is angry with Drew—he sounds too exuberant for that—but something's got him worked up.

"His mother dropped in for a surprise visit. And the bastard didn't tell me, so I was *completely* ambushed when I came home from work. I almost fainted. Thank God it was after school, so I was presentable." Bennie always dresses in a sharp suit for his classes.

I muster a proper response. "Wow. Um...how did it go?"

"She was so...*normal*. I couldn't believe it. She didn't mind taking off her Cucinelli pumps in the entryway, or eating our cup ramen. It was positively surreal."

"So it went well?"

"Uh-huh. So well that I actually thought I dreamed it all! She said she was *thrilled*—a direct quote—that Drew had found someone he loves so much." Bennie lets out a squeal. "She asked me to forgive her for barging in, but she couldn't stand the curiosity. She'd never *seen* Drew so in love before." He takes a breath. "Also a direct quote."

"I'm really happy for you." My breath hitches as a fresh wave of tears fill my eyes, and I bite my lower lip, praying he didn't hear it.

Of course, today isn't my lucky day. "Are you okay?"

"I'm fine." My voice breaks.

"Okaaay... Come on, girl. You can't hide what's going on. Oh shit. It's Thanksgiving, isn't it? Something happened to Darcy and Ray?"

I shake my head then remember he can't see me. "No. Nothing like that." My knees are too weak, and I can't remain standing anymore. I slowly fold until I'm squatting on the concrete. "I'm a mess. You were right about everything."

"What happened?"

I tell him about the dinner—how it was going so well until Faye showed up and dropped the bombshell. "I ruined everything."

"No, you didn't. You were going to tell him. It's just that that bitch had to fuck it up. *Ugh.* This is why I *hate* men with clingy exes! Hetero, homo, bi...it doesn't matter. They're like cockroaches, always coming out when you least want them." He breathes out harshly. "What are you going to do?"

"I don't know."

"Is there anything I can do?"

"Just be yourself. That's more than enough, Bennie." I wipe the tears from my face. Mascara smears my fingers.

"Jesus. I'm a shitty friend, going on about how nice Drew's mom is when you're in crisis."

"Benjamin Kelly Monsanto, you did not just say that!"

"Hey, what's with the attitude?" There's a wince in his voice. He hates it when people use his full name.

"I'm just glad one of us is happy, okay? Don't ever try to lessen your happiness for me. If you're really my friend, you'll relish every second of joy because that's what I want for you."

"Ava..."

"At least one of us, Bennie."

"Thanks." He is subdued. "You know... Just a suggestion..."

"Yeah?"

"When I was too scared to go for it with Drew, you pushed me to do it, right? And he and I had a real heart-to-heart. You know a lot about Lucas—at least a lot of the public stuff. He probably doesn't know much about you, except what you told him."

"Probably not." He knows about how I grew up—sort of—and my parents' utterly dysfunctional lives, but he doesn't know much about me since my first encounter with Blake.

"Give him a day or two to digest it all—just like you needed time to pull things together after you googled him—then talk to him. If he really loves you, he'll give you that chance."

"I didn't."

"You didn't what?"

"I didn't give him a chance to explain when I read about the deal between him and his father."

"That was different," Bennie says loyally.

"No, it wasn't." I wrap an arm around my knees. "Maybe I'm just not worthy of a chance. Lucas deserves somebody better than me, somebody who actually listens and cares about him."

"Don't do that. Look, I was skeptical as hell, but I listened to you and now I have Drew. I know you're hurting, but do as I say and go talk to him after giving him some time to cool off. Got it?"

I bite my lower lip. "Okay," I croak, even though I am not sure if I'm really going to follow through. Unlike Bennie and Drew, Lucas's and my relationship is full of scars, so many of them inflicted by me. At some point, he's going to cut his losses.

And I can't help but think maybe that time is now.

34

LUCAS

IF THIS BLACK FRIDAY GETS ANY DARKER, THEY'LL have to call it Black Hole Friday. I sprawl on Blake's couch and just...stare. I haven't had a drop of alcohol since the bombshell went off, which should make me lucid.

It's not working.

Thoughts spin around my head—not as badly as before—but I can't seem to get a grip on anything. They slip past, elusive as a school of minnows.

The only thing I know is that Mia is mine...and Ava hid her from me all this time.

"Want some vodka? Elizabeth's favorite," Blake says, coming down from his room upstairs with a full bottle clutched in his fist. He's in frayed jeans and a white T-shirt, his feet bare. The circles under his eyes are a deep purple, but he doesn't seem much the worse for wear. But then he never did need a lot of sleep.

"You going to drink again?"

"Why not?" He settles into an armchair, propping his feet on a matching ottoman. "Beats brooding, which is what you're doing."

"I'm not brooding. I'm thinking."

"Yeah, in circles. I can tell. If you need some suggestions—"

"I don't need your advice."

He raises an eloquent eyebrow. "Don't you want to know why she did it?"

I study his posture—arms crossed, eyes watery but steady. "Did you get diagnosed with something terminal? An inoperable brain tumor? Cancer, maybe? This solicitude isn't like you."

Blake snorts. "I'm in perfect health, asshole. I'm trying to get you to quit chasing your tail."

"You said you don't remember being nasty to Ava." She implied her decision had something to do with her encounter with my eldest brother, but... Damn it. Who the hell am I supposed to believe now? Until Faye's announcement, my answer would've been Ava, but now...

Now I don't know.

"I don't." Blake scowls. "But that doesn't... Shit." He runs a hand through his hair.

"What?"

"I might've said something."

I sigh. "Great."

"I was in a bad place, mentally. I wouldn't have come to the hospital if Elliot hadn't said you might die."

"What the hell can put you in a place so bad—mentally—that you can't remember what you said?"

A flush streaks his cheeks. "It involved Dane and a woman."

I straighten. "Dane? Dane Pryce?"

He nods.

"For fuck's sake. Dane's romance can't be worth much mental energy." I've met the man a few times, but he's cold, not an ounce of compassion in his expression or voice. He actually comes off as sociopathic.

"It wasn't about his romance."

It slowly dawns on me. "*Yours?*"

Blake rolls his eyes. "It's an old story. In any case, I could've said something without realizing it. But no, I don't remember."

"What the fuck. You should've told me this before."

"I don't want to even think about that time."

"All of us have stuff we don't want to think about."

"Anyway," Blake says, pointing the bottle at me, "here's the advice. Make her tell you everything."

"How's that going to help?" What if she tells me something I'd rather not know? That she never thought I was good enough? Or maybe she thought I'd make a terrible father. After all, I'm a fuck-up. I might've gotten better over time, but...

I'm like a broken bowl—it can be put back together, but it'll never be as good as it was before.

"You won't be flying blind, for one thing. And there won't be any way for someone like Faye to throw a Molotov cocktail into your relationship. Or, if you're tired of Ava, this is the perfect time to end it. You can be the good guy here—the victim of her scheming ways."

"I'm no fucking victim."

As the words slip out of my lips, I realize that's true. I don't let my mother's poisonous words chip away at me day and night like they used to. The main thing I've been thinking about since the day Ava came to my suite to mend our relationship is our future together—how I'm going to spoil her and treasure her, so she'll never, ever lack for anything. Every smile from her, every contented sigh is a gift.

My phone rings. I pick it up, hoping it's Ava calling. But no, it's some unknown number. Who...?

"Hello?" I answer anyway. Just in case.

"Is this Lucas?"

I tense. It's Ray. "Speaking."

A soft clearing of the throat. "This is Ray McIntire. Am I interrupting anything?"

"Depends on what you got to say." I haven't forgotten the way he pulled Mia out of my reach. Bastard. "How did you get my number?"

"Ava gave it to me when you took her away for the weekend in Charlottesville. I insisted, since I didn't quite trust you."

"Did you think I'd kill her? Leave her body on the side of the road?"

There's a stretch of silence that's all too eloquent. Then he says, "Ava and Darcy left to do some shopping, and I wanted to talk to you without them listening." He draws in air audibly. "Blame me."

"For what?"

"Everything. Ava wanted to tell you about Mia, but I asked her not to."

"Why?"

"I can't lose my daughter."

Anger erupts within me. I jump to my feet, my arm slashing the air. "She's *my* daughter!"

"You weren't even there!" Ray bellows. "Who do you think gave Ava the support and love she needed when she was alone and pregnant? It sure as hell wasn't you!"

"Because I didn't know!"

"And if you had, what would you have done? You didn't bother to tell her who you really were. You had your fancy piece on the side. What could we realistically expect you to have done?"

I glare at the phone. How dare he talk to me that way? The only reason I'm restraining myself with him is that he's the one who took Ava in and raised her as his own after her mother died...

"She couldn't rely on you, not after learning about that other woman. It's unfair to act like she took something from you. Because she didn't."

The phrasing of his comment hits me. When I

showed up in Chiang Mai and mentioned that she'd taken something from me, she almost passed out from shock. She must've assumed I found out about Mia and planned to take her.

"Ava almost lost Mia, and it's partly your fault. She was too stressed and heartbroken. We did everything we could for her, and it's unfair that you pop up now expecting to play father."

"Then why are you calling? To tell me to fuck off?" There's no way I'm listening to this garbage.

"No." Ray's laugh is hollow. "I'm calling because she's hurting so badly. She's hurting worse than she did before, even though she's put on that 'I'm fine' smile of hers. That's why I want you to know where the blame lies—with me." Then he hangs up.

I snarl at the phone.

"Who was that?" Blake asks.

"Ava's foster father."

"What does he want?"

"He says he's the one who told Ava to keep the whole baby thing a secret."

Blake's mouth twists. "You believe that?"

"Do you?"

He shrugs.

"What would you have done?" I ask, even though it's a stupid idea. Blake is the worst relationship person.

"I'm not like you. I never give anyone a second chance to fuck me over."

Of course not. What he's saying is so logical. So normal, but part of me rebels at the idea.

"So don't worry about what I would've done. It isn't important," Blake continues. "What matters is what *you*'re gonna do. Because she's your woman, not mine."

He proffers the bottle again and I shake my head. He shrugs and takes a generous swig.

I go out on the balcony to look at the city below. She's somewhere out there...hurting, if Ray is to be believed. And the notion of Ava in pain sends a pang through my heart. I put a hand on my chest, rubbing as though I can will away the ache.

The hell of it is, I believe Ray's telling the truth. Ava and I promised to be honest with each other, and she wouldn't disregard that unless she had an excellent reason. And Ray and Darcy are her weakness.

I can follow Blake's life philosophy. He might never have experienced love—or even given a shit about such things—but I know he's never suffered the way I have, either. He's always so careful, so strategic about everything. And not giving Ava another chance to shred my soul makes perfect sense.

Except isn't that what almost ended us in Charlottesville?

I stare at the phone. My thoughts are still too jumbled, and I don't know if I'm being smart or stupid, but I know one thing.

Ava didn't give me a chance to explain about the damned deal because she was devastated and had already made up her mind...about me, about us, about everything. Even after all that, she came to me and bared her soul, fighting for me because she couldn't stand to end it.

I want us to have a happy ending, with her loving me the way I love her. If that makes me needy and pathetic, so be it.

I can't let Ava go like this.

35

Ava

Darcy and I go shopping. I'm not really in the mood, but Ray insists that we go have "some girl time," shooing us out the door and promising to watch Mia for the duration.

The malls are packed, every store overflowing with people. Darcy and I snag a few deals after fighting hordes of sale-crazed shoppers, then—thank God—manage to grab a table at Starbucks and get some coffee. I don't know about her, but my feet are killing me, even in sneakers.

"That was fun," Darcy says. "At least I'm done with Christmas gifts for this year."

"A woman with a plan." I smile. She doesn't need to shop Black Friday bargains to be able to afford presents. "And thank you."

"For what?"

"Being sweet. If I'd stayed home, I would've been moping all day."

Darcy sighs. "I'm the one who should be apologizing. I didn't realize Ray asked you to keep it from Lucas. That was...shortsighted."

"He wants to protect you."

She nods. "But Lucas has the right. I'm not going to lie and say that if he decides to take her from us, it won't hurt. It will. Unbearably. But the truth always comes out, and it would have been much worse if he found out later. I much prefer having it out in the open, and then we can make our case for why he should honor the adoption."

I reach out and take her hand. Darcy is always so levelheaded.

"I hope you make up with him," she says.

"I... Yeah. I don't know how."

"Maybe you two could talk...?"

"I don't think he's going to want to hear me out. He was really, *really* angry."

"When you went upstairs at Ryder's house, you didn't have enough time to tell him everything. Maybe you should, from the beginning. How what he did hurt, how it left you no choice. If he's the kind of man who deserves your heart, he'll understand you did the best you could in the situation, Ava."

I hope so. But she's right. No matter how nervous the idea makes me, I need to talk to him. I can't just... give up like this.

My phone rings. *Probably Ray calling for us to come back.* As lovely as Mia is, she can be a handful to—

"Ava."

My mouth dries at the sound of Lucas's voice. I take a quick swallow of my coffee. "Hi."

"Are you busy today?" There's no inflection, nothing in his tone to indicate his mood.

"No. Well, it depends on when. I should be free in about three hours." That should give me enough time to go home and change. I don't want to see him in these old clothes.

"Then is about five thirty good?"

"Yes. Perfect."

"I'll send you a car at four thirty."

"Okay," I say, my voice shaky.

He hangs up. No teasing tone, no "I love you"—and I realize how much that hurts.

"Who was that?" Darcy asks, but she already knows.

I meet her eyes, hoping for some kind of sign. "He wants to talk."

"That's good then."

"Yeah...I guess." I hope so. Oh, how I hope so. "But I need to go back and get ready. Do you mind if we cut our shopping short?"

"Of course not." She loops an arm through mine. "Let's go. You've got a man to win over!"

Ava

THE PENTHOUSE LUCAS'S DRIVER TAKES ME TO IS not the one Lucas and I saw together. Is this the place he's planning to get? I have no idea what the location means.

I vaguely register that it's far more opulent than the place we decided on. The place is like a palace, designed to awe. It's so ostentatious, it's almost embarrassing.

An elevator with one glass wall takes me to the top level. I see L.A., twilit, at my feet, but it only makes my palms clammier. The people below seem to judge me... speculating about my chances of success.

I place a hand over my fluttering belly. Surely I can make this work. I'm in my favorite cornflower dress and matching heels. I didn't do anything special with my hair, just brushed it out, but my face sports fresh makeup. I'm not here to elicit pity or anything like that. I just want a chance to say how sorry I am and explain why I felt I had to do what I did. It isn't easy—I'm not generally an open person.

When the elevator arrives, I take a deep breath. My phone pings with a text from Darcy. *You can do this. Have faith. And I'll do as you asked, and hopefully it'll all be good.*

I swallow, then straighten my shoulders and walk past the foyer into a three-level penthouse. The lofts above are open and tiered, soaring like a cathedral. I feel like a woefully unprepared child about to sing a Christmas carol in front of everyone.

"Ava."

I try a smile. "Lucas."

I drink him in. Standing by the fireplace, he's absolutely gorgeous in a sweater the color of the Pacific and black slacks. He isn't smiling, his expression somber, but he also doesn't seem frigid or angry.

That's something, right?

"Have a seat." He gestures at some couches.

I sit at the edge of a loveseat and fold my hands in my lap, my heart hammering.

Silence stretches, and my gut twists until I don't think it'll ever go back to normal. I lick my dry lips and finally say, "I'm sorry."

"I didn't ask you to come so you can apologize."

My palms are so sweaty now, I'm surprised my skirt isn't soaked.

"Talk to me," he says, his voice almost too soft to hear. "I have the right to know, don't I?"

He doesn't have to specify. I understand exactly what he wants, and I start from the beginning because that's the simplest way.

Stick to the facts, Ava. Don't get overly emotional. It's not that kind of moment here.

I draw in a breath. Then I begin.

36

———

Lucas

I stand by the fireplace because that's all I can do. Ava looks stunning in that blue dress, but she sits on the edge of the loveseat like a prisoner waiting for judgment.

I should go to her, hold her and comfort her as she talks, but I can't. I'm bracing myself for the worst.

Licking her lips, she begins. "The day before your accident, I found out I was pregnant. I'd missed my period and...didn't feel well for a few days. I used two tests, just to be sure. And when they were both positive, I stayed up all night thinking about how I was going to tell you."

"We were so careful," I murmur. Contraceptives aren't a hundred percent effective, I know that...but it's still a shock when one fails.

"I know." She swallows, looking down at her fingers briefly. "But the decision about what to do with the baby couldn't be mine alone. I mean, she was yours, too. So I was going tell you the next day, but then Erin called and said you'd been in an accident. When I went to the hospital, I saw your brothers. Blake didn't take kindly to my being there, and he said some...pretty bad things. You were in surgery."

I already know this part. "You jumped to the worst conclusion."

She nods, her pale cheeks flushing. "I did, and I'm sorry. The whole situation just felt...so *familiar* to what my dad did to my mom. Almost like déjà vu. And then I looked you up, and found out about Faye and every-thing, and...I just couldn't." She shakes her head, her fingers twisting. "I had to cut ties. Completely. But I also had no idea what to do with the baby. I didn't tell anyone I was pregnant. I just kept it all in, wondering and thinking about how I was going to get a job and pay for everything. I heard Erin talk about how much it cost her older sister to have twins, and that was with insur-ance. I didn't have anything."

My hands clench, and it's all I can do to modulate my breathing. My heart constricts at the image of Ava alone...pregnant and hurting and scared. Who gives a shit about my rehab issues? I should've done more to find out what happened. I should've been there for her whether she liked it or not—to grovel, to explain Faye, explain why I did what I did and...

I screwed up. Monumentally.

She continues, "When I was visiting Ray and Darcy a couple months later—I wasn't showing yet—I fainted while getting up from a chair. They took me to the hospital, and that's how they found out. They wanted to know what I planned to do, and when I told them I had no clue, they offered to pay for everything, no strings attached. They were worried I wouldn't get the care I needed, and...I don't know if I could've gotten through the whole thing if it hadn't been for them.

"And when Mia was born... She was too small. I felt like it was my fault for not having had good prenatal care from the beginning."

I can't speak through the lump in my throat. She's wrong. It wasn't her fault Mia was born too small. It was mine. If I hadn't been such an idiot, Ava could've had the best care, the best of everything, and Mia would've been born big and healthy. I know it.

"I had no idea what to do," Ava says. "I was completely unprepared for everything, and it was Ray and Darcy who stepped in and made sure Mia and I got what we needed. Watching them care for Mia made me realize I could never give her the kind of life and opportunities she deserved. I wasn't even working full-time. I couldn't afford daycare without a full-time job, but no one wants to hire a single mom who just had a baby. I knew Darcy and Ray wanted to have children of their own but couldn't, so it made the most sense for me to ask if they'd like to adopt Mia. And they said yes."

She places an elbow on her knee and rests her forehead

in her palm. "When you showed up again, it put me in a complicated situation. I couldn't cut Darcy, Ray and Mia out of my life, but that also meant I had to tell you the truth at some point. I just didn't know when...or how. I wasn't sure how you'd react to the news two years after the fact. I told Ray you and I could have another baby if that's what we decided, but children... They touch us and bring out emotions and drives that we never knew existed. I never thought I'd want to have children, but when I realized I was pregnant...Lucas, I wanted that little girl more than anything."

Ava's version is...abbreviated, but it's more than enough for me to fill in the blanks and feel the pain and conflict she's been under. I push off the mantel, my legs stiff and my gait uneven. She doesn't look up. I rest my weight on the edge of the couch, like her, then reach out and take her cold, clammy hand in mine.

She finally lifts her head, looks at me with eyes darkened by old, painful memories. There's no recrimination or anger, and that only makes me feel worse.

"I'm sorry I put you through that. I should've been braver. Better," I say.

"Lucas..."

"Letting people in is never easy, and I should've realized how my actions would affect you. Back then I was only worried about protecting myself. I assumed our relationship would blow up eventually, because I didn't deserve anything better. But that's all wrong. I ended up hurting you—hurting *us*—because I didn't have faith. I didn't think we could have it all...and so I didn't fight for it." I pause, shame making me unable to go on. I let my mother's toxic words linger, even after cutting her out of my life years ago, and hurt the one woman I want to treasure above all.

Ava reaches out, cups my neck and gently pulls until our foreheads are touching, our breaths mingling.

"I'm not entirely blameless either. I should have fought for what I wanted, told you what you should've heard two years ago," she whispers. "And I'm glad you're giving me a chance to tell you now."

I cradle her beloved face. "I couldn't do anything else. When I was going to propose to Faye, you didn't let me go. You fought for me. I made a very deliberate choice to listen and trust you and accept your love."

Tears start to flow, trailing down her cheeks. I see relief, joy and gratitude in her eyes, and know they're reflected in my heart. I press my lips against hers, but all too soon she pulls back.

"There's...one more thing," she says.

I stiffen, bracing for another lacerating memory. But I deserve this, too—whatever pain is coming will be part of my penance. "What?"

"Hold on." She rises to her feet and goes to the door. Outside are Darcy and Ray, with Mia in tow. Darcy hands Ava the toddler, and she brings the child to me. "You never got to hold her."

I pull back, suddenly unsure. "But..." I can't say the rest...that I'm unworthy of touching something as perfect as this child. I look at Ray.

"I was wrong at the dinner." He nods. "Go ahead."

I take the girl in my arms, feeling her tiny softness. She's in a pretty pink dress with lots of lace and tiny pear buttons. I smell the clean, heartbreakingly lovely scent of a young child, and I can't look away. Her eyes are guileless and bright, her smile sweetly inviting as though asking me to love her because she's awesome and she thinks I'm interesting and just the person to give her the love she wants.

She reaches out and touches my hair and my face.

Manipulation. When you say things like "I love you," you're trying to get the other person to say it back. Putting pressure on someone.

You're being needy.

Needy children are the worst.

My chest swells with emotion, and I can't speak. Mia wants me to love her, and she's reaching out to me. But I already love her so much I'd gladly give up my life for hers. Loving someone and wanting the person to love you back doesn't make you needy. It makes you human.

I don't know why I never realized that. Why it took holding Mia in my arms.

A frown furrows her tiny forehead. "Cwy? Sad?"

I blink, shocked at the tears wetting my cheeks.

"Hurt?"

I shake my head. "No. I just love you so much."

She gives me a blinding smile then babbles. Or at least I think it's babbling; I can't make sense of her baby talk. But maybe that's because she's already smarter than I am.

I see the innocence in her, the absolute conviction that she's deserving of love and care and everything else wonderful and sweet in life, and I know Darcy and Ray have done an incredible job raising Mia. Taking her from them now... It would be a travesty.

I feel Ava's hand on my shoulder. Then I remember we aren't quite finished. I give Mia to Darcy and Ray. "You've done an amazing job with her. She's lucky to have parents like you."

Darcy blinks away tears. "It's our pleasure, Lucas... and thank you."

"No, thank *you*. I'll never be able to repay everything that you've done for Ava and Mia."

"You know you're always welcome to spend time with her. We'd like that," Ray says.

I nod. "Of course. She'll have two sets of parents who adore her."

Ava rests her head against my arm, and I shift to put it around her. Darcy and Ray leave with Mia, giving us some privacy.

When the door closes behind them, Ava pulls away and takes my hands in hers. Her expression is serious. She goes down on one knee and says, "I know it's traditional to have a ring, but engagement rings are usually reserved for women. So I'm asking without any props— Lucas Reed, will you marry me?"

Dropping to my knees, I hold her arms, needing to make sure she isn't saying this out of some momentary emotional overload. "Ava, that's supposed to be my question."

She shakes her head. "Nope. This isn't just a proposal, Lucas. You said you were going to marry me, and I'm thrilled. But what I'm asking you to do is marry me sooner rather than later."

"I already told—"

"I know what you said. You don't want to give me any reason to doubt your love. And I don't. You have the biggest heart in the world and I'm lucky it's mine. But I also want you to know I'm going to be devastated if your...perception...of my insecurity cost you an inheritance. If your siblings are all jumping through hoops, the paintings mean more than just money. So I'm asking you to marry me. Now."

"*Now?*"

"Well...as soon as we can manage."

"But I don't want you to rush into this just to help me get the paint—"

"Don't you understand? I'm doing this because I don't want to wait any more to start my life with you. Over *two years,* Lucas! Don't you think we've waited long enough?"

She has a point. "Yes. And yes."

"Before Darcy and Ray go back to Charlottesville?"

"If that's what you want." There's no way I'm denying this woman anything.

She gifts me with a thousand-candlepower smile, and I know I've found what I've been looking for all my life.

37

AVA

DARCY AND RAY ARE SCHEDULED TO FLY OUT ON Tuesday, so Lucas and I go to the courthouse on Monday. Since it *is* a wedding, after all, I haven't let him see my knee-length white dress, and insisted on arriving separately. It's such short notice that I don't expect anybody else to attend, but somehow all of Lucas's siblings and in-laws except Blake and Elizabeth show up. She sends me a text apologizing that she's out of town. Blake... Well. I don't mind too much that he's unavailable.

"I'm so happy to see you getting married," Darcy says, helping me with my hair. "You look beautiful."

Ray nods. He's in a crisp suit that Ryder sent over. Even though we're doing the ceremony in a courthouse, we're trying to make things as traditional as possible.

My foster father kisses me on the forehead. "You look perfect."

I smile and gaze down at the simple but elegant diamond solitaire Lucas put on my finger. I love it that he knew exactly what I'd want without my having to say anything.

Ray walks with me to the judge's chambers, and Darcy follows with Mia in her arms. The little princess is holding a basket full of pink flower petals and already throwing them around like confetti, while stopping occasionally to blow kisses. When we enter the room, all I see is Lucas in a gorgeous black tux. And all I feel is love.

Our relationship should've never worked. We were such an unlikely pair, too different, too wounded, too guarded.

Yet somehow we're here, about to be bound together in every way.

When Lucas reaches for me and I'm standing by his side, my heart swells with gratitude and adoration.

I'm finally where I'm meant to be.

THANK YOU FOR READING *AN UNLIKELY BRIDE*. Don't miss the final book in Billionaires' Bride of Convenience, *A Final Deal* (Blake & Faith Standalone)!

Would you like to know when my next book is

available? Join my mailing list at http://www.nadia-alee.net/newsletter.

If you enjoyed *An Unlikely Bride*, I'd appreciate it if you would help others enjoy this book, too.

Recommend it. Please help other readers find this book by recommending it to friends, reader's groups and discussion boards.

Review it. Please tell other readers why you liked this book by reviewing it. If you do write a review, please contact me at nadia@nadialee.net so I can thank you with a personal email.

I love to hear from readers! Feel free to write me at nadia@nadialee.net or follow me on Twitter @nadi-alee, or like my Facebook page at http://www.facebook.com/nadialeewrites. Say hello and let me know which one of my characters is your favorite or what you want to see next or anything else you want to talk about! I personally read all my emails, Tweets and Facebook comments.

TITLES BY NADIA LEE

Billionaires' Brides of Convenience

A Hollywood Deal

A Hollywood Bride

An Improper Deal

An Improper Bride

An Improper Ever After

An Unlikely Deal

An Unlikely Bride

A Final Deal

~

The Pryce Family

The Billionaire's Counterfeit Girlfriend

The Billionaire's Inconvenient Obsession

The Billionaire's Secret Wife

The Billionaire's Forgotten Fiancée

The Billionaire's Forbidden Desire

The Billionaire's Holiday Bride

~

Seduced by the Billionaire

Taken by Her Unforgiving Billionaire Boss

Pursued by Her Billionaire Hook-Up

Pregnant with Her Billionaire Ex's Baby

Romanced by Her Illicit Millionaire Crush

Wanted by Her Scandalous Billionaire

Loving Her Best Friend's Billionaire Brother

ABOUT NADIA LEE

New York Times and *USA Today* bestselling author Nadia Lee writes sexy, emotional contemporary romance. Born with a love for excellent food, travel and adventure, she has lived in four different countries, kissed stingrays, been bitten by a shark, ridden an elephant and petted tigers.

Currently, she shares a condo overlooking a small river and sakura trees in Japan with her husband and son. When she's not writing, she can be found reading books by her favorite authors or planning another trip.

To learn more about Nadia and her projects, please visit http://www.nadialee.net. To receive updates about upcoming works from Nadia, please visit http://www.nadialee.net/newsletter to subscribe to her new release alert.

Stalk Me!

nadialee.net/newsletter
facebook.com/nadialeewrites

CPSIA information can be obtained
at www.ICGtesting.com
Printed in the USA
LVOW11s2318080418
572690LV00007B/660/P